Animal Ghosts
Or, Animal Hauntings and the Hereafter

Elliott O'Donnell

Contents

ANIMAL GHOSTS
OR, ANIMAL HAUNTINGS
AND THE HEREAFTER

BY

Elliott O'Donnell

PREFACE

If human beings, with all their vices, have a future life, assuredly animals, who in character so often equal, nay, excel human beings, have a future life also.

Those who in the Scriptures find a key to all things, can find nothing in them to confute this argument. There is no saying of Christ that justifies one in supposing that man is the only being, whose existence extends beyond the grave.

Granted, however, merely for the sake of argument, that we have some ground for the denial of a future existence for animals, consider the injustice such a denial would involve. Take, for example, the case of the horse. Harming no one, and without thought of reward, it toils for man all its life, and when too old to work it is put to death without even the compensation of a well-earned rest. But if compensation be God's law,--as I, for one, believe it to be--and also the raison d'etre of a hereafter, then surely the Creator, whose chief claim to our respect and veneration lies in the fact that He is just and merciful, will take good care that the horse--the gentle, patient, never-complaining horse--is well compensated--compensated in a golden hereafter.

Consider again, the case of another of our four-footed friends--the dog; the faithful, affectionate, obedient and forgiving dog, the dog who is so often called upon to stand all sorts of rough treatment, and is shot or poisoned, if, provoked beyond endurance, he at last rounds on his persecutors, and bites. And the cat--the timid, peaceful cat who is mauled, and all but pulled in two by cruel children, and beaten to a jelly when in sheer agony and fright it scratches. Reflect again, on the cow and the sheep, fed only to supply our wants; shouted at and kicked, if, when nearly scared out of their senses, they wander off the track; and pole-axed, or done to death in some equally atrocious manner when the sickening demand for flesh food is at its height.

And yet, you say, these innocent, unoffending--and, I say, martyred--animals are to have no future, no compensation. Monstrous! Absurd! It is an effrontery to common sense, philosophy--anything, everything. It is a damned lie, damned bigotry, damned nonsense. The whole animal world will live again; and it will be man--spoilt, presumptuous, degenerate man--who will not participate in another life, unless he very much improves.

Think well over this,--you who preach the gospel of man's pre-eminence;--you who prate of God and know nothing whatsoever about Him! The horse, dog, cat,--even the wild animals, whose vices, perchance, pale beside your own, may go to Heaven before you. The Supreme Architect is neither a Nero, nor a Stuart, nor a clown. He will recompense all who deserve recompense, be they great or small--biped or quadruped.

It is to testify to a future existence for animals and to create a wider interest in it that I have undertaken to compile this book; and my object, I think, can best be achieved in my own way, the way of the investigator of haunted places. The mere fact that there are manifestations of "dead" people (pardon the paradox) proves some kind of life after death for human beings; and happily the same proof is available with regard a future life for animals; indeed there are as many animal phantasms as human--perhaps more; hence, if the human being lives again, so do his dumb friends.

Be comforted then, you who love your pets, and have been kind to them. You will see them all again, on the soft undying pasture lands of your Elysium and theirs.

Be warned, you--you who have despised animals, and have been cruel to them. Who knows but that, in your future life, you may be as they are now--in subjection?

*   *   *   *   *

My task in writing this book has been considerably lightened by the extreme courtesy and kindness of Mr. Shirley, Mr. Eveleigh Nash, and the Proprietors of the Review of Reviews, in allowing me to make use of extracts and quotations from their most valuable works.

ELLIOTT O'DONNELL.

CHAPTER I
CATS

In opening this volume on Animals and their associations with the unknown, I will commence with a case of hauntings in the Old Manor House, at Oxenby. My informant was a Mrs. Hartnoll, whom I can see in my mind's eye, as distinctly as if I were looking at her now. Hers was a personality that no lapse of time, nothing could efface; a personality that made itself felt on boys of all temperaments, most of all, of course, on those who--like myself--were highly strung and sensitive.

She was classical mistress at L.'s, the then well-known dame school in Clifton, where for three years--prior to migrating to a Public School--I was well grounded in all the mysticisms of Kennedy's Latin Primer and Smith's First Greek Principia.

I doubt if she got anything more than a very small salary--governesses in those days were shockingly remunerated--and I know,--poor soul, she had to work monstrously hard. Drumming Latin and Greek into heads as thick as ours was no easy task.

But there were times, when the excessive tension on the nerves proving too much, Mrs. Hartnoll stole a little relaxation; when she allowed herself to chat with us, and even to smile--Heavens! those smiles! And when--I can feel the tingling of my pulses at the bare mention of it--she spoke about herself, stated she had once been young--a declaration so astounding, so utterly beyond our comprehension, that we were rendered quite speechless--and told us anecdotes.

Of many of her narratives I have no recollection, but one or two, which interested me more than the rest, are almost as fresh in my mind as when recounted. The one that appealed to me most, and which I have every reason to believe is absolutely true,[1] is as follows:--I give it as nearly as I can in her own somewhat stilted style:--

"Up to the age of nineteen, I resided with my parents in the Manor House, Oxenby. It was an old building, dating back, I believe, to the reign of Edward VI, and had originally served as the residence of noble families. Built, or, rather, faced with split flints, and edged and buttressed with cut grey stone, it had a majestic though very gloomy appearance, and seen from afar resembled nothing so much as a huge and grotesquely decorated sarcophagus. In the centre of its frowning and menacing front was the device of a cat, constructed out of black shingles, and having white shingles for the eyes; the effect being curiously realistic, especially on moonlight nights, when anything more lifelike and sinister could scarcely have been conceived. The artist, whoever he was, had a more than human knowledge of cats--he portrayed not merely their bodies but their souls.

"In style the front of the house was somewhat castellated. Two semicircular bows, or half towers, placed at a suitable distance from each other, rose from the base to the summit of the edifice, to the height of four or five stairs; and were pierced, at every floor, with rows of stone-mullioned windows. The flat wall between had larger windows, lighting the great hall, gallery, and upper apartments. These windows were wholly composed of stained glass, engraved with every imaginable fantastic design--imps, satyrs, dragons, witches, queer-shaped trees, hands, eyes, circles, triangles and cats.[1]

"The towers, half included in the building, were completely circular within, and contained the winding stairs of the mansion; and whoever ascended them when a storm was raging seemed rising by a whirlwind to the clouds.

"In the upper rooms even the wildest screams of the hurricane were drowned in the rattling clamour of the assaulted casements. When a gale of wind took the building in front, it rocked it to the foundations, and, at such times, threatened its instant demolition.

"Midway between the towers there stood forth a heavy stone porch with a Gothic gateway, surmounted by a battlemented parapet, made gable fashion, the apex of which was garnished by a pair of dolphins, rampant and antagonistic, whose corkscrew tails seemed contorted--especially at night--by the last agonies of rage

---

1   I have subsequently met several people who experienced the same phenomena in the house, which was standing a short time ago.

convulsed. The porch doors stood open, except in tremendous weather; the inner ones were regularly shut and barred after all who entered. They led into a wide vaulted and lofty hall, the walls of which were decorated with faded tapestry, that rose, and fell, and rustled in the most mysterious fashion every time there was the suspicion--and often barely the suspicion--of a breeze.

"Interspersed with the tapestry--and in great contrast to its antiquity--were quite modern and very ordinary portraits of my family. The general fittings and furniture, both of the hall and house, were sombre and handsome--truss-beams, corbels, girders and panels were of the blackest oak; and the general effect of all this, augmented, if anything, by the windows, which were too high and narrow to admit of much light, was much the same as that produced by the interior of a sub-terranean chapel or charnel house.

"From the hall proceeded doorways and passages, more than my memory can now particularize. Of these portals, one at each end conducted to the tower stairs, others to reception rooms and domestic offices.

"The whole of the house being too large for us, only one wing--the right and newer of the two--was occupied, the other was unfurnished, and generally shut up. I say generally because there were times when either my mother or father--the servants never ventured there--forgot to lock the doors, and the handles yielding to my daring fingers, I surreptitiously crept in.

"Everywhere--even in daylight, even on the sunniest of mornings--were dark shadows that hung around the ingles and recesses of the rooms, the deep cupboards, the passages, and silent, winding staircases.

"There was one corridor--long, low, vaulted--where these shadows assembled in particular. I can see them now, as I saw them then, as they have come to me many times in my dreams, grouped about the doorways, flitting to and fro on the bare, dismal boards, and congregated in menacing clusters at the head of the sepulchral staircase leading to the cellars. Generally, and excepting at times when the weather was particularly violent, the silence here was so emphatic that I could never feel it was altogether natural, but rather that it was assumed especially for my benefit-- to intimidate me. If I moved, if I coughed, almost if I breathed, the whole passage was filled with hoarse reverberating echoes, that, in my affrighted ears, appeared to terminate in a series of mirthless, malevolent chuckles. Once, when fascinated beyond control, I stole on tiptoe along the passage, momentarily expecting a door to fly open and something grim and horrible to pounce out on me, I was brought to a standstill by a loud, clanging noise, as if a pail or some such utensil were set down very roughly on a stone floor. Then there was the sound of rushing footsteps and of someone hastily ascending the cellar staircase. In fearful anticipation as to what I should see--for there was something in the sounds that told me they were not made by anything human--I stood in the middle of the passage and stared. Up, up, up they came, until I saw the dark, indefinite shape of something very horrid, but which I could not--I dare not--define. It was accompanied by the clanging of a pail. I tried to scream, but my tongue cleaving to the roof of my mouth prevented my uttering a syllable, and when I essayed to move, I found I was temporarily paralysed. The thing came rushing down on me. I grew icy cold all over, and when it was within a few feet of me, my horror was so great, I fainted.

"On recovering consciousness, it was some minutes before I summoned up courage to open my eyes, but when I did so, they alighted on nothing but the empty passage--the thing had disappeared.

"On another occasion, when I was clandestinely paying a visit to the unused wing, and was in the act of mounting one of the staircases leading from the corridor, I have just described, to the first floor, there was the sound of a furious scuffle overhead, and something dashed down the stairs past me. I instinctively looked up, and there, glaring down at me from over the balustrade, was a very white face. It was that of a man, but very badly proportioned--the forehead being low and receding, and the rest of the face too long and narrow. The crown rose to a kind of peak, the ears were pointed and set very low down and far back. The mouth was very cruel and thin-lipped; the teeth were yellow and uneven. There was no hair on the face, but that on the head was red and matted. The eyes were obliquely set, pale blue, and full of an expression so absolutely malignant that every atom of blood in my veins seemed to congeal as I met their gaze. I could not clearly see the body of the thing, as it was hazy and indistinct, but the impression I got of it was that it was clad in some sort of tight-fitting, fantastic garment. As the landing was in semi-darkness, and the face at all events was most startlingly visible, I concluded it brought with it a light of its own, though there was none of that lurid glow attached to it, which I subsequently learned is almost inseparable from spirit phenomena seen under similar conditions.

"For some seconds, I was too overcome with terror to move, but my faculties at length reasserting themselves, I turned round and flew to the other wing of the house with the utmost precipitation.

"One would have thought that after these experiences nothing would have induced me to have run the risk of another such encounter, yet only a few days after the incident of the head, I was again impelled by a fascination I could not withstand to visit the same quarters. In sickly anticipation of what my eyes would alight on, I stole to the foot of the staircase and peeped cautiously up. To my infinite joy there was nothing there but a bright patch of sunshine, that, in the most unusual fashion, had forced its way through from one of the slits of windows near at hand.

"After gazing at it long enough to assure myself it was only sunshine, I quitted the spot, and proceeded on my way down the vaulted corridor. Just as I was passing one of the doors, it opened. I stopped--terrified. What could it be? Bit by bit, inch by inch, I watched the gap slowly widen. At last, just as I felt I must either go mad or die, something appeared--and, to my utter astonishment, it was a big, black cat! Limping painfully, it came towards me with a curious, gliding motion, and I perceived with a thrill of horror that it had been very cruelly maltreated. One of its eyes looked as if it had been gouged out--its ears were lacerated, whilst the paw of one of its hind-legs had either been torn or hacked off. As I drew back from it, it made a feeble and pathetic effort to reach me and rub itself against my legs, as is the way with cats, but in so doing it fell down, and uttering a half purr, half gurgle, vanished--seeming to sink through the hard oak boards.

"That evening my youngest brother met with an accident in the barn at the back of the house, and died. Though I did not then associate his death with the apparition of the cat, the latter shocked me much, for I was extremely fond of animals. I did not dare venture in the wing again for nearly two years.

"When next I did so, it was early one June morning--between five and six, and none of the family, saving my father, who was out in the fields looking after his men, were as yet up. I explored the dreaded corridor and staircase, and was crossing the floor of one of the rooms I had hitherto regarded as immune from ghostly influences, when there was an icy rush of wind, the door behind me slammed to violently, and a heavy object struck me with great force in the hollow of my back.

With a cry of surprise and agony I turned sharply round, and there, lying on the floor, stretched out in the last convulsions of death, was the big black cat, maimed and bleeding as it had been on the previous occasion. How I got out of the room I don't recollect. I was too horror-stricken to know exactly what I was doing, but I distinctly remember that, as I tugged the door open, there was a low, gleeful chuckle, and something slipped by me and disappeared in the direction of the corridor. At noon that day my mother had a seizure of apoplexy, and died at midnight.

"Again there was a lapse of years--this time nearly four--when, sent on an errand for my father, I turned the key of one of the doors leading into the empty wing, and once again found myself within the haunted precincts. All was just as it had been on the occasion of my last visit--gloom, stillness and cobwebs reigned everywhere, whilst permeating the atmosphere was a feeling of intense sadness and depression.

"I did what was required of me as quickly as possible, and was crossing one of the rooms to make my exit, when a dark shadow fell athwart the threshold of the door, and I saw the cat.

*   *   *   *   *

"That evening my father dropped dead as he was hastening home through the fields. He had long suffered from heart disease.

"After his death we--that is to say, my brother, sisters and self--were obliged to leave the house and go out into the world to earn our living. We never went there again, and never heard if any of the subsequent tenants experienced similar manifestations."

This is as nearly as I can recollect Mrs. Hartnoll's story. But as it is a good many years since I heard it, there is just a possibility of some of the details--the smaller ones at all events--having escaped my memory.

When I was grown up, I stayed for a few weeks near Oxenby, and met, at a garden party, a Mr. and Mrs. Wheeler, the then occupants of the Manor House.

I asked if they believed in ghosts, and told them I had always heard their house was haunted.

"Well," they said, "we never believed in ghosts till we came to Oxenby, but we have seen and heard such strange things since we have been in the Manor House that we are now prepared to believe anything."

They then went on to tell me that they--and many of their visitors and ser-
vants--had seen the phantasms of a very hideous and malignant old man, clad in
tight-fitting hosiery of mediaeval days, and a maimed and bleeding big, black cat,
that seemed sometimes to drop from the ceiling, and sometimes to be thrown at
them. In one of the passages all sorts of queer sounds, such as whinings, meanings,
screeches, clangings of pails and rattlings of chains, were heard, whilst something,
no one could ever see distinctly, but which they all felt to be indescribably nasty,
rushed up the cellar steps and flew past, as if engaged in a desperate chase. Indeed,
the disturbances were of so constant and harrowing a nature, that the wing had to
be vacated and was eventually locked up.

The Wheelers excavated in different parts of the haunted wing and found, in
the cellar, at a depth of some eight or nine feet, the skeletons of three men and two
women; whilst in the wainscoting of the passage they discovered the bones of a boy,
all of which remains they had properly interred in the churchyard. According to
local tradition, handed down through many centuries by word of mouth, the house
originally belonged to a knight, who, with his wife, was killed out hunting. He had
only one child, a boy of about ten, who became a ward in chancery. The man appointed by the Crown as guardian to this child proved an inhuman monster, and
after ill-treating the lad in every conceivable manner, eventually murdered him
and tried to substitute a bastard boy of his own in his place. For a time the fraud
succeeded, but on its being eventually found out, the murderer and his offspring
were both brought to trial and hanged.

During his occupation of the house, many people were seen to enter the premises, but never leave them, and the place got the most sinister reputation. Among
other deeds credited to the murderer and his offspring was the mutilation and boiling of a cat--the particular pet of the young heir, who was compelled to witness
the whole revolting process. Years later, a subsequent owner of the property had a
monument erected in the churchyard to the memory of this poor, abused child, and
on the front of the house constructed the device of the cat.

Though it is impossible to determine what amount of truth there may be in
this tradition, it certainly seems to accord with the hauntings, and to supply some
sort of explanation to them. The ghostly head on the banisters might well be that
of the low and brutal guardian, whose spirit would be the exact counterpart of his

mind. The figure seen, and noises heard in the passage, point to the re-enaction of some tragedy, possibly the murder of the heir, or the slaughter of his cat, in either of which a bucket might easily have played a grimly significant part. And if human murderers and their victims have phantasms, why should not animals have phantasms too? Why should not the phenomenon of the cat seen by Mrs. Hartnoll and the Wheelers have been the actual phantasm of an earthbound cat?

No amount of reasoning--religious or otherwise--has as yet annihilated the possibility of all forms of earthly life possessing spirits.

LETTER FROM MY WIFE

I heard the foregoing account from my husband when first I met him years ago, and I know it to be true. I have seen the rooms, etc. in the Old Manor House, Oxenby, where the incidents Mrs. Hartnoll mentions took place.

ADA B. O'DONNELL.
July 2, 1913.

To further substantiate my views with regard to a future existence for animals, I reproduce (by permission of the Editor) the following letters and articles that have appeared from time to time in the Occult Review:--

Letter 1

That other Cat

One evening about four years ago I was in my drawing-room with two friends; we were all standing up on the point of going to bed, and only waiting till the old cook had succeeded in inducing the grey Persian cat to come in for the night. This was sometimes difficult, and then cook came up as on this occasion and called him from the balcony, and the French window was wide open, when a cat rushed in at the window and through the door.

"What was that?" we said, looking at one another. It was not Kitty, the grey Persian, but darker, and was it really a cat, or what? My friend "Ruegen" has written the account of what she saw before seeing what I have said. "Iona" confirms our description. What I saw seemed dark and shadowy and yet unmistakably a cat. It seemed to me like the predecessor of Kitty, which was a black Persian; he had the same habit of coming in at night by this window, and he constantly rushed through the room, and downstairs, being in a hurry for his supper. A moment or two afterwards the grey cat walked slowly in, and though we searched the house, we could find no other.

"THANET."

Letter 2

Fraeulein Mullet's Story

Three or four years ago, Iona and I were sitting in the drawing-room on a Sunday evening, when cook came in to ask for Kitty (a silver-grey Persian cat) to settle him in the kitchen for the night. Kitty was still in the garden, and cook went to the balcony calling him.

Suddenly I saw a black cat flying in and disappearing behind or under a seat. First, I did not take much notice of this. But when a minute after Kitty slowly and solemnly stepped in, followed by cook, it struck me that the dark something could not have been Kitty, and Thanet and Iona made the remark simultaneously. Now we began to look for the dark one all over the place without any result. Cook had not seen any cat passing her on the balcony, but Kitty the grey one. Thanet had had a black Persian cat, which died before Kitty came.

"RUeGEN."

Letter 3

I can entirely corroborate the accounts written by "Thanet" and "Ruegen."

I remember that I saw something like a dark shadow move very quickly and disappear in front of a cottage piano. I exclaimed simultaneously with my friends "What was that?" and shared their surprise when no black cat was found, and the grey Persian walked in unconcernedly through the open window.

"IONA."

Letter 4

What Kitty saw

Cook said, "I wish you would come downstairs and see how strangely Kitty behaves as soon as I open the cupboard. There is nothing in it but the wood; I turned it all out to see what might be the reason--not even a mousehole can I find." Some days previously cook had told me that nothing could induce Kitty to sleep in his basket, and one day he would not eat any food in the kitchen, and his meals had to be given him outside. So I went down to please cook. Kitty was picked up, and while cook petted and stroked him, she knelt down and opened the cupboard. Kitty, stretching his neck and looking with big, frightened eyes into the cupboard's corner, suddenly turned round; struggling out of cook's hold and rushing over her shoulder, he flew out of the kitchen. Getting up, Cook said: "That's always what he does, just as if he was seeing something horrible!"

Next day I encouraged cook to talk of Ruff, the former black cat, which had been a great favourite of hers, and which she had been nursing when he was dying. "Oh, poor thing, when he was ill, he would creep into dark corners, so I put him in his basket into the cupboard, making it very comfortable for him, and there he died"--pointing to the very corner which caused such horror to Kitty.

"RUeGEN."

Letter 5

Captain Humphries's Story--A Materialized Cat

My son had the following experience at the age of four years in our Worcestershire home.

He was an only child and spent much of his time in the company of a cat who shared his tastes and pursuits even to the extent of fishing in the River Weir with him, the cat being far more proficient at the sport than the boy. When the cat died we none of us dared to break the news to the child, and were much surprised when he asked us to say why his cat only came to play with him at nights nowadays. When we questioned him about it, he stoutly maintained that his cat was there in bodily form every night after he went to bed, looking much the same but a little thinner.

At about the same age, one evening after being in bed one hour, I heard him cry out, and going upstairs (his maid also heard and ran up) and asking him what was the matter, he said that an old gentleman with a long grey beard like his grandfather came into his room, and stood at the front of his bed. At the very moment, the former had a seizure in his carriage while driving through the streets of Birmingham, from which he died without regaining consciousness; later on he recognized a photograph of his grandfather as being the person he saw at the foot of his bed. My wife, the maid, and myself can vouch for the accuracy of these statements, also friends to whom we have related these facts.

"MUNSTER."

Letter 6

Mrs. E.J. Ellis's Story--"The Old Woman's Cat"

My wife, writes Mr. Ellis, who was brought up in Germany, and who is not sufficiently confident about her English to attempt to put down anything for publication in that language, tells me the following story for the Occult Review:--

"When I was a little girl living with my family near Michelstadt in the Odenwald, I remember an old woman like an old witch, whose name was Louise, and who was called 'Pfeiffe Louise,' because she exhibited pipes for sale in her cottage window, along with the cheap dress-stuffs, needles and threads, and simple toys for children which were her stock-in-trade. She had a favourite cat which was devoted to her, but its attachment doesn't seem to have been enough to make her happy, for she married a young sergeant named Lautenschlager, who might have been her son--or indeed her grandson--and who, as everyone said, courted her for her money. She died as long ago as 1869, and during her last illness the devoted cat was always with her. It kept watch beside the body when she was dead, and refused to be driven away. In a fit of exasperation Lautenschlager seized it, carried it off, and drowned it in the little River Mumling, at a place where the road from Michelstadt to the neighbouring village Steinbach runs near the water's edge. It was bordered with poplars then, but chestnut trees shade it now.

"Soon after his first wife was buried Lautenschlager married again, and opened an eating-house in Steinbach, where he established his second wife. He had a sister whom he placed in the cottage of poor 'Pfeiffe Louise.' She carried on the business, and every day Lautenschlager used to walk over from Steinbach to see how she was getting on, returning in the evening to his wife, who used to relate to my mother that he frequently came home terrified and bathed in perspiration, for as he passed the place where he had drowned the cat, its ghost used to come out of the river and run beside him along the dark road, sometimes terrifying him still more by jumping in front of him.

"After a few years of married life the second wife died, and Lautenschlager married a third. The little cottage business had prospered, and in its place he now had a considerable draper's shop in Michelstadt. He continued to walk over from Steinbach, where now the third wife lived in the eating-house, and the ghost of the cat continued to frighten him by appearing at nightfall as he walked beside the river.

"I can remember hearing his third wife describe his dread of it, and my mother has told me how both the sister and the second wife used to say the same thing, though I was too young then for them to tell me about it. Lautenschlager used also to complain to the country people who came to dine at his eating-house. He considered himself an ill-used man, and felt that the supernatural powers were treating him very hardly, and subjecting him to a real persecution. I have only the conversation of his wife and the gossip of the village to vouch for his sincerity, and the genuineness of the apparition is supported only by Lautenschlager's word, but his evident anger and agitation were accepted as genuine, and no one dreamed of doubting his word. He was not at all a dreamy or imaginative man, and did not drink. His passion was merely momentary. He was not only a draper and caterer but a usurer, and realized something of a fortune by lending money on good security to peasants and farmers who, it was said, did not consider how they bound themselves when they signed the papers he put before them.

"Lautenschlager continued to be haunted by the cat-ghost at irregular intervals for more than twenty years, and it made a marked change in his character. He became serious, and during the latter part of his life would only talk about religion and read sacred literature. He died about ten years ago."

"FELINE."

Letter 7

A Spectral Fox-terrier

Two or three years ago I visited a medium (Mrs. Davies of 44 Laburnum Grove, Portsmouth). I had been seated only a few minutes when a little pug-dog of hers looked up in the direction of my knees and down towards my feet, growling and howling in a most strange manner.

"What on earth is he looking at?" I exclaimed.

"Oh," said the medium, "there is a little fox-terrier lying across your feet; one half of his face is quite dark and the other half white, but he has such a peculiar black patch over the eye that one would almost think it was a black bruise." Now, sir, I had such a little dog in India, but this lady did not know of him, and would never have known had he not, as I afterwards found, died out there. This is not only a case of the appearance of an animal after death, but also a case in which it was seen by another animal, as also by the medium. I am also told that the pug-dog who had this vision of my dog was once seen to pounce upon what seemed to the medium to be several cats, near the copper in the scullery of the same house. The medium asked a neighbour if the previous occupants had had any cats. "Oh, yes," replied the neighbour, "and badly the poor things were served, for they were cruelly thrown into the copper, which was full of boiling water."

"SIMLA" (M. Conder).

Letter 8

Killed by a Street Car, but walks in at the Front Door

Some five years ago we had a little puppy about six months old. I used to train him to always go round the back way to come into the house. One day he got hurt and run over, being instantly killed by a street car. A day or two after the accident I was going in my front door and I saw the dog go up the steps in front of me, as plain as I ever saw him in my life. It seemed he knew that I had taught him he must not go in the front way, because he would go a few steps and then turn round and look at me, as though he wanted to see how I was taking it, and I positively saw him go to the full length of the hall into the house, a distance of about twenty feet, before he disappeared. I saw him do this at least three times in two months that we stayed in that flat. I told at least a half-dozen people of the incident at the time it happened, and I can vouch for its authenticity.

I remain, yours truly,

"MAJILTON" (Chas. A. Thompson, Chicago, Ill., U.S.A.).

Letter 9

Mrs. Vincent Taylor's Experience. A Spirit Purr

One evening in February, 1906, my son and I were quietly reading, in full gaslight, our small grey cat lying on the sofa a short distance from where I sat. Suddenly I saw on my knee a large red and white cat which belonged to us in India, which was a very dear family friend and as fond of us as a child.

On leaving India we were obliged to give him to a friend, and in the end he shared the usual fate of pets in that country, making a meal for some wild animal.

"Rufie-Oofie," in his spirit shape, purred vigorously, rubbing his head against me and giving every sign of delight at seeing us again. I did not speak, but in a few minutes my son looked up and said, "Mother, Rufie-Oofie is on your knee," when the spirit cat jumped down and went to him to be petted. Then he returned to me, and walked along the sofa to where our present cat, "Kim," was asleep. The spirit cat, with a look of almost human fun, patted Kim's head, the latter awaking with a start. Rufie-Oofie continued to make playful dabs at Kim's ears, Kim following each movement with glaring eyes, distinctly seeing and realizing that another cat was invading his sofa, but not in the least angry with him and quite ready to play. After a few minutes the spirit cat came back to my knee, whereupon the earth cat displayed jealousy which Rufie-Oofie resented, but before they came to actual "words" the spirit cat retired behind the veil.

"ARJUeNA."

Letter 10

SIR,

The following notes of psychological experiences with animals may be of interest:--

I had a collie who lived to a good old age. She was deaf and infirm, and one hind-leg was paralysed, so that it dragged as she walked. I was taken ill, not seriously, nor so as in any way to affect my brain, but as my poor old dog would insist on coming and lying in my room the doctor insisted on her being destroyed. I felt that her life was no pleasure to her, and she was killed with chloroform. Three days afterwards in the afternoon I heard her come upstairs with her dragging hind-leg. I heard her steps come along the long passage which had my room at the end, and lost them about half-way up. On the third day I called her and spoke to her, putting out my hand as if she would come and put her head under it, and told her all was right. I never heard her any more.

I believe that on one occasion she told me by thought transference that she had no water in her pan. The pan was always filled, and I knew that she wanted something, but thought of all other wants but water. She made her eyes protrude, and looked at me intently, and "water" flashed into my mind. I looked and found the pan empty. It is, of course, possible that the suggestion came from my own sub-conscious mind. I never saw the aura of a human being, but I once had a kind of vision of this dog, which experts have told me was her aura. I was sitting by the fire, somewhat somnolent, and he was lying on the hearthrug. All at once his golden brown coat disappeared, and I saw a mass of reddish brown or perhaps I should say brownish red, and on one side of it was an irregular patch of fleecy white, bordered with sapphire blue. I was told that the brownish red represented the dog's animal instincts, the pearly white his animal innocence, and the sapphire blue his devotional instinct, in his case directed to me as his deity. Whether any of your readers have had similar experiences and explain them similarly, I do not know.

I had to go abroad one summer and my dog was ill with eczema, and as I did not very much trust the maid I was leaving in charge, I sent him to the vet's to be treated. As soon as I reached my destination I wrote to a friend to go and inquire how he was. She replied that the dog was perfectly miserable, and that he had an enormous wound on his back, that he had eaten nothing for a week, that he was too weak to stand, and that if he were hers, she would have him put out of his misery at once. I wrote at once to the vet, telling him to telegraph "Curable" or "Hopeless," and to act accordingly. Meanwhile, I sat that afternoon in the Buergerpark by my-self and imagined the dog upon my lap, and myself stroking and healing him. After this I found myself fully believing that he would get better. The telegram I received was "Curable," and my friend wrote a second letter and said it was a miracle, for the dog was quite convalescent. He recovered perfectly. Here, again, however, it may have been that he was breaking his heart for a friend, and that my friend's visit cheered him. Or may not both causes have had their effect?

"AMBROSE ZAIL MARTYN."

Here is another case in the veracity of which I have every confidence. I will call it

The Headless Cat of No. ---- Lower Seedley Road, Seedley, Manchester

It was related to me by Mr. Robert Dane, who was at one time a tenant of No. ---- Lower Seedley Road, Seedley. I quote it as nearly as possible in his words, thus:--

"When we--my wife and I--took No. ---- Lower Seedley Road, no possibility of the place being haunted crossed our minds. Indeed ghosts were the very last things we reckoned on, as neither of us had the slightest belief in them. Like the generality of solicitors, I am stodgy and unimaginative, whilst my wife is the most practical and matter-of-fact little woman you would meet in a day's march. Nor was there anything about the house that in any way suggested the superphysical. It was airy and light--no dark corners nor sinister staircases--and equipped throughout with all modern conveniences. We began our lease in June--the hottest June I remember-- and nothing occurred to disturb us till October.

"It happened then in this wise. I will quote from my diary:--

"Monday, October 11th.--Dick--that is my brother-in-law--and I, at 11 p.m., were sitting smoking and chatting together in the study. All the rest of the household had gone to bed. We had no light in the room--as Dick had a headache--save the fire, and that had burned so low that its feeble glimmering scarcely enabled us to see each other's face. After a space of sudden and thoughtful silence, Dick took the stump of a cigar from his lips and threw it in the grate, where for a few moments it lay glowing in the gloom.

"'Jack,' he said, 'you will think me mad, but there is something deuced queer about this room to-night--something in the atmosphere I cannot define, but which I have never felt here--or indeed anywhere--before. Look at that cigar-end--look!'

"I did so, and received a shock. What I saw was certainly not the stump Dick had had in his mouth, but an eye--a large, red and lurid eye--that looked up at us with an expression of the utmost hate.

"Dick raised the shovel and struck at it, but without effect--it still glared at us. A great horror then seized us, and unable to remove our gaze from the hellish thing, we sat glued to our chairs staring at it. This state of affairs lasted till the clock in the hall outside struck twelve, when the eye suddenly vanished, and we both felt as if some intensely evil influence had been suddenly removed.

"Dick did not like the idea of sleeping alone, and asked if he might keep the electric light on in his room all night. Tremendous extravagance, but under the circumstances excusable. I confess I devoutly wished it was morning.

"Tuesday, October 12th.--I was awakened at 11.30 p.m. by Delia saying to me, 'Oh, Edward, there have been such dreadful noises on the landing, just as if a cat were being worried to death by dogs. Hark! there it is again.' And as she spoke, from apparently just outside the door, came a series of loud screeches, accompanied by savage growls and snarls.

"Not knowing what to make of it, as we had no animals of our own in the house, but concluding that a door or window having been left open, a dog and cat had got in from outside, I lit a candle, and opened the bedroom door. Instantly the sounds ceased and there was dead silence, and although I searched everywhere, not a vestige of any animal was to be seen. Moreover all the doors leading into the garden were shut and locked, and the windows closed. Not wishing to frighten Delia, I laughingly assured her the cat--a black Tom--was all right, that it was sitting on the roof of the summer-house, looking none the worse for its treatment, and that I had sent the dog--a terrier--flying out of the gate with a well-deserved kick. I explained it was my fault about the front door being left open--my brain had been a bit overstrained through excessive work--and asked her on no account to blame the servants. I grow alarmed at times when I realize how easy lawyering makes lying.

"Friday, October 21st.--On my way to bed last night I encountered a rush of icy cold air at the first bend of the staircase. The candle flared up, a bright blue flame, and went out. Something--an animal of sorts--came tearing down the stairs past me, and on peering over the banisters, I saw, looking up at me from the well of darkness beneath, two big red eyes, the counterparts of the one Dick and I had seen on October 11th. I threw a matchbox at them, but without effect. It was only when I switched on the electric light that they disappeared. I searched the house most carefully, but there were no signs of any animal. Joined Delia, feeling nervous and henpecky.

"Monday, November 7th.--Tom and Mable came running into Delia's room in a great state of excitement after tea to-day. 'Mother!' they cried, 'Mother! Do come! Some horrid dog has got a cat in the spare room and is tearing it to pieces.' Delia, who was mending my socks at the time, flung them anywhere, and springing to her feet, flew to the spare room. The door was shut, but proceeding from within was the most appalling pandemonium of screeches and snarls, just as if some dog had got hold of a cat by the neck and was shaking it to death. Delia swung open the door and rushed in. The room was empty--not a trace of a cat or dog anywhere--and the sounds ceased! On my return home Delia met me in the garden. 'Jack!' she said, 'I have probed the mystery at last. The house is haunted! We must leave.'

"Saturday, November 12th.--Sublet house to James Barstow, retired oil merchant, to-day. He comes in on the 30th. Hope he'll like it!

"Tuesday, November 15th.--Cook left to-day. 'I've no fault to find with you, mum,' she condescendingly explained to Delia. 'It's not you, nor the children, nor the food. It's the noises at night--screeches outside my door, which sound like a cat, but which I know can't be a cat, as there is no cat in the house. This morning, mum, shortly after the clock struck two, things came to a climax. Hearing something in the corner and wondering if it was a mouse--I ain't a bit afraid of mice, mum--I sat up in bed and was getting ready to strike a light--the matchbox was in my hand-- when something heavy sprang right on the top of me and gave a loud growl in my ear. That finished me, mum--I fainted. When I came to myself, I was too frightened to stir, but lay with my head under the blankets till it was time to get up. I then searched everywhere, but there was no sign of any dog, and as the door was locked there was no possibility of any dog having got in during the night. Mum, I wouldn't go through what I suffered again for fifty pounds; I've got palpitations even now; and I would rather go without my month's wages than sleep in that room another night.' Delia paid her up to date, and she went directly after tea.

"Friday, November 18th.--As I was coming out of the bathroom at 11 p.m. something fell into the bath with a loud splash. I turned to see what it was--there was nothing there. I ran up the stairs to bed, three steps at a time!

"Sunday, November 20th.--Went to church in the morning and heard the usual Oxford drawl. On the way back I was pondering over the sermon and wishing I could contort the Law as successfully as parsons contort the Scriptures, when Dot--she is six to-day--came running up to me with a very scared expression in her eyes. 'Father,' she cried, plucking me by the sleeve, 'do hurry up. Mother is very ill.' Full of dreadful anticipations, I tore home, and on arriving found Delia lying on the sofa in a violent fit of hysterics. It was fully an hour before she recovered sufficiently to tell me what had happened. Her account runs thus:--

"'After you went to church,' she began, 'I made the custard pudding, jelly and blancmange for dinner, heard the children their collects, and had just sat down with the intention of writing a letter to mother, when I heard a very pathetic mew coming, so I thought, from under the sofa. Thinking it was some stray cat that had got in through one of the windows, I tried to entice it out, by calling "Puss, puss," and making the usual silly noise people do on such occasions. No cat coming out and the mewing still continuing, I knelt down and peered under the sofa. There was no cat there. Had it been night I should have been very much afraid, but I could scarcely reconcile myself to the idea of ghosts with the room filled with sunshine. Resuming my seat I went on with my writing, but not for long. The mewing grew nearer. I distinctly heard something crawl out from under the sofa; there was then a pause, during which you could have heard the proverbial pin fall, and then something sprang upon me and dug its claws in my knees. I looked down, and to my horror and distress, perceived, standing on its hind-legs, pawing my clothes, a large, tabby cat, without a head--the neck terminating in a mangled stump. The sight so appalled me that I don't know what happened, but nurse and the children came in and found me lying on the floor in hysterics. Can't we leave the house at once?'

"Wednesday, November 30th.--Left No. ---- Lower Seedley Road at 2 p.m. Had an awful scurry to get things packed in time, and dread opening certain of the packing-cases lest we shall find all the crockery smashed. Just as we were starting Delia cried out that she had left her reticule behind, and I was despatched in search of it. I searched everywhere--till I was worn out, for I know what Delia is--and was leaving the premises in full anticipation of being sent back again, when there was a loud commotion in the hall, just as if a dog had suddenly pounced on a cat, and the next moment a large tabby, with the head hewn away as Delia had described, rushed up to me and tried to spring on to my shoulders. At this juncture one of the servants cautiously opened the hall door from without, and informed me I was wanted. The cat instantly vanished, and, on my reaching the carriage in a state of breathless haste and trepidation, Delia told me she had found her reticule--she had been sitting on it all the time!"

In a subsequent note in his diary a year or so later Mr. Dane says: "After innumerable enquiries *re* the history of No. ---- Lower Seedley Road prior to our inhabiting it, I have at length elicited the fact that twelve years ago a Mr. and Mrs. Barlowe lived there. They had one son, Arthur, whom they spoilt in the most outrageous fashion, even to the extent of encouraging him in acts of cruelty. To afford him amusement they used to buy rats for his dog--a fox-terrier--to worry, and on one occasion procured a stray cat, which the servants afterwards declared was mangled in the most shocking manner before being finally destroyed by Arthur. Here, then, in my opinion, is a very feasible explanation for the hauntings--the phenomenon seen was the phantasm of the poor, tortured cat. For if human tragedies are re-enacted by ghosts, why not animal tragedies too? It is absurd to suppose man has the monopoly of soul or spirit."

The Cat on the Post

In her Ghosts and Family Legends Mrs. Crowe narrates the following case of a haunting by the phantom of a cat:--

"After the doctor's story, I fear mine will appear too trifling," said Mrs. M., "but as it is the only circumstance of the kind that ever happened to myself, I prefer giving it you to any of the many stories I have heard.

"About fifteen years ago I was staying with some friends at a magnificent old seat in Yorkshire, and our host being very much crippled with the gout, was in the habit of driving about the park and neighbourhood in a low pony phaeton, on which occasions I often accompanied him. One of our favourite excursions was to the ruins of an old abbey just beyond the park, and we generally returned by a remarkably pretty rural lane leading to the village, or rather small town, of C----.

"One fine summer's evening we had just entered this lane when, seeing the hedges full of wild flowers, I asked my friend to let me alight and gather some. I walked before the carriage picking honeysuckles and roses as I went along, till I came to a gate that led into a field. It was a common country gate with a post on each side, and on one of these posts sat a large white cat, the finest animal of the kind I had ever seen; and as I have a weakness for cats I stopped to admire this sleek, fat puss, looking so wonderfully comfortable in a very uncomfortable position, the top of the post, on which it was sitting with its feet doubled up under it, being out of all proportion to its body, for no Angola ever rivalled it in size.

"'Come on gently,' I called to my friend; 'here's such a magnificent cat!' for I feared the approach of the phaeton would startle it away before he had seen it.

"'Where?' said he, pulling up his horse opposite the gate.

"'There,' said I, pointing to the post. 'Isn't he a beauty? I wonder if it would let me stroke it?'

"'I see no cat,' said he.

"'There on the post,' said I, but he declared he saw nothing, though puss sat there in perfect composure during this colloquy.

"'Don't you see the cat, James?' said I in great perplexity to the groom.

"'Yes, ma'am; a large white cat on that post.'

"I thought my friend must be joking, or losing his eyesight, and I approached the cat, intending to take it in my arms and carry it to the carriage; but as I drew near she jumped off the post, which was natural enough, but to my surprise she jumped into nothing--as she jumped she disappeared! No cat in the field--none in the lane--none in the ditch!

"'Where did she go, James?'

"'I don't know, ma'am. I can't see her,' said the groom, standing up in his seat and looking all round.

"I was quite bewildered; but still I had no glimmering of the truth; and when I got into the carriage again my friend said he thought I and James were dreaming, and I retorted that I thought he must be going blind.

"I had a commission to execute as we passed through the town, and I alighted for that purpose at the little haberdasher's; and while they were serving me I mentioned that I had seen a remarkably beautiful cat sitting on a gate in the lane, and asked if they could tell me who it belonged to, adding it was the largest cat I ever saw.

"The owners of the shop, and two women who were making purchases, suspended their proceedings, looked at each other and then looked at me, evidently very much surprised.

"'Was it a white cat, ma'am?' said the mistress.

"'Yes, a white cat; a beautiful creature and----'

"'Bless me!' cried two or three, 'the lady's seen the white cat of C----. It hasn't been seen these twenty years.'

"'Master wishes to know if you'll soon be done, ma'am. The pony is getting restless,' said James.

"Of course I hurried out, and got into the carriage, telling my friend that the cat was well known to the people at C----, and that it was twenty years old.

"In those days, I believe, I never thought of ghosts, and least of all should have thought of the ghost of a cat; but two evenings afterwards, as we were driving down the lane, I again saw the cat in the same position and again my companion could not see it, though the groom did. I alighted immediately, and went up to it. As I approached it turned its head and looked full towards me with its soft mild eyes, and a friendly expression, like that of a loving dog; and then, without moving from the post, it began to fade gradually away, as if it were a vapour, till it had quite disappeared. All this the groom saw as well as myself; and now there could be no mistake as to what it was. A third time I saw it in broad daylight, and my curiosity greatly awakened, I resolved to make further enquiries amongst the inhabitants of C----, but before I had an opportunity of doing so, I was summoned away by the death of my eldest child, and I have never been in that part of the world since.

"However, I once mentioned the circumstance to a lady who was acquainted with that neighbourhood, and she said she had heard of the white cat of C----, but had never seen it."

This is Mrs. M.'s account as related by Mrs. Crowe, and after perusing the authoress's preface to the work, I am inclined to give it full credence.

The Mystic Properties of Cats

The most common forms of animal phenomena seen in haunted houses are undoubtedly those of cats. The number of places reported to me as being haunted by cats is almost incredible--in one street in Whitechapel there are no less than four. This state of affairs may possibly be accounted for by the fact that cats, more than any other animals that live in houses, meet with sudden and unnatural ends, especially in the poorer districts, where the doctrine of kindness to animals has not as yet made itself thoroughly felt. Now I am touching on the subject of cat ghosts, it may not be out of place to reproduce the following article of mine, entitled "Cats and the Unknown," which appeared in the Occult Review for December, 1912:--

"Since, from all ages, the cat has been closely associated with the supernatural, it is not surprising to learn that images and symbols of that animal figured in the temples of the sun and moon, respectively, in ancient Egypt. According to Horapollo, the cat was worshipped in the Temple of Heliopolis, sacred to the sun, because the size of the pupil of the cat's eye is regulated by the height of the sun above the horizon.

"Other authorities suggest a rather more subtle--and, in my opinion, more probable--reason, namely, that the link between the sun and the cat is not merely physical but superphysical, that the cat is attracted to the sun not only because it loves warmth, but because the sun keeps off terrifying and antagonistic occult forces, to the influences of which the cat, above all other animals, is specially susceptible; a fact fully recognized by the Egyptians, who, to show their understanding and appreciation of this feline attachment, took care that whenever a temple was dedicated to the sun an image or symbol of the cat was placed somewhere, well in evidence, within the precincts.

"To make this theory all the more probable, images and symbols of the cat were dedicated to the moon, the moon being universally regarded as the quintessence of everything supernatural, the very cockpit, in fact, of mystery and spookism. The nocturnal habits of the cat, its love of prowling about during moonlight hours, and the spectacle of its two round, gleaming eyes, may, of course, as Plutarch seems to have thought, have suggested to the Egyptians human influence and analogy, and thus the presence of its effigy in temples to Isis would be partially, at all events, accounted for; though, as before, I am inclined to think there is another and rather more subtle reason.

"From endless experiments made in haunted houses, I have proved to my own satisfaction, at least, that the cat acts as a thoroughly reliable psychic barometer.

"The dog is sometimes unaware of the proximity of the Unknown. When the ghost materializes or in some other way demonstrates its advent, the dog, occasionally, is wholly undisturbed--the cat never. I have never yet had a cat with me that has not shown the most obvious signs of terror and uneasiness both before and during a superphysical manifestation.

"Now, although I won't go so far as to say that ghostly demonstrations are actually dependent on the moon--that they occur only on nights when the moon is visible--experience has led me to believe that the moon most certainly does influence them--that moonlight nights are much more favourable to ghostly appearances than other nights. Hence--there is this much in common between the moon and cats--the one influences and the other is influenced by psychic phenomena--a fact that could scarcely have failed to be recognized by so keen observers of the occult as the Ancient Egyptians.

"The presence of the cat's effigy in the temples of Isis might thus be explained. Over and over again we come across the cat in the land of the Pharaohs. It seems to be inseparable from the esoteric side of Egyptian life. The goddess Bast is depicted with a cat's head, holding the sistrum, i.e. the symbol of the world's harmony, in her hand.

"One of the most ancient symbols of the cat is to be found in the Necropolis of Thebes, which contains the tomb of Hana (who probably belonged to the Eleventh Dynasty). There, Hana is depicted standing erect, proud and kingly, with his favourite cat Borehaki--Borehaki, the picture of all things strange and psychic, and from whom one cannot help supposing he may have chosen his occult inspiration--at his feet. So sure were the Egyptians that the cat possessed a soul that they deemed it worthy of the same funeral rites they bestowed on man. Cats were embalmed, and innumerable cat mummies have been discovered in wooden coffins at Bubastis, Speos, Artemidos and Thebes. When a cat died the Egyptians shaved their eyebrows, not only to show grief at the loss of their loved one, but to avert subsequent misfortune.

"So long as a cat was in his house the Egyptian felt safe from inimical supernatural influences, but if there was no cat in the house at night, then any undesirable from the occult world might visit him. Indeed, in such high esteem did the Egyptians hold the cat, that they voluntarily incurred the gravest risks when its life was in peril. No one of them appreciated the cat and set a higher value on its mystic properties than the Sultan El-Daher-Beybas, who reigned in A.D. 1260, and has been compared with William of Tripoli for his courage, and with Nero for his cruelty. El-Daher-Beybas kept his palace swarming with cats, and--if we may give credence to tradition--was seldom to be seen unaccompanied by one of these animals. When he died, he left the proceeds from the product of a garden to support his feline friends--an example that found many subsequent imitators. Indeed, until comparatively recently in Cairo, cats were regularly fed, between noon and sunset, in the outer court of the Mehkemeh.

"In Geneva, Rome and Constantinople, though cats were generally deemed to have souls and to possess psychic properties, they were thought to derive them from evil sources, and so strong was the prejudice against these unfortunate animals on this account, that all through the Middle Ages we find them suffering such barbaric torture as only the perverted minds of a fanatical, priest-ridden people could devise (which treatment, no doubt, partly, at all events, accounts for the many palaces, houses, etc., in those particular countries, stated to have been haunted by the spirits of cats).

"The devil was popularly supposed to appear in the shape of a black Tom in preference to assuming any other guise, and the bare fact of an old woman being seen, once or twice, with a black cat by her side was quite sufficient to earn for her the reputation of a witch. It would be idle, of course, to expect people in these un-meditative times to believe there was ever the remotest truth underlying these so-called phantastic suppositions of the past; yet, according to reliable testimony, there are, at the present moment, many houses in England haunted by phantasms in the form of black cats, of so sinister and hostile an appearance, that one can only assume that unless they are the actual spirits of cats, earthbound through cruel and vicious propensities, they must be vice-elementals, i.e. spirits that have never inhabited any material body, and which have either been generated by vicious thoughts, or else have been attracted elsewhere to a spot by some crime or vicious act once per-petrated there. Vice-elemental is merely the modern name for fiend or demon.

"Apart from his luciferan qualities, the cat was awarded all sorts of other quali-ties, not the least important of which was its prophetic capability. If a cat washed its face, rainy weather was regarded as inevitable; if a cat frolicked on the deck of a ship, it was a sure sign of a storm; whilst if a live ember fell on a cat, an earthquake shock would speedily be felt. Cats, too, were reputed the harbingers of good and bad fortune. Not a person in Normandy but believed, at one time, that the spectacle of a tortoiseshell cat, climbing a tree, foretold death from accident, and that a black cat crossing one's path, in the moonlight, presaged death from an epidemic. Two black cats viewed in the open between 4 and 7 a.m. were generally believed to predict a

death; whereas a strange white cat, heard mewing on a doorstep, was loudly wel-
comed as the indication of an approaching marriage. According to tradition, one
learns that cats were occasionally made use of in medicine; to cure peasants of skin
diseases, French sorcerers sprinkling the afflicted parts with three drops of blood
drawn from the vein under a cat's tail; whilst blindness was treated by blowing into
the patient's eyes, three times a day, the dust made from ashes of the head of a black
cat that had been burned alive.

"Talking of burning cats reminds me of a horrible practice that was prevalent
in the Hebrides as late as 1750. It was firmly believed there that cats were extraor-
dinarily psychic, and that a sure means of getting in close touch with occult powers,
and of obtaining from them the faculty of second sight--such as the cat possessed-
-was to offer up as sacrifices innumerable black cats. The process was very simple.
A black cat was fastened to a spit before a slow fire, and as soon as the wretched
animal was well roasted, another took its place; victims being supplied without in-
termission, until their vociferous screams brought to the scene a number of ghostly
cats who joined in the chorus. The desired climax was reached, when an enormous
phantom cat suddenly appeared, and informed the operator that it was willing to
grant him any one request if he would only refrain from his cruel persecution. The
operator at once demanded the faculty of second sight--a power more highly prized
in the Hebrides than any other--and the moment it was bestowed on him, set free
the remaining cats. Had all races been as barbarously disposed as these occult-hun-
gering Westerners, cats would soon have become extinct; but it is comforting to
think that in some parts of the world a very different value was set on their psychic
properties.

"In various parts of Europe (some districts of England included) white cats were
thought to attract benevolently disposed fairies, and a peasant would as soon have
thought of cutting off his fingers, or otherwise maltreating himself, as being unkind
to an animal of this species. In the fairy lore of half Europe we have instances of
luck-bringing cats--each country producing its own version of Puss in Boots, Dame
Mitchell and her cat, the White Cat, Dick Whittington and his cat, etc. It is the
same in Asia, too; for nowhere are such stories more prolific than in China and
Persia.

"To sum up--in all climes and in all periods of past history, the cat was credited with many propensities that brought it into affinity and sympathy with the supernatural--or to quote the up-to-date term--superphysical world. Let us review the cat to-day, and see to what extent this past regard of it is justified.

"Firstly, with respect to it as the harbinger of fortune. Has a cat insight into the future? Can it presage wealth or death? I am inclined to believe that certain cats can at all events foresee the advent of the latter; and that they do this in the same manner as the shark, crow, owl, jackal, hyena, etc., viz. by their abnormally developed sense of smell. My own and other people's experience has led me to believe that when a person is about to die, some kind of phantom, maybe, a spirit whose special function it is to be present on such occasions, is in close proximity to the sick or injured one, waiting to escort his or her soul into the world of shadows--and that certain cats scent its approach.

"Therein then--in this wonderful property of smell--lies one of the secrets to the cat's mysterious powers, it has the psychic faculty of scent--of scenting ghosts. Some people, too, have this faculty. In a recent murder case, in the North of England, a rustic witness gave it in her evidence that she was sure a tragedy was about to happen because she "smelt death in the house," and it made her very uneasy. Cats possessing this peculiarity are affected in a similar manner--they are uneasy.

"Before a death in a house I have watched a cat show gradually increasing signs of uneasiness. It has moved from place to place, unable to settle in any one spot for any length of time, had frequent fits of shivering, gone to the door, sniffed the atmosphere, thrown back its head and mewed in a low, plaintive key, and shown the greatest reluctance to being alone in the dark.

"This faculty--possessed by certain cats--may in some measure explain certain of the superstitions respecting them. Take, for example, that of cats crossing one's path predicting death.

"The cat is drawn to the spot because it scents the phantom of death, and cannot resist its magnetic attraction.

"From this, it does not follow that the person who sees the cat is going to die, but that death is overtaking someone associated with that person; and it is in connection with the latter that the spirit of the grave is present, employing, as a medium of prognostication, the cat, which has been given the psychic faculty of smell that it might be so used.

"But although I regard this theory as very feasible, I do not attribute to cats, with the same degree of certainty, the power to presage good fortune, simply because I have had no experience of it myself. Yet, adopting the same lines of argument, I see no reason why cats should not prognosticate good as well as evil.

"There may be phantoms representative of prosperity, in just the same manner as there are those representative of death; they, too, may also have some distinguishing scent (flowers have various odours, so why not spirits?) and certain cats, i.e. white cats in particular, may be attracted by it.

"This becomes all the more probable when one considers how very impressionable the cat is--how very sensitive to kindness. There are some strangers with whom the cat will at once make friends, and others whom it will studiously avoid. Why? The explanation, I fancy, lies once more in the occult--in the cat's psychic faculty of smell. Kind people attract benevolently disposed phantoms, which bring with them an agreeably scented atmosphere, that, in turn, attracts cats. The cat comes to one person because it knows by the smell of the atmosphere surrounding him, or her, that it has nothing to fear--that the person is essentially gentle and benignant. On the contrary, cruel people attract malevolent phantoms, distinguishable also to the cat by their smell, a smell typical of cruelty--often of homicidal lunacy (I have particularly noticed how cats have shrunk from people who have afterwards become dangerously insane). Is this sense of smell, then, the keynote to the halo of mystery that has for all times surrounded the cat--that has led to its bitter persecution--that has made it the hero of fairy lore, the pet of old maids? I believe it is--I believe that in this psychic faculty of smell lies, in degree, the solution to the oft-asked riddle--why is the cat uncanny? Having then satisfied oneself on this point, namely, that cats are in the possession of rare psychic properties, is it likely that the Unknown Powers which have so endowed them, should withhold from them either souls or spirits? Is it not contrary to reason, instinct, and observation to suppose that the many thoroughly material and grossly minded people--people whose whole beings are steeped in money worship--we see around us every day should have spirits, and that pretty, refined and artistic-looking cats, whose occult powers place them in the very closest connection with the superphysical, should not? Monstrous--the bare conception of such incongruity in the one case, and such an omission in the other, is inconceivable, wholly irreconcilable with the notion of any other than a mummer of a creator--a mere court fool of a God."

CHAPTER II
APPARITIONS OF DOGS

One of the most extraordinary cases of hauntings by the phantasms of dogs is related in an old Christmas number of the Review of Reviews, edited by the late Mr. W.T. Stead, and entitled "Real Ghost Stories."

"The most remarkable," writes Mr. Stead, "of all the stories which I have heard concerning ghosts which touch is one that reaches me from Darlington. I owe this, as I owe so many of the other narratives in this collection, to the Rev. Harry Kendall, of Darlington, whose painstaking perseverance in the collection of all matters of this kind cannot be too highly praised. Mr. Kendall is a Congregational minister of old standing. He was my pastor when I was editing the Northern Echo, and he is the author of a remarkable book, entitled All the World's Akin. The following narrative is quite unique in its way, and fortunately he was able to get it at first hand from the only living person present. Here we have a ghost which not only strikes the first blow, hitting a man fair in the eye, but afterwards sets a ghostly dog upon his victim and then disappears. The narrative was signed by Mr. James Durham as lately as December 5th, 1890." Mr. Stead then proceeds to quote the account which he had from Mr. Kendall, and which I append ad verbum from the Review of Reviews. It is as follows: "I was night watchman at the old Darlington and Stockton Station at the town of Darlington, a few yards from the first station that ever existed. I was there fifteen years. I used to go on duty about 8 p.m. and come off at 6 a.m. I had been there a little while--perhaps two or three years--and about forty years ago. One night during winter at about 12 o'clock or 12.30 I was feeling rather cold with standing here and there; I said to myself, 'I will away down and get something to eat.' There was a porter's cellar where a fire was kept on and a coal-house was connected with it. So I went down the steps, took off my overcoat, and had just sat down on the bench opposite the fire and turned up the gas when a strange man came out of the coal-house, followed by a big black retriever. As soon as he entered my eye was upon him, and his eye upon me, and we were intently watching each other as he moved on to the front of the fire. There he stood looking at me, and a curious smile came over his countenance. He had a stand-up collar and a cut-away coat with gilt buttons and a Scotch cap. All at once he struck at me, and I had the impression that he hit me. I up with my fist and struck back at him. My fist seemed to go through him and struck against the stone above the fireplace, and knocked the skin off my knuckles. The man seemed to be struck back into the fire, and uttered a strange, unearthly squeak. Immediately the dog gripped me by the calf of my leg, and seemed to cause me pain. The man recovered his position, called off the dog with a sort of click of the tongue, then went back into the coal-house, followed by the dog. I lighted my dark lantern and looked into the coal-house, but there was neither dog nor man, and no outlet for them except the one by which they had entered.

"I was satisfied that what I had seen was ghostly, and it accounted for the fact that when the man had first come into the place where he sat I had not challenged him with any enquiry. Next day, and for several weeks, my account caused quite a commotion, and a host of people spoke to me about it; among the rest old Edward Pease, father of railways, and his three sons, John, Joseph, and Henry. Old Edward sent for me to his house and asked me all particulars. He and others put this question to me: "Are you sure you were not asleep and had the nightmare?" My answer was quite sure, for I had not been a minute in the cellar, and was just going to get something to eat. I was certainly not under the influence of strong drink, for I was then, as I have been for forty-nine years, a teetotaler. My mind at the time was perfectly free from trouble. What increased the excitement was the fact that a man a number of years before, who was employed in the office of the station, had committed suicide, and his body had been carried into this very cellar. I knew nothing of this circumstance, nor of the body of the man, but Mr. Pease and others who had known him, told me my description exactly corresponded to his appearance and the way he dressed, and also that he had a black retriever just like the one which gripped me. I should add that no mark or effect remained on the spot where I seemed to be seized.

JAMES DURHAM. "Dec. 9th, 1890."

Following the above statement Mr. Stead appends Mr. Kendall's reasons for believing that what James Durham experienced was objective psychic phenomena, and neither produced during sleep nor by hallucination.

The arguments used strike me as being so concise and sensible that I think it will not be out of place to reproduce them.

"First," Mr. Kendall says, "he (James Durham) was accustomed as watchman to be up all night, and therefore not likely from that cause to feel sleepy. Secondly, he had scarcely been a minute in the cellar, and, feeling hungry, was just going to get something to eat. Thirdly, if he was asleep at the beginning of the vision, he must have been awake enough during the latter part of it when he had knocked the skin off his knuckles. Fourthly, there was his own confident testimony. I strongly incline to the opinion that there was an objective cause for the vision, and that it was genuinely apparitional."

So interested was Mr. Kendall in the case that he visited the spot some short time later. He was taken into the cellar where the manifestations took place, and his guide, an old official of the North Road Station, informed him he well remembered the clerk--a man of the name of Winter--who committed suicide there, and showed him the exact spot where he had shot himself with a pistol. In dress and appearance Mr. Winter corresponded minutely with the phenomenon described by James Durham, and he had had a black retriever.

Mr. Kendal came away more convinced than ever of the veracity of James Durham's story, though he admits it was not evidential after the high standard of the S.P.R. I do not know whether the S.P.R. published the case, and I certainly do not think Mr. Kendall need have minded if they did not--for after all there is no reason to suppose the judgment of the S.P.R. is always infallible.

Mr. Stead does not comment on the apparition of the dog, which leads one to suppose cases of animal phantasms were by no means uncommon to him.

The Grey Dog of ---- House, Birmingham

According to a story current in the Midlands, a house in Birmingham, near the Roman Catholic Cathedral, was once very badly haunted. A family who took up their abode in it in the 'eighties complained of hearing all sorts of uncanny sounds--such as screams and sighs--coming from a room behind the kitchen. On one occasion the tenant's wife, on entering the sitting-room, was almost startled out of her senses at seeing, standing before the fireplace, the figure of a tall, stout man with a large, grey dog by his side. What was so alarming about the man was his face--it was apparently a mere blob of flesh without any features in it. The lady screamed out, whereupon there was a terrific crash, as if all the crockery in the house had been suddenly clashed on the stone floor; and a friend of the lady's, attracted to the spot by the noise, saw two clouds of vapour, one resembling a man and the other a dog, which, after hovering over the hearth for several seconds, finally dispersed altogether.

A gasfitter, when working in the house, saw the same figures no less than nine times, and so distinctly that he was able to give a detailed description of both the man and dog.

The house seems to have been well known in Birmingham, and was certainly standing as recently as 1885. Many theories were advanced as to its history, the one gaining most credence being that it was occupied, in 1829, by a man who supplied the medical students with human bodies.

It was noticed at the time that many people who were seen to enter the house in the company of the owner were never seen to leave it, which accords well with the theory of resurrection men.

No suggestion has been offered to account for the animal, which may very easily have been the phantom of the murderer's dog, or, what is rather less likely, the dog of one of his numerous victims.

Anyhow, explanation or no explanation, the fact remains the house was haunted in the manner described, and F. Grey, a Warwickshire Chief Constable, in his ***Recollections***, published 1821, alludes to it.

The Dog in the Cupboard

Miss Prettyman, whom I met some years ago in Cornwall, told me she once lived in a house in Westmorland that was haunted by the apparition of a large dog, enveloped in a blueish glow, which apparently emanated from within it. The dog, whilst appearing in all parts of the house, invariably vanished in a big cupboard at the back of the hall staircase. Miss Prettyman, her family, several of their visitors, and the servants all saw the same phantasm, and were, perhaps, more frightened by the suddenness of its advent than by its actual appearance.

The theory was that it was the ghost of some dog that had been cruelly done to death--possibly by starvation--in the cupboard.

How the Ghost of a Dog saved Life

When I was a boy, an elderly friend of mine, Miss Lefanu, narrated to me an anecdote which impressed me much. It was to this effect.

Miss Lefanu was walking one day along a very lonely country lane, when she suddenly observed an enormous Newfoundland dog following in her wake a few yards behind. Being very fond of dogs, she called out to it in a caressing voice and endeavoured to stroke it. To her disappointment, however, it dodged aside, and repeated the manoeuvre every time she tried to touch it. At length, losing patience, she desisted, and resumed her walk, the dog still following her. In this fashion they went on, until they came to a particularly dark part of the road, where the branches of the trees almost met overhead, and there was a pool of stagnant, slimy water, suggestive of great depth. On the one side the hedge was high, but on the other there was a slight gap leading into a thick spinney. Miss Lefanu never visited the spot alone after dusk, and had been warned against it even in the daytime. As she drew near to it, everything that she had ever heard about it flashed across her mind, and she was more than once on the verge of turning back, when the sight of the big, friendly-looking dog plodding behind, reassuring her, she pressed on. Just as she came to the gap, there was a loud snapping of twigs, and, to her horror, two tramps, with singularly sinister faces, sprang out, and were about to strike her with their bludgeons, when the dog, uttering a low, ominous growl, dashed at them. In an instant the expression of murderous joy in their eyes died out, one of abject terror took its place, and, dropping their weapons, they fled, as if the very salvation of their souls depended on it. As may be imagined, Miss Lefanu lost no time in getting home, and the first thing she did on arriving there was to go into the kitchen and order the cook to prepare, at once, a thoroughly good meal for her gallant rescuer--the Newfoundland dog, which she had shut up securely in the back yard, with the laughing remark, "There--you can't escape me now." Judge of her astonishment, however, when, on her return, the dog had gone. As the walls of the back yard were twelve feet high, and the doors had been shut all the while--no one having passed through them--it was impossible for the animal to have escaped, and the only interpretation that could possibly be put on the matter was that the dog was superphysical--a conclusion that was subsequently confirmed by the experiences of various other people. As the result of exhaustive enquiries Miss Lefanu eventually learned that many years before, on the very spot where the tramps had leaped out on her, a pedlar and his Newfoundland dog had been discovered murdered.

This story being true, then, there is one more link in the chain of evidence to show that dogs, as well as men, have spirits, and spirits that can, on occasion, at least, perform deeds of practical service.

A Precentor's Story

The late Mr. W.T. Stead, in his volume of Real Ghost Stories, narrates the following, which by reason of its being witnessed by three people simultaneously, may be regarded as highly evidential.

In reply to Mr. Stead's request to hear the anecdote the precentor says (I quote him ad verbum):

"I was walking, about nine years ago, one night in August, about ten o'clock, and about half a mile from the house where we are now sitting. I was going along the public road between the hamlets of Mill of Haldane and Ballock. I had with me two young women, and we were leisurely walking along, when suddenly we were startled by seeing a woman, a child about seven years old, and a Newfoundland dog jump over the stone wall which was on one side of the road, and walk on rapidly in front of us. I was not in the least frightened, but my two companions were very much startled. What bothered me was that the woman, the child, and the dog, instead of coming over the wall naturally one after the other, as would have been necessary for them to do, had come over with a bound, simultaneously leaping the wall, lighting on the road, and then hurrying on without a word. Leaving my two companions, who were too frightened to move, I walked rapidly after the trio. They walked on so quickly that it was with difficulty that I got up to them. I spoke to the woman, she never answered. I walked beside her for some little distance, and then suddenly the woman, the child, and the Newfoundland dog disappeared. I did not see them go anywhere, they simply were no longer there. I examined the road minutely, at the spot where they had disappeared, to see if it was possible for them to have gone through a hole in the wall on either side; but it was quite impossible for a woman and a child to get over a high dyke on either side. They had disappeared, and I only regret that I did not try to pass my stick right through their bodies, to see whether or not they had any resistance. Finding they had gone, I returned to my lady friends, who were quite unnerved, and who, with difficulty, were induced to go on to the end of their journey."

One of his companions, Mr. Stead goes on to explain, who heard him tell the story at the time, corroborated the fact that it had made a great impression on those who had seen it. Nothing was ever ascertained as to any woman, child, or Newfoundland dog that had ever been in the district before. When they got to Ballock they enquired of the keeper of the bridge whether a woman, a child, and a dog had passed that way, but he had seen nothing. The apparition had disappeared as suddenly as it had appeared. Mr. Stead's article ends here. Of course, one can only surmise as to the nature of the phenomena. No member of the Psychical Research Society could do more--and in the absence of any authentic history of the spot where the manifestations occurred, such a surmise can be of little value. Since the phenomena were seen by three people at the same time, it is quite safe to assume they were objective, but it is impossible to lay down the law as to whether they were actual phantasms of the dead--of a woman, child, and Newfoundland dog who had all three met with some violent end--or phantasms of three living beings, who, happening to think of that locality at the same time, had projected their immaterial bodies there simultaneously. But whichever of these alternatives be true, the same thing holds good in either case, viz. that the Newfoundland dog had a spirit--and what applies to one dog should assuredly apply to the generality, if not, indeed, to all.

Phantom Dog seen on Souter Fell

Miss Harriet Martineau, in her English Lakes, refers to certain strange phenomena seen from time to time on Souter Fell.

In 1745, for example, a Mr. Wren and his servant saw, simultaneously, a man and dog pursuing some horses along a razor-like ridge of rocks, on which it was obviously impossible for any ordinary being to gain a bare foothold, let alone walk. They watched the figures until the latter suddenly vanished, when Mr. Wren and his servant, thinking, perhaps, the man, dog, and horses had really fallen over the cliff, went to look for them. They searched elsewhere, but despite their vigilance, nothing was to be found, and convinced at last that what they had seen was something superphysical, they came away mystified, and no doubt somewhat frightened.

There is no suggestion to make here other than the manifestations may have been the phantasms of a man, dog, and horses that at some former date had been killed, either accidentally or purposely, in or near that spot.

The Jumping Ghost

Mr. George Sinclair, in his work Satan's Invisible World Discovered, gives a detailed account of hauntings in a house in Mary King's Close, Edinburgh.

The house, at the time Mr. Sinclair writes, was occupied by Mr. Thomas Coltheart, a law agent. Seated one afternoon at home reading, Mrs. Coltheart was immeasurably startled at seeing, suspended in mid-air gazing at her, the head of an old man. She uttered some sort of exclamation, most probably a cry, and the apparition at once vanished. Some nights later, when in bed, both she and her husband saw the same head, which was presently joined by the head of a child, and a long, naked arm, which tried to catch hold of them.

On another occasion, a member of the Coltheart family was greatly alarmed by the sudden appearance of a large dog, which leaped on the chair by her side, and as suddenly disappeared.

Every effort was made to lay the ghosts. Ministers--and one knows how pious Scotch clergymen are--were called in, but their exhortations, instead of dispelling or even minimizing the phenomena, only increased them. It was a case of more prayers, more spooks; which state of affairs, however complimentary to the ministers' powers of address, was scarcely as comforting to the Colthearts, who, unable to bear the strange sights and noises any longer, evacuated the premises. As no other tenants could be found, the house was eventually pulled down, and a row of fine modern buildings now occupy the site. As the history of the place could never be traced with any degree of authenticity, one can do no more than speculate as to the cause of the disturbances, which, I am inclined to think, were due to the phantoms of people and animals that had once actually lived and died there.

Dogs seen before a Death

Mrs. Crowe, in her Night Side of Nature, mentions the case of a young lady named P----, who saw a big black dog twice suddenly appear and disappear by her side, immediately before the death of her mother.

In The Unseen World a story is also told of the phantasm of a big black dog appearing on the bed of a Cornish child, doomed to die shortly afterwards, the same dog invariably manifesting itself before the death of any member of the child's family.

There are so many cases of a similar kind--one hears of them nearly everywhere one goes--that one is led to believe some of them, at least, must be true. There is no more reason to believe all ghost-story tellers are liars, than there is to believe all parsons are liars--and this being so, additional proof is afforded of the continuation of the dog's life after death; for these family canine ghosts are more than probably the phantasms of dogs that once belonged to families--maybe centuries ago--and met their fate in some cruel and unnatural manner.

A Dog scared by a Canine Ghost

A friend of mine, Edward Morgan, had a terrier that was found one morning, poisoned in a big stone kennel. Soon afterwards this friend came to me and said, "I have got a new dog--a spaniel--but nothing will induce it to enter the kennel in which poor Zack was poisoned. Come and see!"

I did so, and what he said was true. Mack (Morgan gave all his dogs names that rhymed--Zack, Mack, Jack, Tack, and even Whack and Smack), when carried to the entrance of the kennel, resolutely refused to cross the threshold, barking, whining, and exhibiting unmistakable symptoms of fear. I knelt down, and peering into the kennel saw two luminous eyes and the distinct outlines of a dog's head.

"Morgan!" I exclaimed, "the mystery is easily solved; there's a dog in here."

"Nonsense!" Morgan cried, speaking very excitedly.

"But there is," I retorted, "see for yourself."

Morgan immediately bent down and poked his head into the kennel.

"What rot," he said. "You're having me on, there's nothing here."

"What!" I cried, "do you mean to say you can see no dog?"

"No!" he replied, "there is none!"

"Let me look again!" I said, and kneeling down, I peeped in.

"Do you mean to say you can't see a dog's face and eyes looking straight at us?" I asked.

"No," he answered, "I can see nothing." And to prove to me the truth of what he said, he fetched a pole and raked about the kennel vigorously with it. We both, then, tried to make Mack enter, and Morgan at last caught hold of him and placed him forcibly inside. Mack's terror knew no limit. He gave one loud howl, and flying out of the kennel with his ears hanging back, tore past into the front garden, where we left him in peace. Morgan was still sceptical as to there being anything wrong with the kennel, but two days later wrote to me as follows:--

"I must apologize for doubting you the other day. I have just had, what you declared you saw, corroborated. A friend of my wife's was calling here this afternoon, and, on hearing of Mack's refusal to sleep in the kennel, at once said, 'I know what's the matter. It's the smell. Mack scents the poison which was used to destroy Zack. Have the kennel thoroughly fumigated, and you'll have no more trouble.' At my wife's request she went into the yard to have a look at it, and the moment she bent down, she cried out like you did, 'Why, there's a dog inside--a terrier!' My wife and I both looked and could see nothing. The lady, however, persisted, and, on my handing her a stick, struck at the figure she saw. To her amazement the stick went right through it. Then, and not till then, did we tell her of your experience. 'Well!' she exclaimed, 'I have never believed in ghosts, but I do so now. I am quite certain that what I see is the phantom of Zack! How glad I am, because I am at last assured animals have spirits and can come back to us.'"

In concluding the accounts of phantasms of dead dogs, let me quote two cases taken from my work entitled The Haunted Houses of London, published by Mr. Eveleigh Nash, of Fawside House, King Street, Covent Garden, London, W.C., in 1909. The cases are these:--

The Phantom Dachshund of W---- St., London, W.

In letter No. 1 my correspondent writes:--

"Though I am by no means over-indulgent to dogs, the latter generally greet me very effusively, and it would seem that there is something in my individuality that is peculiarly attractive to them. This being so, I was not greatly surprised one day, when in the immediate neighbourhood of X---- Street, to find myself persistently followed by a rough-haired dachshund wearing a gaudy yellow collar. I tried to scare it away by shaking my sunshade at it, but all to no purpose--it came resolutely on; and I was beginning to despair of getting rid of it, when I came to X---- Street, where my husband once practised as an oculist. There it suddenly altered its tactics, and instead of keeping at my heels, became my conductor, forging slowly ahead with a gliding motion that both puzzled and fascinated me. I furthermore observed that notwithstanding the temperature--it was not a whit less than ninety degrees in the shade--the legs and stomach of the dachshund were covered with mud and dripping with water. When it came to No. 90 it halted, and veering swiftly round, eyed me in the strangest manner, just as if it had some secret it was bursting to disclose. It remained in this attitude until I was within two or three feet of it--certainly not more--when, to my unlimited amazement, it absolutely vanished--melted away into thin air.

"The iron gate leading to the area was closed, so that there was nowhere for it to have hidden, and, besides, I was almost bending over it at the time, as I wanted to read the name on its collar. There being no one near at hand, I could not obtain a second opinion, and so came away wondering whether what I had seen was actually a phantasm or a mere hallucination. No. 90, I might add, judging by the brass plate on the door, was inhabited by a doctor with an unpronounceable foreign name," etc. etc.

I think one cannot help attaching a great deal of importance to what this lady says, as her language is strictly moderate throughout, and because she does not seem to have been biassed by any special views on the subject of animal futurity.

Correspondent No. 2 (who, by the way, is a total stranger to the writer whose letter I have just quoted) is candidly devoted to dogs, regarding them as in every way on a par with, if not actually superior to, most human beings. Still, notwithstanding this partiality, and consequent profusion of terms of endearment, which will doubtless prove somewhat nauseating to many, her letter is, in my opinion, valuable, because it not only refers to the phenomenon I have mentioned, but to a certain extent furnishes a reason for its occurrence. The lady writes as follows:--

"I once had a rough-haired dachshund, Robert, whom I loved devotedly. We were living at the time near H---- Street, which always had a peculiar attraction for dear Robert, who, I am now obliged to confess, had rather too much liberty--more, indeed, than eventually proved good for him. The servants complained that Robert ruled the house, and I believe what they said was true, for my sister and I idolized him, giving him the very best of everything and never having the heart to refuse him anything he wanted. You will probably scarcely credit it, but I have sat up all night nursing him when he had a cold and was otherwise indisposed. Can you therefore imagine my feelings when my darling was absent one day from dinner? Such a thing had never happened before, for, fond of morning 'constitutionals' as poor Robert was, he was always the soul of punctuality at meal times.

"Neither my sister nor I would hear of eating anything. Whilst he was missing, not a morsel did we touch, but slipping on our hats, and bidding the servants do the same, we scoured the neighbourhood instead. The afternoon passed without any sign of Robert, and when bedtime came (he always slept in our room) and still no signs of our pet, I thought we should both have gone mad. Of course, we advertised, selecting the most popular and, accordingly, the most likely papers, and we resorted to other mediums, too, but, alas! it was hopeless. Our darling little Robert was irrevocably, irredeemably lost. For days we were utterly inconsolable, doing nothing but mope morning, noon, and night. I cannot tell you how forlorn we felt, nor how long we should have remained in that state but for an incident which, although revealing the terrible manner of his death, gave us every reason to feel sure we were not parted from him for all time, but would meet again in the great hereafter. It happened in this wise: I was walking along W---- Street one evening when, to my intense joy and surprise, I suddenly saw my darling standing on the pavement a few feet ahead of me, regarding me intently from out of his pathetic brown eyes. A sensation of extreme coldness now stole over me, and I noticed with something akin to a shock that, in spite of the hot, dry weather, Robert looked as if he had been in the rain for hours. He wore the bright yellow collar I had bought him shortly before his disappearance, so that had there been any doubt as to his identity that would have removed it instantly. On my calling to him, he turned quickly round and, with a slight gesture of the head as if bidding me to follow, he glided forward. My natural impulse was to run after him, pick him up and smother him with kisses; but try as hard as I could, I could not diminish the distance between us, although he never appeared to alter his pace. I was quite out of breath by the time we reached H---- Street, where, to my surprise, he stopped at No. 90 and, turning round again, gazed at me in the most beseeching manner. I can't describe that look; suffice it to say that no human eyes could have been more expressive, but of what beyond the most profound love and sorrow I cannot, I dare not, attempt to state. I have pondered upon it through the whole of a mid-summer night, but not even the severest of my mental efforts have enabled me to solve it to my satisfaction. Could I but do that, I feel I should have fathomed the greatest of all mysteries--the mystery of life and death.

"I do not know for how long we stood there looking at one another, it may have been minutes or hours, or, again, but a few paltry seconds. He took the initiative from me, for, as I leaped forward to raise him in my arms, he glided through the stone steps into the area.

"Convinced now that what I beheld was Robert's apparition, I determined to see the strange affair through to the bitter end, and entering the gate, I also went down into the area. The phantom had come to an abrupt halt by the side of a low wooden box, and as I foolishly made an abortive attempt to reach it with my hand, it vanished instantaneously. I searched the area thoroughly, and was assured that there was no outlet, save by the steps I had just descended, and no hole, nor nook, nor cranny where anything the size of Robert could be completely hidden from sight. What did it all mean? Ah! I knew Robert had always had a weakness for exploring areas, especially in H---- Street, and in the box where his wraith disappeared I espied a piece of raw meat!

"Now there are ways in which a piece of raw meat may lie without arousing suspicion, but the position of this morsel strangely suggested that it had been placed there carefully, and for assuredly no other purpose than to entice stray animals. Resolving to interrogate the owner of the house on the subject, I rapped at the front door, but was informed by the manservant, obviously a German, that his master never saw anyone without an appointment. I then did a very unwise thing--I explained the purpose of my visit to this man, who not only denied any knowledge of my dog, but declared the meat must have been thrown into the area by some passer-by.

"'No one in dis house trow away gut meat like dat,' he explained, 'we eat all we can git here, we have nutting for de animals. Please go away at once, or de master will be very angry. He stand no nonsense from anyone.'

"And as I had no alternative--for, after all, who would regard a ghost in the light of evidence?--I had to obey. I found out, however, from a medical friend that No. 90 was tenanted by Mr. K----, an Anglo-German who was deemed a very clever fellow at a certain London hospital, where he was often occupied in vivisection.

"'I dare say,' my friend went on to remark, 'K---- does a little vivisecting in his private surgery, by way of practice, and--well, you see, these foreign chaps are not so squeamish in some respects as we are.'

"'But can't he be stopped?' I asked. 'It is horrible, monstrous that he should be allowed to murder our pets.'

"'You don't know for certain that he has,' was the reply, 'you only suppose so from what you say you saw, and evidence of that immaterial nature is no evidence at all. No, you can do nothing except to be extra careful in future, and if you have another dog make him steer clear of No. 90 H---- Street.'

"I was sensible enough to see that he was right, and the matter dropped. I soon noticed one thing, however, namely, that there were no more pieces of meat temptingly displayed in the box, so it is just possible K---- got wind of my enquiries, and thought it policy to desist from his nefarious practices.

"Poor Robert! To think of him suffering such a cruel and ignominious death, and my being powerless to avenge it. Surely if vivisection is really necessary, and the welfare of mankind cannot be advanced by any less barbarous system, why not operate on creatures less deserving of our love and pity than dogs? On creatures which whilst being nearer allied to man in physiology and anatomy, are at the same time far below the level of brute creation in character and disposition.

"For example, why not experiment on wife-beaters and cowardly street ruffians, and, one might reasonably add, on all those pseudo-humanitarians who, by their constant petitions to Parliament for the abolition of the lash, encourage every form of blackguardism and bestiality?"

This concludes the letter of correspondent No. 2, and with the sentiment in the closing paragraphs I must say I heartily agree--only I should like to add a few more people to the list.

One other case of haunting of this type is taken from my same work.

"One All Hallow E'en," wrote a Mrs. Sebuim, "I was staying with some friends in Hampstead, and we amused ourselves by working spells, to commemorate the night. There is one spell in which one walks alone down a path sowing hempseed, and repeating some fantastic words; when one is supposed to see those that are destined to come into one's life in the near future. Eager to put this spell to the test, I went into the garden by myself and, walking boldly along a path, bordered on each side by evergreens, sprinkled hempseed lavishly.

"Nothing happening, I was about to desist, when suddenly I heard a pattering on the gravel, and turning round I beheld an ugly little black-and-tan mongrel running towards me, wagging its stumpy tail. Not at all prepossessed with the creature, for my own dogs are pure-bred, and thinking it must have strayed into the grounds, I was about to drive it out, and had put down my hand to prevent it jumping on my dress, when, to my astonishment, it had vanished. It literally melted away into fine air beneath my very eyes. Not knowing what to make of the incident, but feeling inclined to attribute it to a trick of the imagination, I rejoined my friends. I did not tell them what had happened, although I made a memorandum of it in one of my innumerable notebooks. Within six months of this incident I was greatly astonished to find a dog, corresponding with the one I have just described, running about on the lawn of my house in Bath. How the animal got there was a complete mystery, and, what is stranger still, it seemed to recognize me, for it rushed towards me, frantically wagging its diminutive tail. I had not the heart to turn it away, as it seemed quite homeless, and so the forlorn little mongrel was permitted to make its home in my house--and a very happy home it proved to be. For three years all went well, and then the end came swiftly and unexpectedly. I was in Blackheath at the time, and the mongrel was in Bath. It was All Hallow E'en, but there was no hempseed sowing, for no one in the house but myself took the slightest interest in anything appertaining to the superphysical or mystic. Eleven o'clock came, and I retired to rest; my bed being one of those antique four-posters, hung with curtains that shine crimson in the ruddy glow of a cheerful fire. All my preparations complete, I had pulled back the hangings, and was about to slip in between the sheets, when, to my unbounded amazement, what should I see sitting on the counterpane but the black-and-tan mongrel. It was he right enough, there could not be another such ugly dog, though, unlike his usual self, he evinced no demonstrations of joy. On the contrary, he appeared downright miserable. His ears hung, his mouth dropped, and his bleared little eyes were watery and sad.

"Greatly perplexed, if not alarmed, at so extraordinary a phenomenon, I nevertheless felt constrained to put out my hand to comfort him--when, as I had half anticipated, he immediately vanished. Two days later I received a letter from Bath, and in a postscript I read that 'the mongrel' (we never called it by any other name) 'had been run over and killed by a motor, the accident occurring on All Hallow E'en, about eleven o'clock.' 'Of course,' my sister wrote, 'you won't mind very much--it was so extremely ugly, and--well--we were only too glad it was none of the other dogs.' But my sister was wrong, for notwithstanding its unsightly appearance and hopeless lack of breed, I had grown to like that little black-and-tan more than any of my rare and choice pets."

The following account, which concludes my notes on hauntings by dog phantasms, was sent me many years ago by a gentleman then living in Virginia, U.S.A. It runs thus:--

The Strange Disappearance of Mr. Jeremiah Dance

"Twenty pounds a year for a twelve-roomed house with large front lawn, good stabling and big kitchen gardens. That sounds all right," I commented. "But why so cheap?"

"Well," the advertiser--Mr. Baldwin by name, a short, stout gentleman, with keen, glittering eyes--replied, "Well, you see, it's a bit of a distance from the town, and--er--most people prefer being nearer--like neighbours and all that sort of thing."

"Like neighbours!" I exclaimed. "I don't. I've just seen about enough of them. Drains all right?"

"Oh, yes! Perfect."

"Water?"

"Excellent."

"Everything in good condition?"

"First rate."

"Loneliness the only thing people object to?"

"That is so."

"Then I'll oblige you to send someone to show me over the house, for I think it is just the sort of place we want. You see, after being bottled up in a theatre all the afternoon and evening, one likes to get away somewhere where it is quiet--somewhere where one can lie in bed in the morning inhaling pure air and undisturbed by street traffic."

"I understand," Mr. Baldwin responded, "but--er--it is rather late now; wouldn't you prefer to see over it in the morning? Everything looks at its worst--its very worst--in the twilight."

"Oh, I'll make allowances for the dusk," I said. "You haven't got any ghosts stowed away there, have you?" And he went off into a roar of laughter.

"No, the house is not haunted," Mr. Baldwin replied. "Not that it would much matter to you if it were, for I can see you don't believe in spooks."

"Believe in spooks!" I cried. "Not much. I would as soon believe in patent hair restorers. Let me see over it at once."

"Very well, sir. I'll take you there myself," Mr. Baldwin replied, somewhat reluctantly. "Here, Tim--fetch the keys of the Crow's Nest and tell Higgins to bring the trap round."

The boy he addressed flew, and in a few minutes the sound of wheels and the jingling of harness announced the vehicle was at the door.

Ten minutes later and I and my escort were bowling merrily over the ground in the direction of the Crow's Nest. It was early autumn, and the cool evening air, fragrant with the mellowness of the luscious Virginian pippin, was tinged also with the sadness inseparable from the demise of a long and glorious summer. Evidences of decay and death were everywhere--in the brown fallen leaves of the oaks and elms; in the bare and denuded ditches. Here a giant mill-wheel, half immersed in a dark, still pool, stood idle and silent; there a hovel, but recently inhabited by hop-pickers, was now tenantless, its glassless windows boarded over, and a wealth of dead and rotting vegetable matter in thick profusion over the tiny path and the single stone doorstep.

"Is it always as quiet and deserted as this?" I asked of my companion, who continually cracked his whip as if he liked to hear the reverberations of its echoes.

"Always," was the reply, "and sometimes more so. You ain't used to the country?"

"Not very. I want to try it by way of a change. Are you well versed in the cry of birds? What was that?"

We were fast approaching an exceedingly gloomy bit of the road where there were plantations on each side, and the trees united their fantastically forked branches overhead. I thought I had never seen so dismal-looking a spot, and a sudden lowering of the temperature made me draw my overcoat tighter round me.

"That--oh, a night bird of some sort," Mr. Baldwin replied. "An ugly sound, wasn't it? Beastly things, I can't imagine why they were created. Whoa--steady there, steady."

The horse reared as he spoke, and taking a violent plunge forward, set off at a wild gallop. A moment later, and I uttered an exclamation of astonishment. Keeping pace with us, although apparently not moving at more than an ordinary walking pace, was a man of medium height, dressed in a panama hat and albert coat. He had a thin, aquiline nose, a rather pronounced chin, was clean-shaven, and had a startlingly white complexion. By the side of him trotted two poodles, whose close-cropped skins showed out with remarkable perspicuity.

"Who the deuce is he?" I asked, raising my voice to a shout on account of the loud clatter made by the horse's hoofs and the wheels.

"Who? what?" Mr. Baldwin shouted in return.

"Why, the man walking along with us!"

"Man! I can see no man!" Mr. Baldwin growled.

I looked at him curiously. It may, of course, have been due to the terrific speed we were going, to the difficulty of holding in the horse, but his cheeks were ashy pale, and his teeth chattered.

"Do you mean to say," I cried, "that you can see no figure walking on my side of the horse and actually keeping pace with it?"

"Of course I can't," Mr. Baldwin snapped. "No more can you. It's an hallucination caused by the moonlight through the branches overhead. I've experienced it more than once."

"Then why don't you have it now?" I queried.

"Don't ask so many questions, please," Mr. Baldwin shouted. "Don't you see it is as much as I can do to hold the brute in? Heaven preserve us, we were nearly over that time."

The trap rose high in the air as he spoke, and then dropped with such a jolt that I was nearly thrown off, and only saved myself by the skin of my teeth. A few yards more the spinney ceased, and we were away out in the open country, plunging and galloping as if our very souls depended on it. From all sides queer and fantastic shadows of objects, which certainly had no material counterparts in the moon-kissed sward of the rich, ripe meadows, rose to greet us, and filled the lane with their black-and-white wavering, ethereal forms. The evening was one of wonders for which I had no name--wonders associated with an iciness that was far from agreeable. I was not at all sure which I liked best--the black, Stygian, tree-lined part of the road we had just left, or the wide ocean of brilliant moonbeams and streaked suggestions.

The figures of the man and the dogs were equally vivid in each. Though I could no longer doubt they were nothing mortal, they were altogether unlike what I had imagined ghosts. Like the generality of people who are psychic and who have never had an experience of the superphysical, my conception of a phantasm was a "thing" in white that made ridiculous groanings and still more ridiculous clankings of chains. But here was something different, something that looked--save, perhaps, for the excessive pallor of its cheeks--just like an ordinary man. I knew it was not a man, partly on account of its extraordinary performance--no man, even if running at full speed, could keep up with us like that; partly on account of the unusual nature of the atmosphere--which was altogether indefinable--it brought with it; and also because of my own sensations--my intense horror which could not, I felt certain, have been generated by anything physical.

I cogitated all this in my mind as I gazed at the figure, and in order to make sure it was no hallucination, I shut first one eye and then the other, covering them alternately with the palm of my hand. The figure, however, was still there, still pacing along at our side with the regular swing, swing of the born walker. We kept on in this fashion till we arrived at a rusty iron gate leading, by means of a weed-covered path, to a low, two-storied white house. Here the figures left us, and as it seemed to me vanished at the foot of the garden wall.

"This is the house," Mr. Baldwin panted, pulling up with the greatest difficulty, the horse evincing obvious antipathy to the iron gate. "And these are the keys. I'm afraid you must go in alone, as I dare not leave the animal even for a minute."

"Oh, all right," I said. "I don't mind, now that the ghost, or whatever you like to call it, has gone; I'm myself again."

I jumped down, and threading my way along the bramble-entangled path, reached the front door. On opening it, I hesitated. The big, old-fashioned hall, with the great, frowning staircase leading to the gallery overhead, the many open doors showing nought but bare, deserted boards within, the grim passages, all moonlit and peopled only with queer flickering shadows, suggested much that was terrifying. I fancied I heard noises, noises like stealthy footsteps moving from room to room, and tiptoeing along the passages and down the staircase. Once my heart almost stopped beating as I saw what, at first, I took to be a white face peering at me from a far recess, but which I eventually discovered was only a daub of whitewash; and, once again, my hair all but rose on end, when one of the doors at which I was looking swung open and something came forth. Oh, the horror of that moment, as long as I live I shall never forget it. The something was a cat, just a rather lean but otherwise material, black Tom; yet, in the state my nerves were then, it created almost as much horror as if it had been a ghost. Of course, it was the figure of the walking man that was the cause of all this nervousness; had it not appeared to me I should doubtless have entered the house with the utmost sang-froid, my mind set on nothing but the condition of the walls, drains, etc. As it was, I held back, and it was only after a severe mental struggle I summoned up the courage to leave the doorway and explore. Cautiously, very cautiously, with my heart in my mouth, I moved from room to room, halting every now and then in dreadful suspense as the wind, soughing through across the open land behind the house, blew down the chimneys and set the window-frames jarring. At the commencement of one of the passages I was immeasurably startled to see a dark shape poke forward, and then spring hurriedly back, and was so frightened that I dared not advance to see what it was. Moment after moment sped by, and I still stood there, the cold sweat oozing out all over me, and my eyes fixed in hideous expectation on the blank wall. What was it? What was hiding there? Would it spring out on me if I went to see? At last, urged on by a fascination I found impossible to resist, I crept down the passage, my heart throbbing painfully and my whole being overcome with the most sickly anticipations. As I drew nearer to the spot, it was as much as I could do to breathe, and my respiration came in quick jerks and gasps. Six, five, four, two feet and I was at the dreaded angle. Another step--taken after the most prodigious battle--and--NOTHING sprang out on me. I was confronted only with a large piece of paper that had come loose from the wall, and flapped backwards and forwards each time the breeze from without rustled past it. The reaction after such an agony of suspense was so great, that I leaned against the wall, and laughed till I cried. A noise, from somewhere away in the basement, calling me to myself, I went downstairs and investigated. Again a shock--this time more sudden, more acute. Pressed against the window-pane of one of the front reception-rooms was the face of a man--with corpse-like cheeks and pale, malevolent eyes. I was petrified--every drop of my blood was congealed. My tongue glued to my mouth, my arms hung helpless. I stood in the doorway and stared at it. This went on for what seemed to me an eternity. Then came a revelation. The face was not that of a ghost but of Mr. Baldwin, who, getting alarmed at my long absence, had come to look for me.

We left the premises together. All the way back to the town I thought--should I, or should I not, take the house? Seen as I had seen it, it was a ghoulish-looking place--as weird as a Paris catacomb--but then daylight makes all the difference. Viewed in the sunshine, it would be just like any other house--plain bricks and mortar. I liked the situation; it was just far enough away from a town to enable me to escape all the smoke and traffic, and near enough to make shopping easy. The only obstacles were the shadows--the strange, enigmatical shadows I had seen in the hall and passages, and the figure of the walker. Dare I take a house that knew such visitors? At first I said no, and then yes. Something, I could not tell what, urged me to say yes. I felt that a very grave issue was at stake--that a great wrong connected in some manner with the mysterious figure awaited righting, and that the hand of Fate pointed at me as the one and only person who could do it.

"Are you sure the house isn't haunted?" I demanded, as we slowly rolled away from the iron gate, and I leaned back in my seat to light my pipe.

"Haunted!" Mr. Baldwin scoffed, "why, I thought you didn't believe in ghosts--laughed at them."

"No more I do believe in them," I retorted, "but I have children, and we know how imaginative children are."

"I can't undertake to stop their imaginations."

"No, but you can tell me whether anyone else has imagined anything there. Imagination is sometimes very infectious."

"As far as I know, then, no; leastways, I have not heard tell of it."

"Who was the last tenant?"

"Mr. Jeremiah Dance."

"Why did he leave?"

"How do I know? Got tired of being there, I suppose."

"How long was he there?"

"Nearly three years."

"Where is he now?"

"That's more than I can say. Why do you wish to know?"

"Why!" I repeated. "Because it is more satisfactory to me to hear about the house from someone who has lived in it. Has he left no address?"

"Not that I know of, and it's more than two years since he was here."

"What! The house has been empty all that time?"

"Two years is not very long. Houses--even town houses--are frequently unoccupied for longer than that. I think you'll like it."

I did not speak again till the drive was over, and we drew up outside the landlord's house. I then said, "Let me have an agreement. I've made up my mind to take it. Three years and the option to stay on."

That was just like me. Whatever I did, I did on the spur of the moment, a mode of procedure that often led me into difficulties.

A month later and my wife, children, servants, and I were all ensconced in the Crow's Nest.

That was in the beginning of October. Well, the month passed by, and November was fairly in before anything remarkable happened. It then came about in this fashion.

Jennie, my eldest child, a self-willed and rather bad-tempered girl of about twelve, evading the vigilance of her mother, who had forbidden her to go out as she had a cold, ran to the gate one evening to see if I was anywhere in sight. Though barely five o'clock, the moon was high in the sky, and the shadows of the big trees had already commenced their gambols along the roadside.

Jennie clambered up the gate as children do, and peering over, suddenly espied what she took to be me, striding towards the house, at a swinging pace, and followed by two poodles.

"Poppa," she cried, "how cute of you! Only to think of you bringing home two doggies! Oh, Poppa, naughty Poppa, what will mum say?" and climbing over into the lane at imminent danger to life and limb, she tore frantically towards the figure. To her dismay, however, it was not me, but a stranger with a horribly white face and big glassy eyes which he turned down at her and stared. She was so frightened that she fainted, and some ten minutes later I found her lying out there on the road. From the description she gave me of the man and dogs, I felt quite certain they were the figures I had seen; though I pretended the man was a tramp, and assured her she would never see him again. A week passed, and I was beginning to hope nothing would happen, when one of the servants gave notice to leave.

At first she would not say why she did not like the house, but when pressed made the following statement:--

"It's haunted, Mrs. B----. I can put up with mice and beetles, but not with ghosts. I've had a queer sensation, as if water was falling down my spine, ever since I've been here, but never saw anything till last night. I was then in the kitchen getting ready to go to bed. Jane and Emma had already gone up, and I was preparing to follow them, when, all of a sudden, I heard footsteps, quick and heavy, cross the gravel and approach the window.

"'The boss,' says I to myself; 'maybe he's forgot the key and can't get in at the front door.'

"Well, I went to the window and was about to throw it open, when I got an awful shock. Pressed against the glass, looking in at me, was a face--not the boss's face, not the face of anyone living, but a horrid white thing with a drooping mouth and wide-open, glassy eyes, that had no more expression in them than a pig. As sure as I'm standing here, Mrs. B----, it was the face of a corpse--the face of a man that had died no natural death. And by its side, standing on their hind-legs, and staring in at me too were two dogs, both poodles--also no living things, but dead, horribly dead. Well, they stared at me, all three of them, for perhaps a minute, certainly not less, and then vanished. That's why I'm leaving, Mrs. B----. My heart was never overstrong. I always suffered with palpitations, and if I saw those heads again, it would kill me."

After this my wife spoke to me seriously.

"Jack," she said, "are you sure there's nothing in it? I don't think Mary would leave us without a good cause, and the description of what she saw tallies exactly with the figure that frightened Jennie. Jennie assures me she never said a word about it to the servants. They can't both have imagined it."

I did not know what to say. My conscience pricked me. Without a doubt I ought to have told my wife of my own experience in the lane, and have consulted her before taking the house. Supposing she, or any of the children, should die of fright, it would be my fault. I should never forgive myself.

"You've something on your mind! What is it?" my wife demanded.

I hesitated a moment or two and then told her. The next quarter of an hour was one I do not care to recollect, but when it was over, and she had had her say, it was decided I should make enquiries and see if there was any possible way of getting rid of the ghosts. With this end in view, I drove to the town, and after several fruitless efforts was at length introduced to a Mr. Marsden, clerk of one of the banks, who, in reply to my questions, said:

"Well, Mr. B----, it's just this way. I do know something, only--in a small place like this--one has to be so extra careful what one says. Some years ago a Mr. Jeremiah Dance occupied the Crow's Nest. He came here apparently a total stranger, and though often in the town, was only seen in the company of one person--his landlord, Mr. Baldwin, with whom--if local gossip is to be relied on--he appeared to be on terms of the greatest familiarity. Indeed, they were seldom apart, walked about the lanes arm-in-arm, visited each other's houses on alternate evenings, called each other "Teddy" and "Leslie." This state of things continued for nearly three years, and then people suddenly began to comment on the fact that Mr. Dance had gone, or at least was no longer visible. An errand-boy, returning back to town, late one evening, swore to being passed on the way by a trap containing Mr. Baldwin and Mr. Dance, who were speaking in very loud voices--just as if they were having a violent altercation. On reaching that part of the road where the trees are thickest overhead, the lad overtook them, or rather Mr. Baldwin, preparing to mount into the trap. Mr. Dance was nowhere to be seen. And from that day to this nothing has ever been heard of him. As none of his friends or relations came forward to raise enquiries, and all his bills were paid--several of them by Mr. Baldwin--no one took the matter up. Mr. Baldwin pooh-poohed the errand-boy's story, and declared that, on the night in question, he had been alone in an altogether different part of the county, and knew nothing whatever of Mr. Dance's movements, further than that he had recently announced his intention of leaving the Crow's Nest before the expiration of the three years' lease. He had not the remotest idea where he was. He claimed the furniture in payment of the rent due to him."

"Did the matter end there?" I asked.

"In one sense of the word, yes--in another, no. Within a few weeks of Dance's disappearance rumours got afloat that his ghost had been seen on the road, just where, you may say, you saw it. As a matter of fact, I've seen it myself--and so have crowds of other people."

"Has anyone ever spoken to it?"

"Yes--and it has vanished at once. I went there one night with the purpose of laying it, but, on its appearing suddenly, I confess I was so startled, that I not only forgot what I had rehearsed to say, but ran home, without uttering as much as a word."

"And what are your deductions of the case?"

"The same as everyone else's," Mr. Marsden whispered, "only, like everyone else, I dare not say."

"Had Mr. Dance any dogs?"

"Yes--two poodles, of which, much to Mr. Baldwin's annoyance (everyone noticed this), he used to make the most ridiculous fuss."

"Humph!" I observed. "That settles it! Ghosts! And to think I never believed in them before! Well, I am going to try."

"Try what?" Mr. Marsden said, a note of alarm in his voice.

"Try laying it. I have an idea I may succeed."

"I wish you luck, then. May I come with you?"

"Thanks, no!" I rejoined. "I would rather go there alone."

I said this in a well-lighted room, with the hum of a crowded thoroughfare in my ears. Twenty minutes later, when I had left all that behind, and was fast approaching the darkest part of an exceptionally dark road, I wished I had not. At the very spot, where I had previously seen the figures, I saw them now. They suddenly appeared by my side, and though I was going at a great rate--for the horse took fright--they kept easy pace with me. Twice I essayed to speak to them, but could not ejaculate a syllable through sheer horror, and it was only by nerving myself to the utmost, and forcing my eyes away from them, that I was able to stick to my seat and hold on to the reins. On and on we dashed, until trees, road, sky, universe were obliterated in one blinding whirlwind that got up my nostrils, choked my ears, and deadened me to everything, save the all-terrorizing, instinctive knowledge, that the figures by my side, were still there, stalking along as quietly and leisurely as if the horse had been going at a snail's pace.

At last, to my intense relief--for never had the ride seemed longer--I reached the Crow's Nest, and as I hurriedly dismounted from the trap, the figures shot past me and vanished. Once inside the house, and in the bosom of my family, where all was light and laughter, courage returned, and I upbraided myself bitterly for this cowardice.

I confessed to my wife, and she insisted on accompanying me the following afternoon, at twilight, to the spot where the ghost appeared to originate. To our intense dismay, we had not been there more than three or four minutes, before Dora, our youngest girl, a pretty, sweet-tempered child of eight, came running up to us with a telegram, which one of the servants had asked her to give us. My wife, snatching it from her, and reading it, was about to scold her severely, when she suddenly paused, and clutching hold of the child with one hand, pointed hysterically at something on one side of her with the other. I looked, and Dora looked, and we both saw, standing erect and staring at us, the spare figure of a man, with a ghastly white face and dull, lifeless eyes, clad in a panama hat, albert coat, and small, patent-leather boots; beside him were two glossy--abnormally glossy--poodles.

I tried to speak, but, as before, was too frightened to articulate a sound, and my wife was in the same plight. With Dora, however, it was otherwise, and she electrified us by going up to the figure, and exclaiming:

"Who are you? You must feel very ill to look so white. Tell me your name."

The figure made no reply, but gliding slowly forward, moved up to a large, isolated oak, and pointing with the index finger of its left hand at the trunk of the tree, seemingly sank into the earth and vanished from view.

For some seconds everyone was silent, and then my wife exclaimed:

"Jack, I shouldn't wonder if Dora hasn't been the means of solving the mystery. Examine the tree closely."

I did so. The tree was hollow, and inside it were three skeletons!

    *   *   *   *   *

Here followed an extract from a local paper:

"Sensational Discovery in a Wood near Marytown

"Whilst exploring in a wood, near Marytown, the other evening, a party of the name of B---- discovered three skeletons--a human being and two dogs--in the trunk of an oak. From the remnant of clothes still adhering to the human remains, the latter were proved to be those of an individual known as Mr. Jeremiah Dance, whose strange disappearance from the Crow's Nest--the house he rented in the neighbourhood--some two years ago, was the occasion of much comment. On closer examination, extraordinary to relate, the remains have been proved to be those of a WOMAN; and from certain abrasions on the skull, there is little doubt she met with a violent end."

A second extract taken from the same paper runs thus:--

"Suicide at Marytown

"Late last night Percy Baldwin, the man who is under arrest on suspicion of having caused the death of the unknown woman, whose skeleton was found on Monday in the trunk of a tree, committed suicide by hanging himself with his suspenders to the ceiling of his cell. Pinned on his coat was a slip of paper bearing these words: 'She was my wife--I loved her. She took to drink--I parted from her. She became a dog-worshipper. I killed her--and her dogs.'"

Phantasms of Living Dogs

I could quote innumerable cases of people who have either seen or heard the spirits of dead dogs. However, as space does not permit of this, I proceed to the oft-raised question, "Do animals as well as people project themselves?" My reply is--yes; according to my experience they do.

Some friends of mine have a big tabby that has frequently been seen in two places at the same time; for example, it has been observed by several people to be sitting on a chair in the dining-room, and, at the same moment, it has been seen by two or more other persons extended at full length before the kitchen fire--the latter figure proving to be its immaterial, or what some designate its astral body, which vanishes the instant an attempt is made to touch it. The only explanation of this phenomenon seems to me to lie in projection--the cat possessing the faculty of separating--in this instance, unconsciously--its spiritual from its physical body--the former travelling anywhere, regardless of space, time and material obstacles. I have often had experiences similar to this with a friend's dog. I have been seated in a room, either reading or writing, and on looking up have distinctly seen the dog lying on the carpet in front of me. A few minutes later a scraping at the door or window--both of which have been shut all the while--and on my rising to see what was there, I have discovered the dog outside! Had I not been so positive I had seen the dog on the ground in front of me, I might have thought it was an hallucination; but hallucinations are never so vivid nor so lasting--moreover, other people have had similar experiences with the same dog. And why not? Dogs, on the whole, are every whit as reasoning and reflective as the bulk of human beings! And how much nobler! Compare, for a moment, the dogs you know--no matter whether mastiffs, retrievers, dachshunds, poodles, or even Pekinese, with your acquaintances--with the people you see everywhere around you--false, greedy, spiteful, scandal-loving women, money-grubbing attorneys, lying, swindling tradesmen, vulgar parvenus, finicky curates, brutal roughs, spoilt, cruel children, hypocrites of both sexes--compare them carefully--and the comparison is entirely in favour of the dog! And if the creating Power (or Powers) has favoured these wholly selfish and degenerate human beings with spirits, and has conferred on certain of them the faculty of projecting those spirits, can one imagine, for one moment, that similar gifts have been denied to dogs--their superiors in every respect? Pshaw! Out upon it! To think so would mean to think the unthinkable, to attribute to God qualities of partiality, injustice and whimsicality, which would render Him little, if anything, better than a James the Second of England, or a Louis the Fifteenth of France.

Besides, from my own experience, and the experiences of those with whom I have been brought in contact, I can safely affirm that there are phantasms (and therefore spirits) of both living and dead dogs in just the same proportion as there are phantasms (and therefore spirits) of both living and dead human beings.

Psychic Properties of Dogs

Some, not all, dogs--like cats--possess the psychic property of scenting the advent of death, and they indicate their fear of it by the most dismal howling. In my opinion there is very little doubt that dogs actually see some kind of phantasm that, knowing when death is about to take place, visits the house of the doomed and stands beside his, or her, couch. I have had this phantasm described to me, by those who declare they have seen it, as a very tall, hooded figure, clad in a dark, loose, flowing costume--its face never discernible. It would, of course, be foolish to say that a dog howling in a house is invariably the sign of death; there are many other and obvious causes which produce something of a similar effect; but I think one may be pretty well assured that, when the howling is accompanied by unmistakable signs of terror, then someone, either in the house at the time, or connected with someone in the house, will shortly die.

Dogs in Haunted Houses

When I investigate a haunted house, I generally take a dog with me, because experience has taught me that a dog seldom fails to give notice, in some way or another--either by whining, or growling, or crouching shivering at one's feet, or springing on one's lap and trying to bury its head in one's coat--of the proximity of a ghost. I had a dog with me, when ghost-hunting, not so very long ago, in a well-known haunted house in Gloucestershire. The dog--my only companion--and I sat on the staircase leading from the hall to the first floor. Just about two o'clock the dog gave a loud growl. I put my hand out and found it was shivering from head to foot. Almost directly afterwards I heard the loud clatter of fire-irons from some-where away in the basement, a door banged, and then something, or someone, began to ascend the stairs. Up, up, up came the footsteps, until I could see--first of all a bluish light, then the top of a head, then a face, white and luminous, staring up at me. A few more steps, and the whole thing was disclosed to view. It was the figure of a girl of about sixteen, with a shock head of red hair, on which was stuck, all awry, a dirty little, old-fashioned servant's cap. She was clad in a cotton dress, soiled and bedraggled, and had on her feet a pair of elastic-sided boots, that looked as if they would fall to pieces each step she took. But it was her face that riveted my attention most. It was startlingly white and full of an expression of the most hopeless misery. The eyes, wide open and glassy, were turned direct on mine. I was too appalled either to stir or utter a sound. The phantasm came right up to where I stood, paused for a second, and then slowly went on; up, up, up, until a sudden bend in the staircase hid it from view. For some seconds there was a continuation of the footsteps, then there came a loud splash from somewhere outside and below--and then silence--sepulchral and omnipotent.

I did not wait to see if anything further would happen. I fled, and Dick, my dog friend, who was apparently even more frightened than I, fled with me. We arrived home--panic-stricken.

Over and over again, on similar occasions, I have had a dog with me, and the same thing has occurred--the dog has made some noise indicative of great fear, re-maining in a state of stupor during the actual presence of the apparition.

Psychic Propensities of Dogs compared with those of Cats

Though dogs are, perhaps, rather more alarmed at the Unknown than cats, I do not think they have a keener sense of its proximity. Still, for the very reason that they show greater--more unmistakable--indications of fear, they make surer psychic barometers. The psychic faculty of scent in dogs would seem to be more limited than that in cats; for, whereas cats can not only detect the advent and presence of pleasant and unpleasant phantoms by their smells, few dogs can do more than detect the approach of death. Dogs make friends nearly, if not quite, as readily with cruel and brutal people as with kind ones, simply because they cannot, so easily as cats, distinguish by their scent the unpleasant types of spirits cruel and brutal people attract; in all probability, they are not even aware of the presence of such spirits.

It would seem, on the face of it, that since dogs are, on the whole, of a gentler disposition than cats, that is to say, not quite so cruel and savage, the phantasms of dogs would be less likely to be earth-bound than those of cats; but, then, one must take into consideration the other qualities of the two animals, and when these are put in the balance, one may find little to choose--morally--between the cat and the dog. Anyhow, after making allowance for the fact that many more cats die unnatural deaths than dogs, there would seem to be small numerical difference in their hauntings--cases of dog ghosts appearing to be just as common as cases of cat ghosts.

Apropos of phantom dogs, my friend Dr. G. West writes to me thus:--

"Of the older English Universities many stories are told of bizarre happenings,--of duels, raggings, suicides and such-like--in olden times; but of K., venerable, illustrious K. of Ireland, few and far between are the accounts of similar occurrences. This is one, however, and it deals with the phantom of a dog:--

"One evening, towards the end of the eighteenth century, John Kelly, a Dean of the College (extremely unpopular on account of his supposed harsh treatment of some of the undergraduates), was about to commence his supper, when he heard a low whine, and looking down, saw a large yellow dog cross the floor in front of him, and disappear immediately under the full-length portrait that hung over the antique chimney-piece. Something prompting him, he glanced at the picture. The eyes that looked into his blinked.

"'It must be the result of an overtaxed brain,' he said to himself. 'Those rascally undergraduates have got on my nerves.'

"He shut his eyes; and re-opening them, stared hard at the portrait. It was not a delusion. The eyes that gazed back at him were alive--alive with the spirit of mockery; they smiled, laughed, jeered; and, as they did so, the knowledge of his surroundings was brought forcibly home to him. The room in which he was seated was situated at the end of a long, cheerless, stone passage in the western wing of the College. Away from all the other rooms of the building, it was absolutely isolated; and had long borne the reputation of being haunted by a dog, which was said to appear only before some catastrophe. The Dean had hitherto committed the story to the category of fables. But now,--now, as he sat all alone in that big silent room, lit only with the reddish rays of a fast-setting August sun, and stared into the gleaming eyes before him--he was obliged to admit the extreme probability of spookdom. Never before had the College seemed so quiet. Not a sound--not even the creaking of a board or the far-away laugh of a student, common enough noises on most nights--fell on his ears. The hush was omnipotent, depressing, unnerving; he could only associate it with the supernatural. Though he was too fascinated to remove his gaze from the thing before him, he could feel the room fill with shadows, and feel them steal through the half-open windows, and, uniting with those already in the corners, glide noiselessly and surreptitiously towards him. He felt, too, that he was under the surveillance of countless invisible visages, all scanning him curiously, and delighted beyond measure at the sight of his terror.

"The moments passed in a breathless state of tension. He stared at the eyes, and the eyes stared back at him. Once he endeavoured to rise, but a dead weight seemed to fall on his shoulders and hold him back; and twice, when he tried to speak--to make some sound, no matter what, to break the appalling silence--his throat closed as if under the pressure of cruel, relentless fingers.

"But the Ultima Thule of his emotions had yet to come. There was a slight stir behind the canvas, a thud, a hollow groan that echoed and re-echoed throughout the room like the muffled clap of distant thunder, and the eyes suddenly underwent a metamorphosis--they grew glazed and glassy like the eyes of a dead person. A cold shudder ran through the Dean, his hair stood on end, his blood turned to ice. Again he essayed to move, to summon help; again he failed. The strain on his nerves proved more than he could bear. A sudden sensation of nausea surged through him; his eyes swam; his brain reeled; there was a loud buzzing in his ears; he knew no more. Some moments later one of the College servants arrived at the door with a bundle of letters, and on receiving no reply to his raps, entered.

"'Good heavens! What's the matter?' he cried, gazing at the figure of the Dean, lolling head downward on the table. 'Merciful Prudence, the gentleman is dead! No, he ain't--some of the young gents will be sorry enough for that--he's fainted.'

"The good fellow poured out some water in a tumbler, and was proceeding to sprinkle the Dean's face with it, when, a noise attracting his attention, he peered round at the picture. It was bulging from the wall; it was falling! And, Good God, what was that that was falling with it--that huge black object? A coffin? No, not a coffin, but a corpse! The servant ran to the door shrieking, and, in less than a minute, passage and room were filled to overflowing with a scared crowd of enquiring officials and undergraduates.

"'What has happened? What's the matter with the Dean? Has he had a fit, or what? And the picture? And--Anderson? Anderson lying on the floor! Hurt? No, not hurt, dead! Murdered!'

"In an instant there was silence, and the white-faced throng closed in on one another as if for protection. In front of them, beside the fallen picture, lay the body of the most gay and popular student in the College--Bob Anderson--Bob Anderson with a stream of blood running from a deep incision in his back made with some sharp instrument, that had been driven home with tremendous force. He had, without doubt, been murdered. But by whom? Then one of the undergraduates, a bright, boyish, fair-haired giant, named O'Farroll, immensely popular both on account of his prowess in sport and an untold number of the most audacious escapades, spoke out:

"'I saw Anderson, about an hour ago, crossing the quadrangle. I asked him where he was going, and he replied, "To old Kelly. I intend paying him out for 'gating' me last week." I enquired how, and he replied: "I've a glorious plan. You know that portrait stuck over his mantel-shelf? Well! In poking about the room the other day, when the old man was out, I had a great find. Directly behind the picture is the door of a secret room, so neatly covered by the designs on the wall that it is not discernible. It was only by the merest fluke I discovered it. I was taking down the picture with the idea of "touching up" the face, when my knuckles bumped against the panels of the wall, touched a spring, and the door flew open, revealing an apartment about six by eight feet large. I at once explored it, and found it could be entered by the chimney. An idea then struck me--I would play a trick upon the Dean by hiding in this secret chamber one evening while he was feeding, cutting out the eyes of the portrait, and peering through the cavities at him. And this,' O'Farroll continued, pointing at the fallen picture, 'is what he evidently did after I left him. You can see the eyes of the portrait have been removed.'

"'That is so, shure,' one of the other undergraduates, Mick Maguire--six feet two in his socks, every inch--exclaimed. 'And, what is more, I knew all about it. Anderson told me yesterday what he was going to do, and I wanted to join him, but he said I would never get up the chimney, I would stick there. And, bedad, I think he was right.'

"At this remark, despite the grimness of the moment, several of those present laughed.

"'Come, come, gentlemen!' one of the officials cried, 'this is no time for levity. Mr. Anderson has been murdered, and the question is--by whom?'

"'Then, if that's the only thing that is troubling you,' O'Farroll put in, 'I fancy the solution is right here at hand,' and he looked significantly at the Dean.

"An ominous silence followed, during which all eyes were fixed on John Kelly, some anxiously, some merely enquiringly, but not a few angrily, for Kelly, as I have said before, had made himself particularly obnoxious just then by his behaviour to the rowdier students; and, as has ever been the case at K., these formed no small portion of the community.

"The Dean hardly seemed to realize the situation. The dignity of office blinded him to danger.

"'What do you mean?' he spluttered. 'I know nothing of what happened to Mr. Anderson! Really, really, O'Farroll, your presumption is preposterous.'

"'There was no one else in here but you and he, Mr. Kelly,' O'Farroll retorted coolly. 'It's only natural we should think you know something of what happened!'

"On the arrival of the police who had been sent for somewhat reluctantly-- for the prestige of the College at that date was very dear to all--the premises were thoroughly searched, and, no other culprit being found, first of all Dean Kelly was apprehended, and then, to make a good job of it, his accuser, Denis O'Farroll.

"All the College was agog with excitement. No one could believe the Dean was a murderer; and it was just as inconceivable to think O'Farroll had committed the deed. And yet if neither of them had killed Anderson, who in God's name had killed him?

"The night succeeding the affair, whilst the Dean and O'Farroll were still in jail awaiting the inquest, a party of undergraduates were discussing the situation in Maguire's rooms, when the door burst open, and into their midst, almost breathless with excitement, came a measly, bespectacled youth named Brady--Patrick Brady.

"'I'm awfully sorry to disturb you fellows,' he stammered, 'but there have been odd noises just outside my room all the evening, and I've just seen a queer kind of dog, that vanished, God knows how. I--I--well, you will call me an ass, of course, but I'm afraid to stay there alone, and that's the long and short of it.'

"'Begorra!' Maguire exclaimed, 'it can't be poor Bob's ghost already! What sort of noises were they?'

"'Noises like laughter!' Brady said. 'Loud peals of horrid laughter.'

"'Someone trying to frighten you,' one of the undergrads observed, 'and faith, he succeeded. You are twice as white as any sheet.'

"'It's ill-timed mirth, anyhow,' someone else put in, 'with Anderson's dead body upstairs. I'm for making an example of the blackguard.'

"'And I,'--'And I,' the others echoed.

"A general movement followed, and headed by Brady the procession moved to the north wing of the College. At that time, be it remembered, a large proportion of K. undergrads were in residence--now it is otherwise. On reaching Brady's rooms the crowd halted outside and listened. For some time there was silence; and then a laugh--low, monotonous, unmirthful, metallic--coming as it were from some adjacent chamber, and so unnatural, so abhorring, that it held everyone spell-bound. It died away in the reverberations of the stone corridor, its echoes seeming to awake a chorus of other laughs hardly less dreadful. Again there was silence, no one daring to express his thoughts. Then, as if by common consent, all turned precipitately into Brady's room and slammed the door.

"'That is what I heard,' Brady said. 'What does it mean?'

"'Is it the meaning of it you're wanting to know?' Maguire observed. 'Sure 'tis the devil, for no one but him could make such a noise. I've never heard the like of it before. Who has the rooms on either side of you?'

"'These?' Brady replied, pointing to the right. 'No one. They were vacated at Easter, and are being repainted and decorated. These on the left--Dobson, who is,

I happen to know, at the present moment in Co. Mayo. He won't be back till next week.'

"'Then we can search them,' a student called Hartnoll intervened.

"'To be sure we can,' Brady replied, 'but I doubt if you'll find anyone.'

"A search was made, and Brady proved to be correct. Not a vestige of anyone was discovered.

"Much mystified, Maguire's party was preparing to depart, when Hartnoll, who had taken the keenest interest in the proceedings, suddenly said, 'Who has the rooms over yours, Brady? Sound, as you know, plays curious tricks, and it is just as likely as not that laugh came from above.'

"'Oh, I don't think so,' Brady answered. 'The man overhead is Belton, a very decent sort. He is going in for his finals shortly, and is sweating fearfully hard at present. We might certainly ask him if he heard the noise.'

"The students agreeing, Brady led the way upstairs, and in response to their summons Belton hastily opened the door. He was a typical book-worm--thin, pale and rather emaciated, but with a pleasant expression in his eyes and mouth, that all felt was assuring.

"'Hulloa!' he exclaimed, 'it isn't often I'm favoured with a surprise party of this sort. Come in'; and he pressed them so hard that they felt constrained to accept his hospitality, and before long were all seated round the fire, quaffing whisky and puffing cigars as if they meant to make a night of it. At two o'clock someone suggested that it was high time they thought of bed, and Belton rose with them.

"'Before we turn in, let's have another search,' he said. 'It's strange you should all hear that noise except me--unless, of course, it came from below.'

"'But there's nothing under me,' Brady remarked, 'except the Dining Hall.'

"'Then let's search that,' Belton went on. 'We ought to make a thorough job of it now we've once begun. Besides, I don't relish being in this lonely place with that laugh "knocking" around, any more than you do.'

"He went with them, and they completely overhauled the ground floor--hall, dining-room, studies, passages, vestibules, everywhere that was not barred to them; but they were no wiser at the end of their search than at the beginning; there was not the slightest clue as to the author of the laugh.

    *   *   *   *   *

"On the morrow there was a fresh shock. One of the College servants, on entering Mr. Maguire's rooms to call him, found that gentleman half dressed and lying on the floor.

"Terrified beyond measure, the servant bent over him and discovered he was dead, obviously stabbed with the same weapon that had put an end to Bob Anderson.

"The factotum at once gave the alarm. Everyone in the College came trooping to the room, and for the second time within three days a general hue and cry was raised. All, again, to no purpose--the murderer had left no traces as to his identity. However, one thing at least was established, and that was the innocence of Dean Kelly and Denis O'Farroll. They were both liberated.

"Then Hartnoll, who seems to have been a regular Sherlock Holmes, got to work in grim earnest. On the floor in Maguire's room he picked up a diminutive silver-topped pencil, which had rolled under the fender and had so escaped observation. He asked several of Maguire's most intimate friends if they remembered seeing the pencil-case in Maguire's possession, but they shook their heads. He enquired in other quarters, too, but with no better result, and finally resolved to ask Brady, who belonged to quite a different set from himself. With that object in view he set off to Brady's room shortly after supper. As there was no response to his raps, he at length opened Brady's door. In front of the hearth in a big easy chair sat a figure.

"'Brady, by all that's holy,' Hartnoll exclaimed. 'By Jupiter, the beggar's asleep. That's what comes of swotting too hard! Brady!'

"Approaching the chair he called again, 'Brady!' and getting no reply, patted the figure gently on the back.

"'Be jabbers, you sleep soundly, old fellow!' he said. 'How about that!' and he shook him heartily by the shoulder. The instant he let go the figure collapsed. In order to get a closer view Hartnoll then struck a light with the tinder box.

"The flickering of the candle flame fell on Brady's face. It was white--ghastly white; there was no animation in it; the jaw dropped.

"With a cry of horror Hartnoll sprang back, and as he did so a great yellow dog dashed across the hearth in front of him, whilst from somewhere close at hand came a laugh--long, low and satirical. A cold terror gripped Hartnoll, and for a moment or so he was on the verge of fainting. However, hearing voices in the quadrangle, he pulled himself together, approached the window on tiptoe, and, peering through the glass, perceived to his utmost joy two of his friends directly beneath him. 'I say, you fellows,' he called in low tones, 'come up here quickly--Brady's rooms. I've seen the phantom dog. There's been another tragedy, and the murderer is close at hand. Come quietly and we may catch him!'

"He then retraced his steps to the centre of the room and listened. Again there came the laugh--subtle, protracted, hellish--and it seemed to him as if it must originate in the room overhead.

"A noise in the direction of the hearth made him look round. Some loose plaster had fallen, and whilst he still gazed, more fell. The truth of the whole thing then dawned on him. The murderer was in the chimney.

"Hartnoll was a creature of impulse. In the excitement of the moment he forgot danger, and the dastardly nature of the crimes gave him more than his usual amount of courage. He rushed at the chimney, and, regardless of soot and darkness, began an impromptu ascent.

"Half-way up something struck him--once, twice, thrice,--sharply, and there was a soft, malevolent chuckle.

"At this juncture the two undergraduates arrived in Brady's room. No one was there--nothing save a hunched-up figure on a chair.

"'Hartnoll!' they whispered. 'Hartnoll!' No reply. They called again--still no reply. Again and again they called, until at length, through sheer fatigue, they desisted, and seized with a sudden panic fled precipitately downstairs and out into the quadrangle.

"Once more the alarm was given, and once again the whole College, wild with excitement, hastened to the scene of the outrage.

"This time there was a double mystery. Brady had been murdered--Hartnoll had disappeared. The police were summoned and the whole building ransacked; but no one thought of the chimney till the search was nearly over, and half the throng--overcome with fatigue--had retired. O'Farroll was the discoverer. Happening to glance at the hearth he saw something drop.

"'For Heaven's sake, you fellows!' he shouted. 'Look! Blood! You may take it from me there's a corpse in the chimney.'

"A dozen candles invaded the hearth, and a herculean policeman undertook the ascent. In breathless silence the crowd below waited, and, after a few seconds of intense suspense, two helpless legs appeared on the hob. Bit by bit, the rest of the body followed, until, at length, the whole figure of Hartnoll, black, bleeding, bloodstained, was disclosed to view.

"At first it was thought that he was dead; but the surgeon who had hurried to the scene pronouncing him still alive, there arose a tremendous cheer. The murderer had at all events been foiled this time.

"'Begorrah!' cried O'Farroll, 'Hartnoll was after the murderer when he was struck, and shure I'll be after him the same way myself.' And before anyone could prevent him O'Farroll was up the chimney. Up, up, up, until he found himself going down, down, down; and then--bedad--he stepped right out on to the floor of Belton's room.

"'Hulloa!' the latter exclaimed, looking not a bit disconcerted, 'that's a curious mode of making your entrance into my domain! Why didn't you come by the door?'

"'Because,' O'Farroll replied, pointing to a patch of soot near the washstand, 'I followed you. Own up, Dicky Belton. You're the culprit--you did for them all.' And Belton laughed.

            *   *   *   *   *

"Yes, it was true; overwork had turned Belton's brain, and he was subsequently sent to a Criminal Lunatic Asylum for the rest of his life. But there were moments when he was comparatively sane, and in these interims he confessed everything. Anderson had told him that he was going to hoax the Dean, and filled with indignation at the idea of such a trick being played on a College official--for he, Belton, was a great favourite with the 'Beaks'--he had accompanied Anderson on the plea of helping him, intending, in reality, to frustrate him. It was not till he was in the chimney, crouching behind Anderson, that the thought of killing his fellow-students had entered his mind. The heat of his hiding-place, acting on an already overworked brain, hastened on the madness; and his fingers closing on a clasped knife in one of his pockets, inspired him with a desire to kill.

"The work once begun, he had argued with himself, would have to be continued, and he had then and there decided that all unruly undergraduates should be exterminated.

"With what measure of success this determination was carried out need not be recapitulated here; but with regard to the phantom dog a few words may be added. Since it appeared immediately before the committal of each of the three murders I have just recorded (it was seen by Mr. Kelly before the death of Bob Anderson; by Brady, before the murder of Maguire; and by Hartnoll, before Brady was murdered), I think there can neither be doubts as to its existence nor as to the purport of its visits.

"Moreover, its latest appearance in the University, reported to me quite recently, preceded a serious outbreak of fire."

National Ghosts in the form of Dogs

One of the most notorious dog ghosts is the Gwyllgi in Wales. This apparition, which is of a particularly terrifying appearance, chiefly haunts the lane leading from Mousiad to Lisworney Crossways.

Belief in a spectral dog, however, is common all over the British Isles. The apparition does not belong to any one breed, but appears equally often as a hound, setter, terrier, shepherd dog, Newfoundland and retriever. In Lancashire it is called the "Trash" or "Striker"; Trash, because the sound of its tread is thought to resemble a person walking along a miry, sloppy road, with heavy shoes; Striker, because it is said to utter a curious screech which may be taken as a warning of the approaching death of some relative or friend. When followed the phantom retreats, glaring at its pursuer, and either sinks into the ground with a harrowing shriek, or disappears in some equally mysterious manner.

In Norfolk and Cambridgeshire this spectre is named the "Shuck," the local name for Shag--and is reported to haunt churchyards and other dreary spots.

In the parish of Overstrand, there used to be a lane called "Shuck's Lane," named after this phantasm.

Round about Leeds the spectre dog is called "Padfoot," and is about the size of a donkey, with shaggy hair and large eyes like saucers. My friend Mr. Barker tells me there was, at one time, a ghost in the Hebrides called the Lamper, which was like a very big, white dog with no tail. It ran sometimes straight ahead, but usually in circles, and to see it was a prognostication of death. Mr. Barker, going home by the sea-coast, saw the Lamper in the hedge. He struck at it, and his stick passed right through it. The Lamper rushed away, whining and howling alternately, and disappeared. Mr. Barker was so scared that he ran all the way home. On the morrow, he learned of his father's death.

In Northumberland, Durham, and various parts of Yorkshire, the ghost-dog, which is firmly believed in, is styled Barguest, Bahrgeist, or Boguest; whilst in Lancashire it is termed the Boggart. Its most common form in these counties is a large, black dog with flaming eyes; and its appearance is a certain prognostication of death.

According to tradition there was once a "Barguest" in a glen between Darlington and Houghton, near Throstlenest. Another haunted a piece of waste land above a spring called the Oxwells, between Wreghorn and Headingley Hill, near Leeds. On the death of any person of local importance in the neighbourhood the creature would come forth, followed by all the other dogs, barking and howling. (Henderson refers to these hauntings in his Folk-lore of Northern Counties.)

Another form of this animal spectre is the Capelthwaite, which, according to common report, had the power of appearing in the form of any quadruped, but usually chose that of a large, black dog.

"The Mauthe Doog"

One of the most famous canine apparitions is that of the "Mauthe Doog," once said--and, I believe, still said--to haunt Peel Castle, Isle of Man.

Its favourite place, so I am told, was the guard-chamber, where it used to crouch by the fireside. The sentry, so the story runs, got so accustomed to seeing it, that they ceased to be afraid; but, as they believed it to be of evil origin, waiting for an opportunity to seize them, they were very particular what they said or did, and refrained from swearing in its presence. The Mauthe Doog used to come out and return by the passage through the church, by which the sentry on duty had to go to deliver the keys every night to the captain. These men, however, were far too nervous to go alone, and were invariably accompanied by one of the retainers. On one occasion, however, one of the sentinels, in a fit of drunken bravado, swore he was afraid of nothing, and insisted on going alone. His comrades tried to dissuade him, upon which he became abusive, cursed the Mauthe Doog, and said he would d----d well strike it. An hour later, he returned absolutely mad with horror, and speechless; nor could he even make signs, whereby his friends could understand what had happened to him. He died soon after--his features distorted--in violent agony. After this the apparition was never seen again.

As to what class of spirits the spectre dog belongs, that is impossible to say. At the most we can only surmise, and I should think the chances of its being the actual phantasm of some dead dog or an elemental are about equal. It is probably sometimes the one and sometimes the other; and its origin is very possibly like that of the Banshee.

Spectral Hounds

As with the spectre dog, so with packs of hounds, stories of them come from all parts of the country.

Gervase of Tilbury states that as long ago as the thirteenth century a pack of spectral hounds was frequently witnessed, on nights when the moon was full, scampering across forest and downs. In the twelfth century the pack was known as "the Herlething" and haunted, chiefly, the banks of the Wye.

Roby, in his Traditions of Lancashire; Hardwick, in his Traditions, Superstitions, and Folk-lore; Homerton, in his Isles of Loch Awe; Wirt Sykes, in his British Goblins; Sir Walter Scott, and others, all refer to them. In the North of England they are known as "Gabriel's Hounds"; in Devon as the "Wisk," "Yesk," "Yeth," or "Heath Hounds"; in Wales as the "Cwn Annwn" or "Cyn y Wybr"; in Cornwall as the "Devil and his Dandy-Dogs"; and in the neighbourhood of Leeds as the "Gabble Retchets." They are common all over the Continent. In appearance they are usually described as monstrous, human-headed dogs, black, with fiery eyes and teeth, and sprinkled all over with blood. They make a great howling noise, which is very shrill and mournful, and appear to be in hot pursuit of some unseen quarry. When they approach a house, it may be taken as a certain sign someone in that house will die very shortly.

According to Mr. Roby, a spectre huntsman known by the name Gabriel Ratchets, accompanied by a pack of phantom hounds, is said to hunt a milk-white doe round the Eagle's Crag in the Vale of Todmorden every All Hallows Eve.

These hounds were also seen in Norfolk. A famous ecclesiast, when on his way to the coast, was forced to spend the night in the King's Lynn Inn, owing to a violent snowstorm. Retiring to bed directly after supper, he tried to forget his disappointment in reading a volume of sermons he had bought at a second-hand shop in Bury St. Edmunds.

"I think I can use this one," he said to himself. "It will do nicely for the people of Aylesham. They are so steeped in hypocrisy that nothing short of violent denunciation will bring it home to them. This I think, however, will pierce even their skins."

A sudden noise made him spring up.

"Hounds!" he exclaimed. "And at this time of night! Good heavens!"

He flew to the window, and there, careering through the yard, baying as they ran, were, at least, fifty luminous, white hounds. Instead of leaping the stone wall, they passed right through it, and the bishop then realized that they were Gabriel Hounds. The following evening he received tidings of his son's--his only son's--death.

I have heard that the "Yeth Hounds" were seen, not so long ago, in a parish in Yorkshire by an old poacher called Barnes. Barnes was walking in the fields one night, when he suddenly heard the baying of the hounds, and the hoarse shouts of the huntsman. The next moment the whole pack hove in view and tore past him so close that he received a cut from "the whip" on his leg. To his surprise, however, it did not hurt him, it only felt icy cold. He then knew that he had seen the "Yeth Hounds."

A Spectral Pack of Hounds in Russia

A gentleman of the name of Rappaport whom I once met in Southampton told me of an experience he had once had with a spectral pack of hounds on the slope of the Urals. "It was about half-past eleven one winter's night," he said, "and I was driving through a thick forest, when my coachman suddenly leaned back in his seat and called out, 'Do you hear that?' I listened, and from afar came a plaintive, whining sound. 'It's not Volki, is it?' I asked. 'I'm afraid so, master,' the coachman replied, 'they're coming on after us.'

"'But they are some way off still!' I said.

"'That is so,' he responded, 'but wolves run quick, and our horses are tired. If we can reach the lake first we shall be all right, but should they overtake us before we get there--' and he shrugged his great shoulders suggestively. 'Not another word,' I cried. 'Drive--drive as if 'twere the devil himself. I have my rifle ready, and will shoot the first wolf that shows itself.'

"'Very good, master,' he answered. 'I will do everything that can be done to save your skin and mine.' He cracked his whip, and away flew the horses at a break-neck speed. But fast as they went, they could not outstrip the sound of the howling, which gradually drew nearer and nearer, until around the curve we had just passed shot into view a huge gaunt wolf. I raised my rifle and fired. The beast fell, but another instantly took its place, and then another and another, till the whole pack came into sight, and close behind us was an ocean of white, tossing, foam-flecked jaws and red gleaming eyes.

"I emptied my rifle into them as fast as I could pull the trigger, but it only checked them momentarily. A few snaps, and of their wounded brethren there was nothing left but a pile of glistening bones. Then, hie away, and they were once again in red-hot pursuit. At last our pace slackened, and still I could see no signs of the lake. A great grey shape, followed by others, then rushed by us and tried to reach the horses' flanks with their sharp, gleaming teeth. A few more seconds, and I knew we should be both fighting, back to back, the last great fight for existence. Indeed I had ceased firing, and was already beginning to strike out furiously with the butt end of my rifle, when a new sound arrested my attention. The baying of dogs! 'Dogs!' I screamed, 'Dogs, Ivan!' (that was the coachman's name) 'Dogs!' and, in my mad joy, I brained two wolves in as many blows. The next moment a large pack of enormous white hounds came racing down on us. The wolves did not wait to dispute the field; they all turned tail and, with loud howls of terror, rushed off in the direction they had come. On came the hounds--more beautiful dogs I had never seen; as they swept by, more than one brushed against my knees, though I could feel nothing save intense cold. When they were about twenty yards ahead of us, they slowed down, and maintained that distance in front of us till we arrived on the shores of the lake. There they halted, and throwing back their heads, bayed as if in farewell, and suddenly vanished. We knew then that they were no earthly hounds, but spirit ones, sent by a merciful Providence to save us from a cruel death."

CHAPTER III
HORSES AND THE UNKNOWN

As in my chapters on cats and dogs, I will preface this chapter on horses with instances of alleged haunted localities.

I take my first case from Mr. W.T. Stead's Real Ghost Stories, published in 1891. It is called "A Weird Story from the Indian Hills," and Mr. Stead preludes it thus: The "tale is told by General Barter, C.B., of Careystown, Whitegate, Co. Cork. At the time he witnessed the spectral cavalcade he was living on the hills in India, and when one evening he was returning home he caught sight of a rider and attendants coming towards him. The rest of the story, given in the General's own words, is as follows:--

"At this time the two dogs came, and, crouching at my side, gave low, frightened whimpers. The moon was at the full--a tropical moon--so bright that you could see to read a newspaper by its light, and--I saw the party before me advance as plainly as it were noon day. They were above me some eight or ten feet on the bridle-road, the earth thrown down from which sloped to within a pace or two of my feet. On the party came, until almost in front of me, and now I had better describe them. The rider was in full dinner dress, with white waistcoat, and wearing a tall chimney-pot hat, and he sat a powerful hill pony (dark brown, with mane and tail) in a listless sort of way, the reins hanging loosely from both hands. A Syce led the pony on each side, but their faces I could not see, the one next to me having his back to me and the one farthest off being hidden by the pony's head. Each held the bridle close by the bit, the man next me with his right and the other with his left hand, and the hands were on the thighs of the rider, as if to steady him in his seat. As they approached, I knowing they could not get to any place other than my own, called out in Hindustani, 'Quon hai?' (Who is it?). There was no answer, and on they came until right in front of me, when I said, in English, 'Hullo, what the d----l do you want here?' Instantly the group came to a halt, the rider gathering the bridle reins up in both hands, turned his face, which had hitherto been looking away from me, towards me, and looked down upon me. The group was still as in a tableau, with the bright moon shining upon it, and I at once recognized the rider as Lieutenant B., whom I had formerly known. The face, however, was different from what it used to be; in the place of being clean-shaven, as when I used to know it, it was now surrounded by a fringe (what used to be known as a Newgate fringe), and it was the face of a dead man, the ghastly waxen pallor of it brought out more distinctly in the moonlight by the dark fringe of hair by which it was encircled; the body, too, was much stouter than when I had known it in life.

"I marked this in a moment; and then resolved to lay hold of the thing, whatever it might be. I dashed up the bank, and the earth which had been thrown on the side giving under my feet, I fell forward up the bank on my hands, recovering myself instantly. I gained the road, and stood in the exact spot where the group had been, but which was now vacant, there was not the trace of anything; it was impossible for them to go on, the road stopped at a precipice about twenty yards further on, and it was impossible to turn and go back in a second. All this flashed through my mind, and I then ran along the road for about 100 yards, along which they had come, until I had to stop for want of breath, but there was no trace of anything, and not a sound to be heard. I then returned home, where I found my dogs, who, on all other occasions my most faithful companions, had not come with me along the road.

"Next morning I went up to D., who belonged to the same regiment as B., and gradually induced him to talk of him. I said, 'How very stout he had become lately, and what possessed him to allow his beard to grow with that horrid fringe?' D. replied, 'Yes, he became very bloated before his death. You know he led a very fast life, and while on the sick list he allowed the fringe to grow, in spite of all that we could say to him, and I believe he was buried with it.' I asked him where he got the pony I had seen, describing it minutely. 'Why,' said D., 'how do you know anything about all this? You hadn't seen B. for two or three years, and the pony you never saw. He bought him at Peshawur, and killed him one day riding in his reckless fashion down the hill to Trete.' I then told him what I had seen the night before.

"Once, when the galloping sound was very distinct, I rushed to the door of my house. There I found my Hindoo bearer, standing with a tattie in his hand. I asked him what he was there for. He said that there came a sound of riding down the hill, and 'passed him like a typhoon,' and went round the corner of the house, and he was determined to waylay it, whatever it was."

In commenting on the case, Mr. Stead remarks, "That such a story as this, gravely told by a British General in the present day, helps us to understand how our ancestors came to believe in the wonderful story of Herne the Hunter." I do not know about Herne the Hunter, but it is at all events good testimony that horses as well as men have spirits, for one of the ghosts the General saw was, undoubtedly, that of the pony murdered by B. Why it was still ridden by the phantom of its former master is another question.

The next case I narrate is also taken from Mr. Stead's same work. It was sent him by one of the leading townsmen of Cowes, in the Isle of Wight, and runs thus:--

"On a fine evening in April, 1859, the writer was riding with a friend on a country road. Twilight was closing down on us, when, after a silence of some minutes, my friend suddenly exclaimed:

"'No man knows me better than you do, J. Do you think I am a nervous, easily frightened sort of man?'

"'Far from it,' said I, 'among all the men I know in the wild country I have lived and worked in, I know none more fearless or of more unhesitating nerve.'

"'Well,' said he, 'I think I am that, too, and though I have travelled these roads all sorts of hours, summer and winter, for twenty years, I never met anything to startle me, or that I could not account for, until last Monday evening. About this time it was. Riding old Fan' (a chestnut mare) 'here on this cross-' (a four-way cross) 'road, on my near side was a man on a grey horse, coming from this left-hand road. I had to pull my off-rein to give myself room to pass ahead of him; he was coming at a right angle to me. As I passed the head of the horse I called out "Good night." Hearing no reply, I turned in my saddle to the off-side, to see whether he appeared to be asleep as he rode, but to my surprise I saw neither man nor horse. So sure was I that I had seen such, that I wheeled old Fan round, and rode back to the middle of the cross, and on neither of the four roads could I see a man or horse, though there was light enough to see two hundred or three hundred yards, as we can now. Well, I then rode over that gate' (a gate at one corner opening into a grass field), 'thinking he might have gone that way; looking down by each hedge, I could see nothing of my man and horse; and then--and not until then--I felt myself thrill and start with a shuddering sense that I had seen something uncanny, and, Jove! I put the mare down this hill we are on now at her very best pace. But the strangest part of my story is to come,' said he, continuing.

"'After I had done my business at the farmhouse here, at foot of this hill, I told the old farmer and his wife what I had seen, as I have now told you. The old man said:

"'"For many years I have known thee, M----, on this road, and have you never seen the like before on that cross?"

"'"Seen what before?" I said.

"'"Why, a man in light-coloured clothes on a grey horse," said he.

"'"No, never," said I, "but I swear I have this evening."

"'The farmer asked, "Had I never heard of what happened to the Miller of L---- Mills about forty years ago?"

"'"No, never a word," I told him.

"'"Well," he said, "about forty years ago this miller, returning from market, was waylaid and murdered on that cross-road, pockets rifled of money and watch. The horse ran home, about a mile away. Two serving-men set out with lanterns and found their master dead. He was dressed, as millers often do in this part of the country, in light-coloured clothes, and the horse was a grey horse. The murderers were never found. These are facts," continued the farmer. "I took this farm soon after it all happened, and, though I have known all this, and have passed over that cross several thousands of times, I never knew anything unusual there myself, but there have been a number of people who tell the same story you have told mother and me, M----, and describe the appearance as you have done to us to-night."'"

Mr. Stead goes on to add: "Four evenings after all this occurred my friend related it to me as we were riding along the same road. He continued to pass there many times every year for ten years, but never a day saw anything of that sort."

My next case, a reproduction of a letter in the Occult Review of September, 1906, reads thus:--

"A Phantom Horse and Rider--Mrs. Gaskin Anderston's Story

"The following story is, I think, very remarkable, and I give it exactly as it was told to me, and written down at the time.

"A number of members of a gentleman's club were talking and discussing, amongst other subjects, the possibility of there being a future state for animals. One of the members said:

"'I firmly believe there is. In my early youth I had a practice as a medical man in one of the Midland Counties. One of my patients was a very wealthy man, who owned large tracts of land and had a stud composed entirely of bay horses with black points--this was a hobby of his, and he would never have any others. One day a messenger came summoning me to Mr. L----, as he had just met with a very bad accident, and was on the point of death. I mounted my horse and started off without delay. As I was riding through the front gates to the house, I heard a shot, and to my amazement the very man I was going to visit rode past at a furious pace, riding a wretched-looking chestnut with one white forefoot and a white star on its forehead. Arrived at the house the butler said:

""'He has gone, sir; they had to shoot the horse--you would hear the shot--and at the same moment my master died."

"'He had had this horse sent on approval; whilst riding it, it backed over a precipice, injuring Mr. L---- fatally, and on being taken to the stables it was found necessary to shoot it.'--Alpha."

The next case I append (I published it in a weekly journal some years ago) was related to me by a Captain Beauclerk.

The White Horse of Eastover

When I came down to breakfast one morning I found amongst several letters awaiting me one from Colonel Onslow, the Commanding Officer of my regiment when I first joined. He had always been rather partial to me, and the friendship between us continued after his retirement. I heard from him regularly at more or less prolonged intervals, and either at Christmas or Easter invariably received an invitation to spend a few days with him. On this occasion he was most anxious that I should accept.

"Do come to us for Easter," he wrote. "I am sure this place will interest you--it is haunted."

The cunning fellow! He knew I was very keen on Psychical Research work, and would go almost anywhere on the bare chance of seeing a ghost.

At that time I was quite open-minded, I had arrived at no definite conclusion as to the existence or non-existence of ghosts. But to tell the truth, I doubted very much if the Colonel's word, in these circumstances, could be relied upon. I had grave suspicions that this "haunting" was but an invention for the purpose of getting me to Eastover. However, as it was just possible that I might be mistaken--that there really was a ghost, and as I had not seen Colonel Onslow for a long time, and indulged in feelings of the warmest regard both for him and his wife, I resolved to go.

Accordingly I set out early in the afternoon of the Good Friday. The weather, which had been muggy in London, grew colder and colder the further we advanced along the line, and by the time we reached Eastover there was every prospect of a storm.

As I expected, a closed carriage had been sent to meet me; for the Colonel, carrying conservatism--with more conservatism than sense, perhaps--to a fine point, cherished a deep-rooted aversion to innovations of any sort, and consequently abhorred motors. His house, Eastover Hall, is three miles from the station, and lies at the foot of a steep spine of the Chilterns.

The grounds of Eastover Hall were extensive; but, in the ordinary sense, far from beautiful. To me, however, they were more than beautiful; there was a grandeur in them--a grandeur that appealed to me far more than mere beauty--the grandeur of desolation, the grandeur of the Unknown. As we passed through the massive iron gates of the lodge, I looked upon countless acres of withered, undulating grass; upon a few rank sedges; upon a score or so of decayed trees; upon a house--huge, bare, grey and massive; upon bleak walls; upon vacant, eye-like windows; upon crude, scenic inhospitality, the very magnitude of which overpowered me. I have said it was cold; but there hung over the estate of Eastover an iciness that brought with it a quickening, a sickening of the heart, and a dreariness that, whilst being depressing in the extreme, was, withal, sublime. Sublime and mysterious; mysterious and insoluble. A thousand fancies swarmed through my mind; yet I could grapple with none; and I was loth to acknowledge that, although there are combinations of very simple material objects which might have had the power of affecting me thus, yet any attempt to analyse that power was beyond--far beyond--my mental capability.

The house, though old--and its black oak panellings, silent staircases, dark corridors, and general air of gloom were certainly suggestive of ghosts--did not affect me in the same degree. The fear it inspired was the ordinary fear inspired by the ordinary superphysical, but the fear I felt in the grounds was a fear created by something out of the way--something far more bizarre than a mere phantom of the dead.

The Colonel asked me if I had experienced any unusual sensations the moment I entered the house, and I told him, "Yes."

"Nearly everyone does," he replied, "and yet, so far as I know, no one has ever seen anything. The noises we hear all round the house have lately been more frequent. I won't describe them; I want to learn your unbiassed opinion of them first."

We then had tea, and whilst the rest--there was a large house-party--indulged in music and cards, the Colonel and I had a delightful chat about old times. I went to bed in the firm resolution of keeping awake till at least two; but I was very tired, and the excessive cold had made me extremely sleepy; consequently, despite my heroic efforts, I gradually dozed off, and knew no more till it was broad daylight and the butler entered my room with a cup of tea. When I came down to breakfast I found everyone in the best of spirits. The Onslows are "great hands" at original entertainments, and the announcement that there would be a masked ball that evening was received with tremendous enthusiasm.

"To-night we dance, to-morrow we feed on Easter eggs and fancy cakes," one of the guests laughingly whispered. "What a nicely ordered programme! I hear, too, we are to have a real old-fashioned Easter Day--heaving and lifting, and stool-ball. Egad! The Colonel deserves knighthood!"

Soon after breakfast there was a general stampede to Seeton and Dinstable to buy gifts; for in that respect again the Onslows stuck to old customs, and there was a general interchange of presents on Easter morning. My purchases made, I joined one or two of the house-party at lunch in Seeton, cycled back alone to Eastover in time for tea; and, at five o'clock, commenced my first explorations of the grounds. The sky having become clouded my progress was somewhat slow. I did the Park first, and I had not gone very far before I detected the same presence I had so acutely felt the previous afternoon. Like the scent of a wild beast, it had a certain defined track which I followed astutely, eventually coming to a full stop in front of a wall of rock. I then perceived by the aid of a few fitful rays of suppressed light, which at intervals struggled successfully through a black bank of clouds, the yawning mouth of a big cavern, from the roof of which hung innumerable stalactites. I now suddenly realized that I was in a very lonely, isolated spot, and became immeasurably perturbed. The Unknown Something in the atmosphere which had inspired me with so much fear was here conglomerated--it was no longer the mere essence--it was the whole Thing. The whole Thing, but what was that Thing? A hideous fascination made me keep my gaze riveted on the gaping hole opposite me. At first I could make out nothing--nothing but jagged walls and roof, and empty darkness; then there suddenly appeared in the very innermost recesses of the cave a faint glow of crimson light which grew and grew, until with startling abruptness it resolved itself into two huge eyes, red and menacing. The sight was so unexpected, and, by reason of its intense malignity, so appalling, that I was simply dumbfounded. I could do nothing but stare at the Thing--paralysed and speechless. I made a desperate effort to get back my self-possession; I strove with all my might to reason with myself, to assure myself that this was the supreme moment of my life, the moment I had so long and earnestly desired. But it was in vain; I was terrified--helplessly, hopelessly terrified. The eyes moved, they drew nearer and nearer to me, and as they did so they became more and more hostile. I opened my mouth to shout for help, I could feel my lungs bursting under the tension; not a sound came; and then--then, as the eyes closed on me, and I could feel the cold, clammy weight pressing me down, there rang out, loud and clear, in the keen and cutting air of the spring evening, a whole choir of voices--the village choral society.

I am not particularly fond of music--certainly not of village music, however well trained it may be; but I can honestly affirm that, at that moment, no sounds could have been more welcome to me than those old folk-songs piped by the rustics, for the instant they commenced the spell that so closely held me prisoner was broken, my faculties returned, and reeling back out of the clutches of the hateful Thing, I joyfully turned and fled.

I related my adventure to the Colonel, and he told me that the cave was generally deemed to be the most haunted spot in the grounds, that no one cared to venture there alone after dark.

"I have myself many times visited the cave at night--in the company of others," he said, "and we have invariably experienced sensations of the utmost horror and repulsion, though we have seen nothing. It must be a devil."

I thought so, too, and exclaimed with some vehemence that the proper course for him to pursue was to have the cave filled in or blasted. That night I awoke at about one o'clock with the feeling very strong on me that something was prowling about under my window. For some time I fought against the impulse to get out of bed and look, but at last I yielded. It was bright moonlight--every obstacle in the grounds stood out with wonderful clearness--and directly beneath the window, peering up at me, were the eyes--red, lurid, satanical. A dog barked, and they vanished. I did not sleep again that night, not until the daylight broke, when I had barely shut my eyes before I was aroused by decidedly material bangings on the doors and hyper-boisterous Easter greetings.

After breakfast a few of the party went to church, a few into the nursery to romp with the children, whilst the rest dispersed in different directions. At luncheon all met again, and there was much merry-making over the tansy cakes--very foolish, no doubt, but to me at least very delightful, and perhaps a wise practice, at times, even for the most prosaic. In the afternoon the Colonel took me for a drive to a charmingly picturesque village in the Chilterns, whence we did not set out on our way back till it was twilight.

The Colonel was a good whip, and the horse, though young and rather high-spirited, was, he said, very dependable on the whole, and had never caused him any trouble. We spun along at a brisk trot--the last village separating us from the Hall was past, and we were on a high eminence, almost within sight of home, when a startling change in the atmosphere suddenly became apparent--it turned icy cold. I made some sort of comment to the Colonel, and as I did so the horse shied.

"Hulloa!" I exclaimed. "Does she often do this?"

"No, not often, only when we are on this road about this time," was the grim rejoinder. "Keep your eyes open and sit tight."

We were now amid scenery of the same desolate type that had so impressed me the day of my arrival. Gaunt, barren hills, wild, uncultivated levels, sombre valleys, inhabited only by grotesque enigmatical shadows that came from Heaven knows where, and hemmed us in on all sides.

A large quarry, half full of water and partly overgrown with brambles, riveted my attention, and as I gazed fixedly at it I saw, or fancied I saw, the shape of something large and white--vividly white--rise from the bottom.

The glimpse I caught of it was, however, only momentary, for we were moving along at a great pace, and I had hardly seen the last of it before the quarry was left behind and we were descending a long and gradual declivity. There was but little wind, but the cold was benumbing; neither of us spoke, and the silence was unbroken save by the monotonous patter, patter of the horse's hoofs on the hard road.

We were, I should say, about half-way down the hill, when away in our rear, from the direction of the quarry, came a loud protracted neigh. I at once looked round, and saw standing on the crest of the eminence we had just quitted, and most vividly outlined against the enveloping darkness, a gigantic horse, white and luminous.

At that moment our own mare took fright; we were abruptly swung forward, and, had I not--mindful of the Colonel's warning--been "sitting tight," I should undoubtedly have been thrown out. We dashed downhill at a terrific rate, our mare mad with terror, and on peering over my shoulder I saw, to my horror, the white steed tearing along not fifty yards behind us. I was now able to get a vivid impression of the monstrous beast. Although the night was dark, a strong, lurid glow, which seemed to emanate from all over it, enabled me to see distinctly its broad, muscular breast; its panting, steaming flanks; its long, graceful legs with their hairy fetlocks and shoeless, shining hoofs; its powerful but arched back; its lofty, colossal head with waving forelock and broad, massive forehead; its snorting nostrils; its distended, foaming jaws; its huge, glistening teeth; and its lips, wreathed in a savage grin. On and on it raced, its strides prodigious, its mighty mane rising and falling, and blowing all around it in unrestrained confusion.

A slip--a single slip, and we should be entirely at its mercy.

Our own horse was now out of control. A series of violent plunges, which nearly succeeded in unseating me, had enabled her to get the check of the bit between her teeth so as to render it utterly useless; and she had then started off at a speed I can only liken to flying. Fortunately we were now on a more or less level ground, and the road, every inch of which our horse knew, was smooth and broad.

I glanced at the Colonel convulsively clutching the reins; he was clinging to his seat for dear life, his hat gone. I wanted to speak, but I knew it was useless--the shrieking of the air as it roared past us deadened all sounds. Once or twice I glanced over the side of the trap. The rapidity with which we were moving caused a hideous delusion--the ground appeared to be gliding from beneath us; and I experienced the sensation of resting on nothing. Despite our danger, however, from natural causes--a danger which, I knew, could not have been more acute--my fears were wholly of the superphysical. It was not the horror of being dashed to pieces I dreaded--it was the horror of the phantom horse--of its sinister, hostile appearance--of its unknown powers. What would it do if it overtook us? With each successive breath I drew I felt sure the fateful event--the long-anticipated crisis--had come.

At last my expectations were realized. The teeth of the gigantic steed closed down on me, its nostrils hissed resistance out of me--I swerved, tottered, fell; and as I sank on the ground my senses left me.

On coming to I found myself in a propped-up position on the floor of a tiny room with someone pouring brandy down my throat. Happily, beyond a severe shock, I had sustained no injury--a sufficiently miraculous circumstance, as the trap had come to grief in failing to clear the lodge gates, the horse had skinned its knees, and the Colonel had fractured his shoulder. Of the phantom horse not a glimpse had been seen. Even the Colonel, strange to relate, though he had managed to peep round, had not seen it. He had heard and felt a Presence, that was all; and after listening to my experience, he owned he was truly thankful he was only clair-audient.

"A gift like yours," he said, with more candour than kindness, "is a curse, not a blessing. And now I have your corroboration, I might as well tell you that we have long suspected the ghost to be a horse, and have attributed its hauntings to the fact that, some time ago, when exploring in the cave, several prehistoric remains of horses were found, one of which we kept, whilst we presented the others to a neighbouring museum. I dare say there are heaps more."

"Undoubtedly there are," I said, "but take my advice and leave them alone--re-inter the remains you have already unearthed--and thus put a stop to the hauntings. If you go on excavating and keep the bones you find, the disturbances will, in all probability, increase, and the hauntings will become not only many but multiform."

Needless to say the Colonel carried out my injunctions to the letter. Far from continuing his work of excavation he lost no time in restoring the bones he had kept to their original resting-place; after which, as I predicted, the hauntings ceased.

This case, to me, is very satisfactory, as it testifies to what was unquestionably an actual phantasm of the dead--of a dead horse--albeit that horse was prehistoric; and such horses are all the more likely to be earth-bound on account of their wild, untamed natures.

Here is another account of a phantom horse taken from Mr. Stead's Real Ghost Stories. It is written by an Afrikander who, in a letter to Mr. Stead, says:

"I am not a believer in ghosts, nor never was; but seeing you wanted a census of them, I can't help giving you a remarkable experience of mine. It was some three summers back, and I was out with a party of Boer hunters. We had crossed the Northern boundary of the Transvaal, and were camped on the ridges of the Sembombo. I had been out from sunrise, and was returning about dusk with the skin of a fine black ostrich thrown across the saddle in front of me, in the best of spirits at my good luck. Making straight for the camp, I had hardly entered a thick bush when I thought that I heard somebody behind me. Looking behind, I saw a man mounted on a white horse. You can imagine my surprise, for my horse was the only one in camp, and we were the only party in the country. Without considering I quickened my pace into a canter, and on doing so my follower appeared to do the same. At this I lost all confidence, and made a run for it, with my follower in hot pursuit, as it appeared to my imagination; and I did race for it (the skin went flying in about two minutes, and my rifle would have done the same had it not been strapped over my shoulders). This I kept up until I rode into camp right among the pals cooking the evening meal. The Boers about the camp were quick in their enquiries as to my distressed condition, and regaining confidence, I was putting them off as best I could, when the old boss (an old Boer of some sixty-eight or seventy years), looking up from the fire, said:

"'The white horse! The Englishman has seen the white horse.'

"This I denied, but to no purpose. And that night round the camp fire I took the trouble to make enquiries as to the antecedents of the white horse. And the old Boer, after he had commanded silence, began. He said:

"'The English are not brave, but foolish. We beat them at Majuba, some twenty-five seasons back. There was an Englishman here like you; he had brought a horse with him, against our advice, to be killed with the fly, the same as yours will be in a day or two. And he, like you, would go where he was told not to go; and one day he went into a bush (that very bush you rode through to-night), and he shot seven elephants, and the next day he went in to fetch the ivory, and about night his horse came into camp riderless, and was dead from the fly before the sun went down. The Englishman is in that bush now; anyway, he never came back. And now anybody who ventures into that bush is chased by the white horse. I wouldn't go into that bush for all the ivory in the land. The English are not brave, but foolish; we beat them at Majuba.'

"Here he ran into a torrent of abuse of all Englishmen in general, and in particular. And I took the opportunity of rolling myself up in my blankets for the night, sleeping all the better for my adventure.

"Now, Mr. Stead, I don't believe in ghosts, but I was firmly convinced during that run of mine, and can vouch for the accuracy of it, not having heard a word of the Englishman or his white horse before my headlong return to the camp that night. I shortly hope to be near that bush again, but, like the old Boer, I can say I wouldn't go into that bush again for all the ivory in the land.

"P.S.--A few days after we dropped across a troop of elephants without entering the fatal bush, and managed to bag seven, photographs of which I took, and shall be pleased to send for your inspection, if desired."

There can be very little doubt that the phantom the Afrikander saw was the actual spirit of a dead horse.

Another experience of haunting by the same animal was told me by a Chelsea artist who assured me it was absolutely true. I append it as nearly as possible in his own words.

Heralds of Death

"It is many years ago," he began, "since I came into my property, Heatherleigh Hall, near Carlisle, Cumberland. It was left me by my great-uncle, General Wimpole, whom I had never seen, but who had made me his heir in preference to his other nephews, owing to my reputed likeness to an aunt, to whom he was greatly attached. Of course I was much envied, and I dare say a good many unkind things were said about me, but I did not care--Heatherleigh Hall was mine, and I had as much right to it as anyone else. I came there all alone--my two brothers, Dick and Hal, the one a soldier and the other a sailor, were both away on foreign service, whilst Beryl, my one and only sister, was staying with her fiance's family in Bath.

Never shall I forget my first impressions. Depict the day--an October afternoon. The air mellow, the leaves yellow, and the sun a golden red. Not a trace of clouds or wind anywhere. Everything serene and still. A broad highway; a wood; a lodge in the midst of the wood; large iron gates; a broad carriage drive, planted on either side with lofty pines and elms, whose gnarled and forked branches threw grotesque and not altogether pleasing shadows on the pale gravel.

"At the end of the avenue, at least a quarter of a mile long, wide expanses of soft, velvety grass, interspersed at regular intervals with plots of flowers--dahlias, michaelmas daisies--no longer in their first bloom--chrysanthemums, etc. Beyond the lawn, the house, and beyond that again, and on either side, big, old-fashioned gardens full of fruit--fruit of all kinds, some, such as grapes and peaches, in monster green-houses, and others--luscious pears, blenheim oranges, golden pippins, etc.--in rich profusion in the open, the whole encompassed by a high and solid brick wall, topped with a bed of mortar and broken glass. The house, which was built, or, rather, faced with split flints, and edged and buttressed with cut grey stone, had a majestic but gloomy appearance. Its front, lofty and handsome, was somewhat castellated in style, two semicircular bows, or half-moons, placed at a suitable distance from each other, rising from the base to the summit of the edifice; these were pierced, at every floor, with rows of stone-mullioned windows, rising to the height of four or five stories. The flat wall between had larger windows, lighting the great hall, gallery, and upper apartments. These windows were abundantly ornamented with stained glass, representing the arms, honours, and alms-deeds of the Wimpole family.

"The towers, half included in the building, were completely circular within, and contained the winding stair of the mansion; and whoso ascended them, when the winter wind was blowing, seemed rising by a tornado to the clouds. Midway between the towers was a heavy stone porch, with a Gothic gateway, surmounted by a battlemented parapet, made gable fashion, the apex of which was garnished by a pair of dolphins, rampant and antagonistic, whose corkscrew tails seemed contorted by the last agonies of rage convulsed.

"The porch doors thrown open to receive me, led into a hall, wide, vaulted and lofty, and decorated here and there with remnants of tapestry and grim portraits of the Wimpoles. One picture in particular riveted my attention. Hung in an obscure corner, where the light rarely penetrated, it represented the head and shoulders of a young man with a strikingly beautiful face--the features small and regular like those of a woman--the hair yellow and curly. It was the eyes that struck me most--they followed me everywhere I went with a persistency that was positively alarming. There was something in them I had never seen in canvas eyes before, something deeper and infinitely more intricate than could be produced by mere paint--something human and yet not human, friendly and yet not friendly; something baffling, enigmatical, haunting. I enquired of my deceased relative's aged housekeeper, Mrs. Grimstone--whom I had retained--whose portrait it was, and she replied with a scared look, 'Horace, youngest son of Sir Algernon Wimpole, who died here in 1745.'

"'The face fascinates me,' I said. 'Is there any history attached to it?'

"'Why, yes, sir!' she responded, her eyes fixed on the floor, 'but the late master never liked referring to it.'

"'Is it as bad as that?' I said, laughing. 'Tell me!'

"'Well, sir,' she began, 'they do say as how Sir Algernon, who was a thorough country squire--very fond of hunting and shooting and all sorts of manly exercises--never liked Mr. Horace, who was delicate and dandified--what the folk in those days used to style a macaroni. The climax came when Mr. Horace took up with the Jacobites. Sir Algernon would have nothing more to do with him then and turned him adrift. One day there was a great commotion in the neighbourhood, the Government troops were hunting the place in search of rebels, and who should come galloping up the avenue with a couple of troopers in hot pursuit but Mr. Horace. The noise brought out Sir Algernon, and he was so infuriated to think that his son was the cause of the disturbance, a "disgraceful young cub," he called him, that despite Mr. Horace's entreaties for protection, he ran him through with his sword. It was a dreadful thing for a father to do, and Sir Algernon bitterly repented it. His wife, who had been devoted to Mr. Horace, left him, and at last, in a fit of despondency, he hanged himself--out there, on one of the elms lining the avenue. It is still standing. Ever since then they do say that the wood is haunted, and that before the death of any member of the family Mr. Horace is seen galloping along the old carriage drive.'

"'Pleasant,' I grunted. 'And how about the house--is it haunted too?'

"'I daresn't say,' she murmured. 'Some will tell you it is, and some will tell you it isn't.'

"'In which category are you included?' I asked.

"'Well!' she said 'I have lived here happy and comfortable forty-five years the day after to-morrow, and that speaks for itself, don't it?' And with that she hobbled off and showed me the way to the dining-room.

"What a house it was! From the hall proceeded doorways and passages, more than the ordinary memory could retain. Of these portals, one at each end conducted to the tower stairs, others, to the reception-rooms and domestic offices. In the right wing, besides bedrooms galore, was a lofty and spacious picture gallery; in the left--a chapel; for the Wimpoles were, formerly, Roman Catholics. The general fittings and furniture, both of the hall and house in general, were substantial, venerable and strongly corroborative of what Mrs. Grimstone hinted at--they suggested ghosts.

"The walls, lined with black oak panels, or dark hangings that fluttered mysteriously each time the wind blew, were funereal indeed; and so high and narrow were the windows, that little was to be discerned through them but cross-barred portions of the sky. One spot in particular appealed to my nerves--and that, a long, vaulted stone passage leading from a morning room to the foot of the back staircase. Here the voice and even the footsteps echoed with a hollow, low response, and often when I have been hurrying along it--I never dared walk slowly--I have fancied--and maybe it was more than fancy--I have been pursued.

"Time passed, and from being merely used to my new environments, I grew to take a pride in them, to love them. I made the acquaintance of several of my neighbours, those I deemed the most desirable, and on returning from wintering abroad, brought home a bride, a young Polish girl, who added lustre to the surroundings, and in no small degree helped to dissipate the gloom. Indeed, had it not been for the picture in the hall, and for the twilight shadows and twilight footsteps in the stone passage, I should soon have ceased to think of ghosts. Ghosts, forsooth! When all around me vibrated with the sounds of girlish laughter, and the summer sunshine, sparkling on the golden curls of my child-wife, saw itself reflected a millionfold in the alluring depths of her azure eyes. In halcyon days like these who thinks of ghosts and death?

"And yet! It is in just such times as these that hell is nearest. There came a night in August when the air was so hot and sultry that I could scarcely breathe, and unable to bear the atmosphere of the house and gardens any longer, I sought the coolness of the wood. Olga--my wife--did not accompany me, as she was suffering from a slight--thank God, it was only slight--sunstroke. It was close on midnight, and there was a dead stillness abroad that seemed as if it must be universal--as if it enveloped the whole of nature. I tried to realize London--to depict the Strand and Piccadilly, aglow with artificial light and reverberating with the roll of countless traffic and the tread of millions of feet.

"I failed. The incongruity of such imaginings here--here amidst omnipotent silence--rendered such thoughts impossible. A leaf rustled, and its rustling sounded to my ears like the gentle closing of some giant door. A twig fell, and I turned sharply round, convinced I should see a pile of broken debris. I love all trees, but I love them best by day--to me it seems that night utterly metamorphizes them--brings out in them a subtler, darker side one would little suspect. Here, in this oak, for instance, was an example. In the morning one sees in it nought but quiet dignity, venerable old age, benevolence, and, by reason of the ample protection its branches afford from the sun, charity and philanthropy. Its leaves are bright, dainty, pretty; its trunk suggests nothing but a cosy and soothing retreat for students and lovers. But now--see how different! These great spreading, gnarled branches are hands, claws--monstrous and menacing; those leaves no longer bright remind me of a hearse's plumes; their rustling--of the rustling and switching of a pall or winding-sheet. The trunk, black, sinuous, towering, is assuredly no piece of timber, but something pulpy, something intangible, something antagonistic, mystic, devilish. I turn from it and shudder. Then my mind reverts to the elm--the elm on which Sir Algernon hanged himself. I remember it is not more than twenty yards from where I stand. I stare down at the soil, at the clumps of crested dog's-tail and stray blades of succulent darnel; I force my attention on a toadstool, whose soft and lowly head gleams sickly white in the moonbeams. I glance from it to a sleeping close-capped dandelion, from it to a thistle, from it again to a late bush vetch, and then, willy-nilly, to the accursed elm. My God! What a change. It wasn't like that when I passed it at noon. It was just an ordinary tree then, but now, now--and what is that--that sinister bundle--suspended from one of its curling branches? A cold sweat bursts out on me, my knees tremble, my hair begins to rise on end. Swinging round, I am about to rush away--blindly rush away--hither, thither, anywhere--anywhere out of sight of that tree and of all the hideous possibilities it promises to materialize for me. I have not taken five strides, however, before I am pulled sharply up by the sounds of horse's hoofs--of hoofs on the hard gravel, away in the distance. They speedily grow nearer. A horse is galloping, galloping towards me along the broad carriage drive. Nearer, nearer and nearer it comes! Who is it? WHAT is it? A deadly nausea seizes me, I swerve, totter, reel, and am only prevented from falling by the timely interference of a pine. The concussion with its leviathan trunk clears my senses. All my faculties become wonderfully and painfully alert. I would give my very soul if it were not so--if I could but fall asleep or faint. The sound of the hoofs is very much nearer now, so near indeed that I may see the man--Heaven grant it may be only a man after all--any moment. Ah! my heart gives a great sickly jerk. Something has shot into view. There, not fifty yards from me, where the road curves, and the break in the foliage overhead admits a great flood of moonlight. I recognize the "thing" at once; it's not a man, it's nothing human, it's the picture I know so well and dread so much, the portrait of Horace Wimpole, that hangs in the main hall--and it's mounted on a coal-black horse with wildly flying mane and foaming mouth. On and on they come, thud, thud, thud! The man is not dressed as a rider, but is wearing the costume in the picture--i.e. that of a macaroni! A nut! More fit for a lady's seminary than a fine, old English mansion.

"Something beside me rustles--rustles angrily, and I know, I can feel, it is the bundle on the branch--the ghastly, groaning, creaking, croaking caricature of Sir Algernon. The horseman comes up to me--our eyes meet--I am looking in those of a dead--of a long since dead man--my blood freezes.

"He flashes past me--thud, thud, thud! A bend in the road, and he vanishes from sight. But I can still hear him, still hear the mad patter of his horse's hoofs as they bear him onward, lifeless, fleshless, weightless, to his ancient home. God pity the souls that know no rest.

"How I got back to the house I hardly know. I believe it was with my eyes shut, and I am certain I ran all the way.

"About four o'clock the following afternoon I received a cablegram from Malta. Intuition warned me to prepare for the worst. Its contents were unpleasantly short and pithy--'Hal drowned at two o'clock this morning.--Dick.'

"Two years passed--again an August night, hot and oppressive as before, and again--though surely against my will, my better judgment, if you like--I visited the wood. Horse's hoofs just the same as before. The same galloping, the same figure, the same EYES! the same mad, panic-stricken flight home, and, early in the succeeding afternoon, a similar cablegram--this time from Sicily. 'Dick died at midnight. Dysentery.--Andrews.'

"Jack Andrews was Dick's pal--his bosom friend. So once again the phantom rider had brought its grisly message--played its ghoulish role. My brothers were both dead now, and only Beryl remained. Another year sped by and the last night in October--a Monday--saw me, impelled by a fascination I could not resist, once again in the wood. Up to a point everything happened as before. As the monotonous church clock struck twelve, from afar came the sound of hoofs. Nearer, nearer, nearer, and then with startling abruptness the rider shot into view. And now, mixed with the awful, indescribable terror the figure always conveyed with it, came a feeling of intense rage and indignation. Should Beryl--Beryl whom I loved next best to my wife--be torn from me even as Dick and Hal had been? No! Ten thousand times no! Sooner than that I would risk anything. A sudden inspiration, coming maybe from the whispering leaves, or from the elm, or from the mysterious flickering moonbeams, flashed through me. Could I not intercept the figures, drive them back? By doing so something told me Beryl might be saved. A terrible struggle at once took place within me, and it was only after the most desperate efforts that I at length succeeded in fighting back my terror and flung myself out into the middle of the drive. No words of mine can describe all I went through as I stood there anticipating the arrival of the phantoms. At length they came, right up to me; and as, with frantic resolution, I screwed up courage to plant myself directly in their path, and stared up into the rider's eyes, the huge steed halted, gave one shrill neigh, and turning round, galloped back again, disappearing whither it had emerged.

"Two days afterwards I received a letter from my brother-in-law.

"'I have been having an awful time,' he wrote. 'My darling Beryl has been frightfully ill. On Monday night we gave up all hope of her recovery, but at twelve o'clock, when the doctor bid us prepare for the end, the most extraordinary thing happened. Turning over in bed, she distinctly called out your name, and rallied. And now, thank God, she is completely out of danger. The doctor says it is the most astonishing recovery he has ever known.'

    *   *   *   *   *

"That is twenty years ago, and I've not seen the phantom rider since. Nor do I fancy he will appear again, for when I look into the eyes of the picture in the hall, they are no longer wandering, but at rest."

    *   *   *   *   *

Perhaps, one of the most interesting accounts of the phantasm of a horse in my possession is that recorded by C.E. G----, a friend of my boyhood. Writing to me from the United States some months ago, he says:

"Knowing how interested you are in all cases of hauntings, and in those relating to animal ghosts especially, I am sending you an account of an 'experience' that happened to my uncle, Mr. John Dale, about six months ago. He was returning to his home in Bishopstone, near Helena, Montana, shortly after dark, and had arrived at a particularly lonely part of the road where the trees almost meet overhead, when his horse showed signs of restlessness. It slackened down, halted, shivered, whinnied, and kept up such a series of antics, that my uncle descended from the trap to see if anything was wrong with it. He thought that, perhaps, it was going to have some kind of fit, or an attack of ague, which is not an uncommon complaint among animals in his part of the country, and he was preparing to give it a dose of quinine, when suddenly it reared up violently, and before he could stop it, was careering along the road at lightning speed. My uncle was now in a pretty mess. He was stranded in a forest without a lantern, ten miles, at least, from home. Feeling too depressed to do anything, he sat down by the roadside, and seriously thought of remaining there till daybreak. A twinge of rheumatism, however, reminded him the ground was little warmer than ice, and made him realize that lying on it would be courting death. Consequently, he got up, and setting his lips grimly, struck out in the direction of Bishopstone. At every step he took the track grew darker. Shadows of trees and countless other things, for which he could see no counterpart, crept out and rendered it almost impossible for him to tell where to tread. A peculiar, indefinable dread also began to make itself felt, and the darkness seemed to him to assume an entirely new character. He plodded on, breaking into a jog-trot every now and then, and whistling by way of companionship. The stillness was sepulchral--he strained his ears, but could not even catch the sound of those tiny animals that are usually heard in the thickets and furze-bushes at night; and all his movements were exaggerated, until their echoes seemed to reverberate through the whole forest. A turn of the road brought him into view of something that made his heart throb with delight. Standing by the wayside was an enormous coach with four huge horses pawing the ground impatiently. My uncle rushed up to the driver, who was so enveloped in wraps, he could not see his face, and in a voice trembling with emotion begged for the favour of a lift--if not to Helena itself, as far in that direction as the coach was going. The driver made no reply, but with his hand motioned my uncle to get in. The latter did not need a second bidding, and the moment he was seated, the vehicle started off. It was a large, roomy conveyance, but had a stifling atmosphere about it that struck my uncle as most unpleasant; and although he could see no one, he intuitively felt he was not alone, and that more than one pair of eyes were watching him.

"The coach did not go as fast as my uncle expected, but moved with a curious gliding motion, and the wheels made no noise whatever. This added to my uncle's apprehensions, and he almost made up his mind to open the carriage door and jump out. Something, however, which he could not account for restrained him, and he maintained his seat. Outside, all was still profoundly dark. The trees were scarcely distinguishable as deeper masses of shadow, and were recognizable only by the resinous odour, that, from time to time, sluggishly flowed in at the open window as the coach rolled on.

"At length they overtook some other vehicle, and for the first time for some hours my uncle heard the sound of solid wheels, which were as welcome to him as any joy bells. Just as they were passing the conveyance--a small wagonette drawn by a pair of horses, the latter took fright; there were loud shouts and a great stampede, and my uncle, who leaned out of the coach window, caught a glimpse of the vehicle dashing along ahead of them at a frightful speed. The driver of the coach, apparently totally unconcerned, continued his journey at the same regular, mechanical pace.

"Presently my uncle heard the sound of rushing water, and knew they must be nearing the Usk, a tributary of the Battle, which was only five miles from his house.

"The forest now ceased, and they crossed the road over the bridge in a brilliant burst of moonlight. About a mile or so further on the coach halted, and, to my uncle's surprise, he found himself in front of a house he had no recollection of seeing before. He got out, and to his horror saw that instead of riding in a coach he had been riding in a hearse, and that the horses had on their heads gigantic sable plumes.

"While he was standing gazing at the extraordinary equipage, the door of the house slowly opened, and two figures came out carrying a small coffin, which they placed inside the vehicle. He then heard loud peals of mad, hilarious laughter, and coach and horses immediately vanished. My uncle arrived home safely, but the shock of what he had experienced kept him in bed for some days. He learned that a phantom coach similar to the one he had ridden in had been seen in the forest twenty years previously, and that it was supposed to be a prognostication of some great misfortune, which supposition, in my uncle's case at least, proved true, as his wife died of apoplexy a few days after this adventure."

Yet another case of haunting by the phantasms of a horse comes to me from a gentleman in Marseilles, who told it me thus:--

"It was 9 p.m. when I left my friend Maitland's hotel in Chateauborne, and, facing north, set out on my way to Liffre, where my headquarters had been for the past fortnight. Liffre is in the hills, and the road which separated it from Chateauborne, wild and lonely enough in daylight and when the weather is fair, is almost untraversable in winter. The night in question was Christmas Eve; the snow had fallen heavily during the day, and with the wind blowing in icy draughts from the northeast, there was every prospect of another downfall. Maitland pressed me to stay in his hotel. 'It is sheer folly,' he said, 'for you to attempt to get home in weather like this. It is pitch dark, you are not familiar with the route, and if you don't wander off the track and tumble over a precipice, you will walk into a snowdrift. Be sensible--sleep here!'

"Much, however, as I should have liked to follow his counsel, I did not feel justified in doing so, as I had a lot of correspondence to attend to, and I realized it was most necessary for me to get back to Liffre without any further delay.

"It was true the night was inky black; but, with the aid of a lamp, I hadn't the slightest doubt I could find my way. Maitland bartered for a candle lantern with his host, and armed with this, a flagon of brandy and water and a thick stick, I said good-bye to Chateauborne.

"A couple of hundred yards saw me beyond the outskirts of the town, wherein I was the sole pedestrian, and silence reigned supreme. On and on I plodded, the feeble, yellow light of my lantern just preventing me--but only just--from wandering from the track. The road, which for the first mile or so was tolerably level, gradually began to rise, and, as it did so, I noticed for the first time indistinct images of gigantic, naked trees that becoming more and more numerous, and closer and closer together, at length united their long and grotesquely shaped branches overhead, and I found myself in the depths of a vast forest. The snow, which had up to the present held off, now recommenced to fall, and presently the wind, which had for some time been slowly acquiring strength, came howling through the trees with the utmost fury, the first blast swishing the lantern out of my hands and hurling me with considerable force into an undergrowth of thorns and brambles, out of which I extricated myself with no little difficulty.

"I was now in the sorriest of plights--enveloped on all sides in Stygian darkness I was unable to discover my lantern, and was thus totally at the mercy of the ruthless elements. There were only two courses before me--either I must remain where I was and be frozen to death, or, making a guess at the route, I must push on ahead and run the risk of ending my life at the bottom of a ravine. I chose the latter. Groping about with my feet, until I at length discovered what I thought must be the right track, I pushed ahead, and, staggering and stumbling forward, managed to make some sort of progress, terribly slow though it was. The blinding darkness of the snowy night, the intense silence and utter solitude of the place, combined with the knowledge that on all sides of me lay holes and chasms, dampened my spirits and raised strange phantoms in my imagination. The wind now rose, and the dismal sighing of the trees speedily grew into a series of the most perturbing screeches, as the branches and trunks swayed to and fro like reeds before the violence of the hurricane.

"At this juncture I gave myself up for lost, and, coming to a standstill up to my knees in snow, was preparing to lie down and die, when, to my great joy, a light suddenly appeared ahead of me, and the next moment a man, mounted on a big white horse, rode noiselessly up to me. He was wrapped in a shaggy great-coat, and a slouch hat worn low over his eyes completely hid his face from me. In his disengaged hand he carried a lantern.

"'By Jove!' I exclaimed, 'I am glad to see you, for I've lost the track to Liffre. Can you tell me, or, better still, show me, the way to some house where I can put up for the remainder of the night?'

"The stranger made no reply, but bidding me follow with a wave of his hand, rode silently in front of me, and although I tried to keep up with him, I could not; and the odd thing was, that without apparently increasing his pace, he always maintained his distance. After proceeding in this manner for possibly ten minutes, we suddenly turned to the left, and I found myself in a big clearing in the wood, with a long, low-built house opposite me.

"My guide then paused, and indicating the front door of the house with an emphatic gesture of his hand, seemed suddenly to melt away into thin air, for although I peered about me on all sides to try to find some indications of him, neither he nor his horse was anywhere to be seen. Thinking this was rather queer, but quite ready to attribute it to natural causes, I approached the building, and, making use of my knuckles in lieu of a knocker, beat a loud tattoo on the woodwork. There was no response. Again I rapped, and the door slowly opening revealed a pair of gleaming, dark eyes. 'What do you want?' enquired a harsh voice in barbarous accents. 'A night's lodging,' I replied; 'and I'm willing to pay a good price for it, for I'm more than half frozen.'

"At this the door opened wider, and I found myself confronted by a woman with a candle. She had not the most prepossessing of expressions, though her hair, eyes and features were decidedly good. She was dressed with tawdry smartness-- earrings, necklace, and rings, and very high-heeled buckle shoes. Indeed, her costume was so out of keeping with the rusticity of her surroundings as to be quite extraordinary. This fact struck me at once, as did her fingers, which, though spatulate and ugly, had been manicured, and of course very much over-manicured, for effect. Had this not been the case, I probably should not have noticed them. But the unnatural gloss on them, exaggerated by the candlelight, made me look, and I was at once impressed with the criminal formation of the fingers--the club-shaped ends denoted something very bad--something homicidal--and as my eyes wandered from the hands to the face, I saw with a thrill of horror that the ears were set low down and far back on the head, and that the eyes gleamed with the sinister glitter of the wolf.

"Still, I must take my chance--the woman or the wood--it had to be one of the two. 'If you'll step inside, monsieur,' she said, 'I'll see what can be done for you. We have only recently come here, and the house is anyhow at present. Still, if you don't mind roughing it a little, we can let you have a bed, and you can rely upon me that it is clean and well-aired.' I followed her eagerly, and she led me down a narrow passage into a big room with a low ceiling, traversed with a ponderous oak beam, blackened with the smoke of endless peat fires.

"Before the blazing faggots on the hearth sat a burly-looking individual in a blue blouse. On our arrival he arose, and as his huge form towered above me, I thought I had never seen anyone quite so hideous, nor so utterly unlike the ortho-dox Frenchman. Obeying his injunction--for I can scarcely call it an invitation--to sit down, I took a seat by the fire, and warming my half-frozen limbs, waited impa-tiently whilst the woman made up my bed and prepared supper.

"The storm had now reached cyclonic dimensions, and under its stupendous fury the whole house--stoutly built though it was--swayed on its foundations. The howling of the wind in the rude, old-fashioned chimney and along the passage, and the frenzied beating of the snow against the diamond window-panes, deadened all other noises, and rendered any attempt at conversation absolutely abortive. So I ate my meal in silence, pretending not to notice the subtle interchange of glances that constantly took place between the strangely assorted pair. Whether they were husband and wife, what the man did for a living, were questions that continually occurred to me, and I found my eyes incessantly wandering to the numerous pack-ing-cases, piles of carpets, casks and other articles, which corroborated the woman's statement that they had but recently 'moved in.' Once I attempted to empty the coffee (which was black and peculiarly bitter) under the table, but had to desist, as I saw the man's devilish eyes fixed searchingly on me. I then pushed aside the cup, and on the woman asking if it was not to my liking, I shouted out that I was not in the least thirsty. After this incident the covert looks became more numerous, and my suspicions increased accordingly.

"At the first opportunity I got up, and signalling my intention to go to bed, was preparing to leave my seat, when my host, walking to a cupboard, fetched out a bottle of cognac, and pouring out a tumbler, handed it me with a mien that I dare not refuse.

"The woman then led me up a flight of rickety, wooden steps and into a sepulchral-looking chamber with no other furniture in it save a long, narrow, iron bedstead, a dilapidated washstand, a very unsteady, common deal table, on which was a looking-glass and a collar stud, and a rush-bottomed chair. Setting the candlestick on the dressing-table, and assuring me again that the bed was well aired, my hostess withdrew, observing as she left the room that she would get me a nice breakfast and call me at seven. At seven! How I wished it was seven now! As I stood in the midst of the floor shivering--for the room was icy cold, I suddenly saw a dark shadow emerge from a remote corner of the room and slide surreptitiously towards the door, where it halted. My eyes then fell on the lock, and I perceived that there was no key. No key! And that evil-looking pair below! I must barricade the door somehow. Yet with what? There was nothing of any weight in the room! Nothing! I began to feel horribly tired and sleepy--so sleepy that it was only with supreme effort I could prevent my eyelids closing. Ah! I had it--a wedge! I had a knife. Of wood there was plenty--a piece off the washstand, table, or chair. Anything would suffice. I essayed to struggle to the chair, my limbs tottered, my eyelids closed. Then the shadow from the doorway moved towards and THROUGH me, and with the coldness of its passage I revived! With desperate energy I cut a couple of chunks off the washstand, and paring them down, eventually succeeded in slipping them in the crack of the door, and rendering it impossible to open from the outside. That done, I staggered to the bed, and falling, dressed as I was, on the counterpane, sank into a deep sleep. How long I slept I cannot say. I suddenly heard the loud neighing of a horse which seemed to come from just under my window, and, as in a vision, saw by my side in the bed a something which gradually developed into the figure of a man, the counterpart of the mysterious being in the shaggy coat who had guided me to the house. He was fully dressed, sound asleep and breathing heavily. As I was looking a dark shadow fell across the sleeper's face, and on glancing up I perceived, to my horror, a black something crawling on the floor. Nearer and nearer it came, until it reached the side of the bed, when I immediately recognized the evil, smirking face of my hostess. In one hand she held a lamp and in the other a horn-handled knife. Setting the lamp on the floor, she coolly undid the collar of the sleeping man, and I saw a stud, the counterpart of the one on the dressing-table, fall on the bare boards with a sharp tap, and disappear in the surrounding darkness. Then the woman felt the edge of the knife with her repulsive thumb, and calmly cut the helpless man's throat. I screamed--and the murderess and her victim instantly vanished--and I realized I was alone in the room and very much awake. Whether all that had occurred was a dream, I cannot say with certainty, though I am inclined to think not.

"For some minutes my heart pulsated painfully, and then as the sound of its throbbing grew fainter and fainter, I heard a curious noise outside my room--some-one was ascending the stairs. I endeavoured to rise, but could not--fear, an aw-ful, ungovernable fear, held me spellbound. The steps paused outside the door, the handle of which was gently turned. Then there was a suggestive silence, then whis-pering, then another turning of the handle, and then--my state of coma abruptly ended, and I stepped noiselessly out of bed and crept to the window. I was heard. 'Stop him,' the woman cried out, 'he's trying to escape. Use the gun.' She hurled herself against the door as she spoke, whilst the man tore downstairs.

"It was now a matter of seconds, the slightest accident, a hesitation, and I was lost. Swinging open the window, I scrambled on the ledge, and without the slightest idea of the distance--dropped! There was a brief rushing through air and I alighted--safe and sound--on the snow. Blessed snow! Had it not been for the snow I should in all probability have hurt myself! I alighted not an instant too soon, for hardly had I touched the ground before my gigantic host came tearing round the angle of the wall with a lantern in one hand and gun in the other. I immediately dashed away, and, thanks to the intense darkness of the morning--for it must have been two o'clock--had no difficulty in evading my pursuer, who fired twice in rapid suc-cession.

"On and on I went, sometimes falling up to my armpits in the snowdrift, and sometimes stunning myself against a low-hanging branch of a tree. With the first rays of sunlight, however, my troubles came to an end. The snow had ceased falling, and I quickly alighted on a track, which brought me to a village, whence I obtained a conveyance into Liffre.

"I reported the affair to the local police, and a party of gendarmes at once set off to arrest the miscreants. But, alas, they had fled. The house was pulled down, and, on the soil being excavated, a dozen or more skeletons of men and women--all showing unmistakable signs of foul play--together with the remains of a horse, were found in various parts of the premises. The place was a veritable Golgotha. I suppose the phantom horse and rider had appeared to me with the sole purpose of making their fate known. If so, they at all events partly achieved their end, though the mystery surrounding their identity was never solved. All the remains, both human and animal, were removed elsewhere, and accorded a decent burial. The site of their original interment, however, is, I believe, still haunted, and maybe will remain so till the miscreants are brought to book."

Brief Summary

After a little consideration I am inclined to think there are quite as many authentic cases of hauntings by the phantasms of horses as by the phantasms of cats and dogs. Innumerable horses die unnatural deaths. Apart from those killed in war, many,--more particularly, it is true, in the olden times,--have been murdered in the highways along with their masters; whilst all but the comparative few, when no longer of use to their owners, are butchered in the slaughter-house, and subsequently despatched to the Zoological Gardens, to be eaten by lions and tigers. So much for Christianity, and for man's gratitude. How much better would the promoters of the White Slave Traffic Act be employed, if,--instead of trying to pass a bill which obviously cannot cure the evil it aims at, but can only, by diverting the course of that evil, drive from pillar to post thousands of defenceless, albeit erring women,--they were to labour to secure a peaceful ending for our four-footed toilers, who work for us all their lives, never strike, never think of a pension for old age, and never even dream of a vote. Alas! If only our poor horses could vote, what a different attitude would our pharisaical politicians at once adopt towards them!

Phantasms of Living Horses

From what I have experienced and have been told, I am of the opinion that horses possess the same faculty of separating their immaterial from their material bodies, as cats and dogs. I knew a Virginian lady who had a piebald horse that frequently appeared simultaneously in two places. She lived in an old country house near Winchfield, and one morning when she went into the breakfast-room, she was surprised to see the piebald horse standing on the gravel path, outside the window, looking in at her. When she called it by name, it immediately melted into fine air. Going round to the stables she found the horse in its stall, and on enquiry was informed that it had been there all the time.

The same thing frequently occurred, other members of the household besides herself witnessing it, and so like, in all its details, was the immaterial horse to the material, that they were often at a loss to tell which was which. The phenomenon sometimes occurring when the real horse was awake, and sometimes when it was asleep, proves that the animal possessed the faculty of projecting its spiritual ego-- astral body, or whatever you like to call it--both consciously and unconsciously. I know of many similar instances.

Horses and the Psychic Faculty of Scent

Horses, in a rather less degree than cats, and in much the same degree as dogs, possess the property of scenting the advent and presence of spirits. On more than one occasion, when I have been riding after dusk, my horse has suddenly come to an abrupt halt and shown unmistakable signs of terror. I have not been able to see anything to account for its conduct, but on subsequent enquiry have learned, either that a tragedy was actually known to have taken place there, or that the spot had long borne a reputation for being haunted. And my experiences are the experiences of countless other people.

Before a death a horse will often neigh repeatedly outside the house of the doomed person, and not infrequently show evidences of terror in passing close to it, from which I deduce the horse can at all events scent the proximity of the phantom of death. Like the dog, however, I think it only possesses this peculiar psychic property in a limited degree. It can, for example, readily detect the whereabouts of phantasms haunting localities, but not so easily those haunting people.

It shows little or no discrimination on sight, between cruel and brutal people and those who are kind, giving the same amount of passing space to the one as it does to the other. Yet, on the other hand, I have watched horses at night, standing in the fields, their heads thrown back, a transfixed, far-off expression in their eyes, sniffing the atmosphere--and snuffling it in a manner that strongly suggested to me they were carrying on, by means of some silent, secret code, a conversation with some superphysical presence, which they either saw or scented, very likely both.

Scent, I am convinced, is the medium of conversation, not only between superphysical animals, but between material animals, and if we ever wish to converse with spirits we must employ cats, dogs, and horses to teach us.

Phantom Coaches

There are few parts of the British Isles--few countries in Europe--which have not their phantom coaches. Perhaps the most famous are those that haunt a road near Newport, South Wales, and an old highway in Devon.

A Spectre Coach and Horses in Pembrokeshire

Miss Mary L. Lewes, in an article called "Some More Welsh Ghosts," that appeared in the Occult Review for December, 1907, writes thus:--

"In common with several other districts in Great Britain and Ireland, Pembrokeshire possesses a good 'phantom coach' legend, localized in the southern part of the county, at a place where four roads meet, called Sampson Cross. In old days the belated farmer driving home in his gig from market was apt to cast a nervous glance over his shoulder as his pony slowly climbed the last pitch leading up to the Cross. For tradition says that every night a certain Lady Z. (who lived in the seventeenth century, and whose monument is in the church close by) drives over from Tenby, ten miles distant, in a coach drawn by headless horses, guided by a headless coachman. She also has no head, and arriving by midnight at Sampson Cross, the whole equipage is said to disappear in a flame of fire, with a loud noise of explosion."

Miss Mary L. Lewes goes on to add:--

"A clergyman living in the immediate neighbourhood, who told the writer the story, said that some people believed the ghostly traveller had been safely 'laid' many years ago in the waters of the lake not far off. He added, however that might be, it was an odd fact that his sedate and elderly cob, when driven home past the Cross after nightfall, would invariably start as if frightened there, a thing which never happened by daylight."

What these kinds of spectral horses are no one can say. At the most--despite what theosophists and occultists may declare to the contrary--one can only theorize--and the speculations of one person, be he who he may, seem to me to be of no more consequence than those of another.

For my own part I am inclined to think that whereas, in some cases, the ghostly coach horses are the phantoms of horses that were killed on the highways, in others they are either Vice-Elementals, or Elementals whose particular function it is to prognosticate death,--either the death of those who see them, or the death of someone connected with those who see them.

A Phantom Horse and Policeman

According to one of my correspondents, Mr. T---- P----, a comparatively modern phantom rider has been seen in Canada. Writing to me from C----, where he lives, he says: "It is stated that this town is periodically haunted by the phantom of a tall, fair policeman mounted on a white horse and clothed in the uniform of the 'forties--namely, tail coat, tight trousers, and tall hat. His 'phantom' beat extends from a gateway at the commencement of Cod Hill, along the Park side of Pablo Street to Sutton Street, and Adam Street, down Dane Street, and back, through Pablo Street, to the gateway on Cod Hill."

A gentleman well known in the art world, who, in order to avoid publicity, wishes to be designated Mr. Bates, gave me his experience of the phenomena as follows:--

"Yes, I have seen the ghostly policeman and his milk-white horse. I was walking along Pablo Street on the Park side, one grey afternoon in November, with the express intention of meeting a friend at my Club in Royal Street, when to my surprise, just as I was about a hundred yards from the gateway on Cod Hill, I was overtaken by a tall, fair-haired man, riding a white horse. He was so dressed that I stared in astonishment. He was wearing the costume of seventy or eighty years ago, and reminded me of the policemen in Cruikshank's illustrations of Dickens. I was not frightened, because I thought he must be someone masquerading; and, in my curiosity to see his face, I hastened my steps to overtake him. I failed; for although he appeared to be riding slowly, hardly moving at all, I could not draw an inch nearer to him. This made me think, and I examined him more critically. Then I noticed several things about him, that, at first, had escaped my notice. They were these: (one) that although he was mounted he was wearing walking clothes--he had on long trousers and thick, clumsy boots; (two) that his ears and neck were perfectly colourless, of an unnatural and startling white; (three) that despite the incongruity of his attire, no one but myself seemed to see him. On he rode, neither looking to the left nor to the right, until he came to Sutton Street, when, without paying the slightest attention to the traffic, he began to cross over. There were crowds of vehicles passing at the time, and one of them rushed right on him. Making sure he would be killed, I uttered an ejaculation of horror. Judge, then, of my amazement, when, instead of seeing him lying on the ground, crushed out of all shape, I saw him still riding on, as leisurely and unconcernedly as if he had been on a country road. THE VEHICLE HAD PASSED RIGHT THROUGH HIM. Though I had hitherto scoffed at ghosts, I was now certain I had seen one, and suddenly becoming conscious how very cold it was, I tore on, not feeling at all comfortable till I had reached the warm, cheery, and thoroughly material quarters of my Club."

To corroborate the evidence of "Mr. Bates," I append a narrative given me verbally by Miss Hartly, who, like Mr. Bates, had, up to the time of her experience, posed as a pronounced and somewhat bitter sceptic. She was an emphatic freethinker, and had then no belief whatsoever in a future life. Now she believes "a sight" more than most people.

"One afternoon, in February, 1911," she stated, "just as twilight was commencing, I left the Park, where I had been exercising my dog, and turning into Pablo Street, made for Bright Street. At the corner of Wolf Street I saw something so strange that I involuntarily halted. Riding slowly along on a big white horse, a few paces ahead of me, was an enormous policeman in the quaint attire of the 'forties-top hat, tail coat, tight trousers, just as I had so often seen portrayed in old books. He was riding stiffly, as if unaccustomed to the saddle, and kept looking rigidly in front of him. Thinking it was someone doing it either for a joke or a wager, I was greatly tickled, and kept saying to myself, 'Well, you are a sport, an A1 sport.' I tried to catch him up, to see how he made up his face, but could not, for although the horse never seemed to quicken its pace--a mere crawl--and I ran, it nevertheless maintained precisely the same distance in front of me. When we had progressed in this fashion some hundred or so yards, I perceived a City policeman advancing towards us.

"'Come, now,' I said to myself, 'we shall see some fun--the 1911 copper meeting the peeler of 1840. I wonder what he will think of him.'

"To my intense astonishment, however, neither even as much as gave the other a fleeting glance, but passed by unmoved, and, to all appearance, wholly unconscious of each other.

"A few yards further, I espied a negro looking intently in a store window. Just as the strange policeman came up to him, he gave a violent start, turned round and stared at him, gasped, his cheeks ashy pale, his eyes bulging, made some exclamation I could not catch, and, dashing past me, fled. Then, and not till then, did I begin to feel funny. Further on still we came to a crossing. A carriage and pair with a coronet on the panels of the door was standing waiting. Directly the policeman approached, both the horses reared so violently, they all but threw the coachman off the box. One of the men cried out, 'Heavens, Bill, what's that?' But the other and older of the two, who was clinging to the reins with all his might, merely swore.

"Convinced now that I was on the trail of something not human--something in all probability superphysical, and, impelled by a fascination I could not resist, I followed.

"At the top of Wolf Street the policeman paused, then crossing slowly over, turned into Dane Street, down which he continued to ride with the same mechanical and automatic tread. At length, when within a few feet of a certain shop, over which is a flat that has long borne a reputation for being haunted, the horse came to a dead halt, and horse and rider, veering slowly round, looked at me. What I saw I shall never forget. I saw the faces of the DEAD--the LONG SINCE dead. For some moments they confronted me, and then--vanished, vanished where they stood. I saw them again, under precisely the same conditions, two days later, and I have seen them once since. I am not an imaginative or highly-strung person, but am, on the contrary, exceedingly practical and matter-of-fact, no better proof of which I can give than this fact--I am engaged to be married to a Quebec solicitor!"

An Irish Haunting

Mr. Reginald B. Span, in a most interesting article called "Some Glimpses of the Unseen," that appeared in the Occult Review for February, 1906, writes as follows:--

"Another strange incident, which also occurred in Ireland, was told me by a coachman in my cousin's employ at Kilpeacon, near Limerick. This man had previously been a park-keeper to Lord Doneraile in Co. Cork. One bright moonlight night, he was coming across Lord Doneraile's park, having been round to see that the gates were shut, when his attention was drawn to the distant baying of hounds, and he stopped to listen, as the sounds seemed to proceed from within the park walls, and he knew there were no hounds kept on the estate. His young son was with him, and also heard the noise, which was getting louder and clearer, and was evidently moving rapidly in their direction. His first idea was that a pack of hounds which were kept in the hunting kennels a few miles away, had escaped and had somehow got into the park, although he had seen that the gates were closed, and there was really no way by which they could have entered. The baying of hounds, as if in 'full cry,' sounded closer and closer, and suddenly, out of the shadow of some trees, a number of foxhounds, running at full speed, appeared in the clear light of the moon. They raced past the amazed spectators (a whole pack of them), followed closely by an elderly man on a large horse. Although they came very near, no sound could be heard but the baying of one or two of the hounds. The galloping of the horse was not heard at all. They swung across the grass at a tremendous pace, and were lost to view round the end of a plantation. The park-keeper knew that all the gates were shut, and that it would be impossible for a pack of hounds to pass out, and he thought the mystery might be solved the next day. However, it never was explained--by any natural cause. No hounds or horseman had been in the park. The mansion was closed, Lord Doneraile being away, and no one had the right of entering the grounds within the park walls. He heard later that there was a story in the neighbourhood about 'the ghost' of a former Lord Doneraile 'haunting' the park-- and possibly the spectral horseman was he. I questioned the man and his son closely about it, and am convinced they were not deceived by hallucination, and that their account is perfectly true."

To this account Mr. Span adds this note:--

"The apparition of hounds and huntsman was witnessed on an estate belonging to Lord Doneraile, in the South of Ireland (Doneraile Park); the man who told me the incident was coachman in the service of my cousin, near Limerick. His young son confirmed his father's account, as he also saw it.

"Yours faithfully,

"REGINALD B. SPAN."

To throw additional light on the matter Mr. Ralph Shirley, editor of the Occult Review, published the following letter, written to him by Lord Doneraile:--

"DEAR SHIRLEY,

"It is rather a curious thing that neither Lady Castletown nor Lady Doneraile has ever heard of the story of the moonlight vision of Lord Doneraile and the pack of hounds. However, there is a man at Doneraile called Jones, a chemist, who is a most enthusiastic antiquarian and a dabbler in the occult sciences, and he takes the greatest interest in all that concerns the St. Legers. Lady Castletown wrote to him, and the reply comes from his brother (I suppose he is away), and that I send you.

"Lady Doneraile says it must refer to the third Lord Doneraile of the first creation, who was killed in a duel afterwards; and there appear to be a lot of stories which Jones has ferreted out or been told. Of course, I don't know how far you could say Jones was authentic. All I can say is that he believes the things himself.

"Yours sincerely,

"DONERAILE."

"Dec. 27, 1905."

"I should explain," adds Mr. Shirley, "that Lady Castletown is daughter to the late Lord Doneraile, and present owner of Doneraile House. Here follows the enclosure, i.e. the extract made by Walter A. Jones, Doneraile, from his MS. notes on the Legends of Peasantry in connection with Doneraile branch of the St. Leger family. Dated December 21, 1905.

"I have heard," so it runs, "the following story respecting the Lord Doneraile, who pursues the chase from Ballydineen through Gloun-na-goth Wilkinson's Lawn, through Byblox, across the ford of Shanagh aha Keel-ahboobleen into Waskin's Glen into the old Deer Park at Old Court, thence into the Horse Close, and from thence into the park. He appears to take particular delight in Wilkinson's Lawn according to tradition, for it was there that the noble stag was lost sight of, and of course it was there he was most searched for. It was only last autumn that two gentlemen were going to a fair, as I heard, and leading a very fine horse behind the trap. The night being fine and moonlight, they stopped at the iron gate there to light their pipes, when a gentleman dressed in old style, with buckskin leggings, walked through the iron gate, though closed, and patted the led horse on the neck. They both agreed that he was most like to gentlemen of the St. Leger family whom they had known. The Radiant Boy also appears here, and for years in the early part of last century no one would pass there after nightfall. The Lord Doneraile, who is believed by the peasantry to stand under Lord Doneraile's Oak, it has been told me positively, was third Viscount.

"There is an old man called Reardon here now who saw a gentleman riding a powerful black horse along Lord Doneraile's route in the middle of the day, and his sister who was with him failed to see the horseman, though her brother had to pull her out of his way.

"I went up to Saffron Hill last winter to see the ostrich-like ghost which is there, and I heard a great sweep as of hounds and horses going past me. Paddy Shea, late herd to Lord Doneraile, also would swear he saw the phantom Lord Doneraile pursuing the chase often. I have heard that James Mullaine also saw him in Wilkinson's Lawn, but have not any further proof.

"It is very few people will admit having seen these things. George Buckley, present keeper of the Doneraile Park, got a great fright one night which might have been from the same cause."

In this case it seems more than likely the huntsman, horse and hounds were all bona fide phantasms of the dead.

Wild Darrell

Littlecote, as everyone knows, is haunted by the spirits of the notorious "Wild Will Darrell" and the horse he invariably rode, and which eventually broke his neck.

But there are many Wild Darrells; all Europe is overrun by them. They nightly tear, on their phantom horses, over the German and Norwegian forests and moorlands that echo and re-echo with their hoarse shouts and the mournful baying of their grisly hounds.

Many travellers in Russia and Germany journeying through the forests at night have caught the sound of wails,--of moans that, starting from the far distance, have gradually come nearer and nearer. Then they have heard the winding of a horn, the shouting and cursing of the huntsman, and in a biting cold wind have seen the whole cavalcade sweep by.

According to various authorities on the subject this spectral chase goes by different names. In Thuringia and elsewhere, it is "Hakelnberg" or "Hackelnbarend,"--the story being that Hakelnberg, a German knight, who had devoted his whole life to the chase, on his death-bed had told the officiating priest that he cared not a jot for heaven, but only for hunting; the priest losing patience and exclaiming, "Then hunt till Doomsday."

So, in all weathers, in snow and ice, Hakelnberg, his horse and hounds, are seen careering after imaginary game.

There are similar stories current in the Netherlands, Denmark, Russia, and practically all over Europe, and not only Europe, but in many of the states and departments of the New World. This being so, I think there must be a substantial substratum of truth underlying the beliefs, phantastic as they may appear, and yet, are no more phantastic than many of the stories we are asked to give absolute credence to in the Bible.

In Old Castile the spirit of a Moorish leader who won many victories over the Spaniards, and was drowned by reason of his heavy armour in a swamp of the River Duero, still haunts his burial-place, a piece of marshy ground, near Burgos. There, weird noises, such as the winding of a huntsman's horn and the neighing of a horse, are heard, and the phantasm of the dead Moor is seen mounted on a white horse followed by twelve huge, black hounds.

In Sweden many of the peasants say, when a noise like that of a coach and horses is heard rumbling past in the dead of night, "It is the White Rider," whilst in Norway they say of the same sounds, "It is the hunt of the Devil and his four horses." In Saxony the rider is believed to be Barbarossa, the celebrated hero of olden days. Near Fontainebleau, Hugh Capet is stated to ride a gigantic sable horse to the palace, where he hunted before the assassination of Henry IV; and in the Landes the rider is thought to be Judas Iscariot. In other parts of France the wild huntsman is known as Harlequin or Henequin, and in some parts of Brittany he is "Herod in pursuit of the Holy Innocents." (Alas, that no such Herod visits London! How welcome would he be, were he only to flout a few of the brawling brats who, allowed to go anywhere they please, make an inferno of every road they choose to play in.)

Here my notes on horses end; and although the evidence I have offered may have failed to convince many, I myself am fully satisfied that these noble and indispensable animals do not terminate their existence in this world, but pass on to another, and, let us all sincerely hope, far happier, plane.

CHAPTER IV
BULLS, COWS, PIGS, ETC.

From the Hebrides there comes to me a case of the phantasm of a black bull, that, on certain nights in the year, is heard bellowing inside the shed where it was killed.

There are many accounts of ghostly cows heard "mooing" in the moors and bog-lands of Scotland and Ireland respectively, and not a few cases of whole herds of phantom cattle seen, gliding along, one behind the other, with silent, noiseless tread. Though I have never had the opportunity of experimenting with cows to see if they are sensitive to the superphysical, I see no reason why they should not be, and I feel quite certain they will participate in "the future life."

Apropos of pigs, Mr. Dyer, in his Ghost World, says, "Another form of spectre animal is the kirk-grim, which is believed to haunt many churches. Sometimes it is a pig, sometimes a horse, the haunting spectre being the spirit of an animal buried alive in the churchyard for the purpose of scaring away the sacrilegious."

Mr. Dyer goes on to say that it was the custom of the old Christian churches to bury a lamb under the altar; and that if anyone entered a church out of service time and happened to see a little lamb spring across the choir and vanish, it was a sure prognostication of the death of some child; and if this apparition was seen by the grave-digger the death would take place immediately. Mr. Dyer also tells us that the Danish kirk-grim was thought to hide itself in the tower of a church in preference to any other place, and that it was thought to protect the sacred buildings. According to the same writer, in the streets of Kroskjoberg, a grave sow, or, as it was called, a "gray-sow," was frequently seen, and it was said to be the apparition of a sow formerly buried alive; its appearance foretelling death or calamity.

Phantasm of a Goat

Mrs. Crowe, in her Night Side of Nature, relates one case of a house near Philadelphia, U.S.A., that was haunted by a variety of phenomena, among others that of a spectre resembling a goat.

"Other extraordinary things happened in the house," she writes, "which had the reputation of being haunted, although the son had not believed it, and had thereupon not mentioned the report to the father.

"One day the children said they had been running after 'such a queer thing in the cellar; it was like a goat, and not like a goat, but it seemed to be like a shadow.'"

This explanation does not appear to be very satisfactory, but as I have heard of one or two other cases of premises being haunted by what, undoubtedly, were the phantasms of goats, I think it highly probable it was the ghost of a goat in this instance, too.

The Phantom Pigs of the Chiltern Hills

A good many years ago there was a story current of an extraordinary haunting by a herd of pigs. The chief authority on the subject was a farmer, who was an eye-witness of the phenomena. I will call him Mr. B.

Mr. B., as a boy, lived in a small house called the Moat Grange, which was situated in a very lonely spot near four cross-roads, connecting four towns.

The house, deriving its name from the fact that a moat surrounded it, stood near the meeting point of the four roads, which was the site of a gibbet, the bodies of the criminals being buried in the moat.

Well, the B----s had not been living long on the farm, before they were awakened one night by hearing the most dreadful noises, partly human and partly animal, seemingly proceeding from a neighbouring spinney, and on going to a long front window overlooking the cross-roads, they saw a number of spotted creatures like pigs, screaming, fighting and tearing up the soil on the site of the criminals' cemetery.

The sight was so unexpected and alarming that the B----s were appalled, and Mr. B. was about to strike a light on the tinder-box, when the most diabolical white face was pressed against the outside of the window-pane and stared in at them.

This was the climax, the children shrieked with terror, and Mrs. B., falling on her knees, began to pray, whereupon the face at the window vanished, and the herd of pigs, ceasing their disturbance, tore frantically down one of the high roads, and disappeared from view.

Similar phenomena were seen and heard so frequently afterwards, that the B----s eventually had to leave the farm, and subsequent enquiries led to their learning that the place had long borne the reputation of being haunted, the ghosts being supposed to be the earth-bound spirits of the executed criminals. Whether this was so or not must, of course, be a matter of conjecture--the herd of hogs may well have been the phantasms of actual earth-bound pigs--attracted to the spot by a sort of fellow-feeling for the criminals, whose gross and carnal natures would no doubt appeal to them.

A lane in Hertfordshire was--and, perhaps, still is--haunted by the phantasm of a big white sow which had accidentally been run over and killed. It was occasionally heard grunting, and had the unpleasant knack of approaching one noiselessly from the rear, and of making the most unearthly noise just behind one's back.

Sheep

Lambs and sheep, possessing finer natures than goats and pigs, would appear to be less earth-bound, and, in all probability, only temporarily haunt the spots that witnessed their usually barbarous ends.

Most slaughter-houses are haunted by them--as, indeed, by many other animals. A Scottish moor long bore the reputation for being haunted by a phantom flock of sheep, which were always heard "baaing" plaintively before a big storm.

It was supposed they were the ghosts of a flock that had perished in the memorable severe weather of Christmas, 1880. Here is a case that may be regarded as typical of hauntings by sheep, presumably the earth-bound spirits of sheep, overwhelmed in some great storm or unexpected catastrophe.

"The Spectre Flock of Sheep in Germany"

"During the seven years' war in Germany," writes Mrs. Crowe, in her Night Side of Nature, "a drover lost his life in a drunken squabble on the high road.

"For some time there was a sort of rude tombstone, with a cross on it, to mark the spot where his body was interred, but this has long fallen, and a milestone now fills its place. Nevertheless, it continues to be commonly asserted by the country people, and also by various travellers, that they have been deluded on that spot by seeing, as they imagine, herds of beasts, which on investigation prove to be merely visionary. Of course, many people look upon this as a superstition; but a very regular confirmation of the story occurred in the year 1826, when two gentlemen and two ladies were passing the spot in a post-carriage. One of these was a clergyman, and none of them had ever heard of the phenomenon said to be attached to the place. They had been discussing the prospects of the minister, who was on his way to a vicarage, to which he had just been appointed, when they saw a large flock of sheep, which stretched quite across the road, and was accompanied by a shepherd and a long-haired black dog. As to meet cattle on that road was nothing uncommon, and indeed they had met several droves in the course of one day, no remark was made at the moment, till suddenly each looked at the other, and said, 'What's become of the sheep?' Quite perplexed at their sudden disappearance, they called to the postilion to stop, and all got out, in order to mount the little elevation and look around, but still unable to discover them, they now bethought themselves of asking the postilion where they were; when, to their infinite surprise, they learned that he had not seen them. Upon this, they bade him quicken his pace, that they might overtake a carriage that had passed them shortly before, and enquire if that party had seen the sheep; but they had not.

"Four years later a postmaster, named J., was on the same road, driving a carriage, in which were a clergyman and his wife, when he saw a large flock of sheep near the same spot. Seeing they were very fine wethers, and supposing them to have been bought at a sheep-fair that was then taking place a few miles off, J. drew up his reins and stopped his horses, turning at the same time to the clergyman to say that he wanted to enquire the price of the sheep, as he intended going next day to the fair himself. Whilst the minister was asking him what sheep he meant, J. got down and found himself in the midst of the animals, the size and beauty of which astonished him. They passed him at an unusual rate, whilst he made his way through them to find the shepherd; when, on getting to the end of the flock, they suddenly disappeared. He then first learnt that his fellow-travellers had not seen them at all."

So writes Mrs. Crowe, and I quote the case in support of my argument that sheep, like horses, cats, dogs and all other kinds of animals, possess spirits, and consequently have a future state of existence.

I have not yet experimented with sheep, goats, or pigs, but I do not doubt but that they are more or less sensitive to superphysical influences, and possess the psychic faculty of scenting the Unknown--though not, perhaps, in so great a degree as any of the other animals I have enumerated.

PART II
WILD ANIMALS AND THE UNKNOWN

CHAPTER V
WILD ANIMALS AND THE UNKNOWN

Apes

The following case of animal hauntings was recorded in automatic writing:--

"I sank wearily into my easy chair before the fire, which burned with a fitful and sullen glow in the tiny grate of my one room--bare and desolate as only the room of an unsuccessful author can be.

"My condition was pitiable. For the past twelve months I had not earned a cent, and of my small capital there now remained but two pounds to ward the hound of starvation from my door. In the moonlight I could perceive all the bareness of the apartment. Would to God Fancy would ride to me on this moonbeam and give me inspiration! 'Twas indeed weird--this silver ethereal path connecting the moon with the earth, and the more I gazed along it, the more I wished to leave my body and escape to the star-lighted vaults. Certainly, from a conversation I had once had with a member of the New Occult Society, I believed it possible by concentrating all the mental activities in one channel, so to overcome the barriers which prevent the soul visiting scenes of the ethereal world, as to pass materialized to the spot upon which the ideas are fixed. But although I had essayed--how many times I do not like to confess--to gain that amount of concentration necessary for the separation of the soul from the body, up to the present all my attempts had been fruitless. Doubtless there had been a something--too minute even for definition--that had interrupted my self-abstraction--a something that had wrecked my venture, just when I felt it to be on the verge of completion. And was it likely that now, when my ideas were misty and vague, I should be more successful? I wanted to quit the cruel bonds of nature and be free--free to roam and ramble. But where?

"At length, as I gazed into the moonlight, I lost all cognizance of the objects around me, and my eyes became fixed on the mountains of the moon, which I discovered, with a start, were no longer specks. I found, to my amazement, I had left my body and was careering swiftly through space--infinite space. The range opened up in front of me, spreading out far and wide, winding, black and awful--their solemn grandeur lost in that terrible desolation which makes the moon appear like a hideous nightmare. I could see with amazing clearness the sides of the mountains; there were enormous black fissures, some of them hundreds of feet in width--and the more I gazed the more impressed I grew with the silence. There was no life. There were no seas, no lakes, no trees, no grass, no sighing nor moaning of the wind, nothing to remind me of the earth I now found to my terror I had actually quitted. Everything around me was black--the sky, the mountains, the vast pits, the dried-up mouths of which gaped dismally.

"With the movements of a man in a fit, I essayed to hinder the finis of my mad plunge. I waved my limbs violently, kicking out and shrieking in the agonies of fear. I cursed and prayed, wept and laughed alternately, did everything, yet nothing, that could save me from contact with the lone desert so horribly close. Nearer and nearer I approached, until at last my feet rested on the hard caked soil. For the first few minutes after my arrival I was too overwhelmed with fear to do other than remain stationary. The ground beneath my feet swarmed with myriads of foul and long-legged insects, things with unwieldy pincers and protruding eyes; things covered with scaly armour; hybrids of beetles and scorpions. I have a distinct recollection of one huge-jointed centipede making a vicious grab at my leg; he failed to make his teeth meet in anything tangible, and emitting a venomous hiss disappeared in a circular pit.

"Whilst I was the victim of this insect's ferocity the horizon had become darkened by the shadowy outline of an enormous apish form. I wanted to run away, but could not, and was compelled, sorely against my will, to witness its approach. Never shall I forget the agonies of doubt I endured during its advance. No man in a

tiger's den, nor deer tied to a tree awaiting its destroyer, could have suffered more than I did then, and my terror increased tenfold when I recognized in the monster-
-Neppon--a young gorilla that had been under my charge and had given me no end of trouble when I was head keeper in the Zoological Gardens at Berne.

"I never hated anything so much as I had hated that baboon. At my hands it had undergone a thousand subtle torments. I had pinched it, poked it, pulled its hair, frightened it by putting on masks and making all sorts of queer noises, and finally I had secretly poisoned it. And now we stood face to face without any bars between us. Never shall I forget the look of intense satisfaction in its hideous eyes, as its gaze encountered mine.

"In that strange forlorn world we faced each other; I, the tyrant once, now the quarry. In the wildness of its glee it capered about like a mad thing, executing the most exaggerated antics that augmented my terror. Every second I anticipated an assault, and the knowledge of my fears lent additional fierceness to its gambols. A sudden change in my attitude at length made it cease. The use had returned to my limbs; my muscles were quivering, and before it could stop me I had fled! The wildest of chases then ensued. I ran with a speed that would have shamed a record-beater on earth. With extraordinary nimbleness I vaulted over titanic boulders of rocks; jumped across dykes of infinite depth, scurried like lightning over tracts of rough, lacerating ground, and never for one instant felt like flagging.

"Suddenly, to my horror, I came to an abrupt standstill, and the cry of some hunted animal burst from my lips. Unwittingly I had run against a huge wall of granite, and escape was now impossible. Again and again I clawed the hard rock, until the skin hung in shreds from my fingers, and the blood pattered on the dark soil, that in all probability had never tasted moisture before. All this amused my pursuer vastly; it watched with the leisure of one who knows its fish will be landed in safety, and there suddenly came to me, through my olfactory nerves, a knowl-edge that it was speaking to me in the language of scents--the language I never understood till now was the language of all animals.

"'Reach, a little higher,' it said; 'there are niches up there, and you must stretch your limbs. Ha! ha! Do you remember how you used to make me stretch mine? You do! Well, you needn't shiver. Explain to me how it is I find you here.'

"'I cannot comprehend,' I gasped with a gesticulation that was grotesque.

"The great beast laughed in my face. 'How so?' it queried. 'You used to quibble me upon my dull wits; must I now return the compliment? Ha! There's blood on your hands. Blood! I will lick it up.' And with a mocking grin it advanced.

"'Keep off! Keep off!' I shouted. 'My God, will this dream never cease?'

"'The dream, as you call it,' the gorilla jeered, 'has only just begun; the climax of your horrors has yet to come. If you cannot tell me the purport of your visit I will tell you mine. Can your lordship spare the time to listen?'

"I gave no answer. I clutched the wall and uttered incoherent cries like some frightened madman.

"The gorilla felt the muscles in its hairy fingers, and showed its huge teeth. I looked eagerly at my enemy.

"'Come, you haven't yet guessed my riddle; you are dull to-night,' it said lightly. 'That old wine of yours made you sleep too soundly. Don't let me disturb you. I will explain. This moon is now my home--I share it with the spirits of all the animals and insects that were once on your earth. And now that we are free from such as you--free to wander anywhere we like without fear of being shot, or caught and caged--we are happy. And what makes us still happier is the knowledge that the majority of men and women will never have a joyous after-state like ours. They will be earth-bound in that miserable world of theirs, and compelled to keep to their old haunts, scaring to death with their ugly faces all who have the misfortune to see them. There is another fate in store for you, however. Do you know what it is?'

"It paused. No sound other than that occasioned by his bumping on the soil broke the impressive hush.

"'Do you know?' it said again. 'Well, I will tell you. I'm going to kill you right away, so that your spirit--it's all nonsense to talk about souls, such as you have no soul--will be earth-bound here--here for ever--and will be a perpetual source of amusement to all of us animal ghosts.'

"It then began to jabber ferociously, and, crouching down, prepared to spring.

"'For Heaven's sake,' I shrieked, 'for Heaven's sake.'

"But I might as well have appealed to the wind. It had no sense of mercy.

"'He, he!' it screamed. 'What a joke--what a splendid joke. Your wit never seems to degenerate, Hugesson! I'm wondering if you will be as funny when you're a ghost. Get ready. I'm coming, coming,' and as the sky deepened to an awe-inspiring black, and the stars grew larger, brighter, fiercer; and the great lone deserts appealed to me with a force unequalled before, it sprang through the air.

"A singing in my ears and a great bloody mist rose before my eyes. The wailing and screeching of a million souls was borne in loud protracted echoings through the drum of my ears. Men and women with evil faces rose up from crag and boulder to spit and tear at me. I saw creatures of such damning ugliness that my soul screamed aloud with terror. And then from the mountain tops the bolt of heaven was let loose. Every spirit was swept away like chaff before the burst of wind that, hurling and shrieking, bore down upon me. I gave myself up for lost. I felt all the agonies of suffocation, my lungs were torn from my palpitating body; my legs wrenched round in their sockets; my feet whirled upwards in that gust of devilish air. All--excruciating, damning pain--and pro tempore--I knew no more."

> *   *   *   *   *

N.B.--It was subsequently ascertained, by my friend the late Mr. Supton, that a man named Hugesson, who had been for a short time head keeper at the Zoological Gardens, had been found dead, in bed, by his landlady, with a look on his face so awful that she had fled shrieking from the room. The death was, of course, attributed to syncope, but my friend--who, by the way, had never heard of Hugesson before he received the foregoing account through the medium of planchette--told me, and I agreed with him, that from similar cases that had come within his experience, it was most probable that Hugesson had in reality projected himself, and had perished in the manner described.

No more improbable than the above story is that sent me by my old school friend Martin Tristram, who died last year.

I style it "The Case of Martin Tristram." It is reproduced from a magazine published some three years ago.

After Martin Tristram once took up spiritualism his visits to me became most erratic, and I not only never knew when to expect him, but I was not always sure, when he did come, that it was he.

This sounds extraordinary--to see a man is assuredly to recognize him! Not always--by no means always!

There are circumstances in which a man loses his identity, when his "ego" is supplanted by another ego, when he ceases to be himself, and assumes an individuality which is entirely different from himself.

This is undoubtedly the case in madness, imbecility, epilepsy, so-called total loss of memory through cerebral injury, hypnotism, sometimes in projection when the astral body gets detained, and also not infrequently in investigating peculiar instances of psychic phenomena.

But if the astral body has been evicted from its carnal home, whither has it gone? and what is the nature of the thing that has taken its place?

Ah! These are indeed puzzles--puzzles I am devoting a lifetime to solve.

There have been moments when unseen hands have gradually begun to pull aside the obscuring veil, when the identity of the usurping spirit has seemed on the verge of being disclosed to me, and I have been about to be initiated into the greatest and most zealously guarded of all secrets.

There have been times, I say, when my occult researches have actually brought me to this climax; but up to the present I have invariably been disappointed--the curtain has suddenly fallen, the esoteric ego has shrunk into its shell, and the mystery surrounding it has remained impenetrable.

This is but one, albeit perhaps the most striking, of the many methods through which the superphysical endeavours to get in immediate contact with the physical.

I was unpleasantly reminded of it when Martin Tristram's carnal body came to visit me one night several years ago. I was aware that it was not Tristram. His mannerisms were the same, his voice had not altered; but there was an expression in his eyes that told of a very different spirit from Martin's dwelling within that body.

The night being cold, he closed the door carefully, and crossing the room to where I sat by the fire, threw himself in an easy chair, and gazed meditatively at me.

My rooms in Bloomsbury were not lonely. They had more than their share of "brawling brats" on either side; there were no gloomy recesses or ghost-suggestive cupboards, and I never once experienced in them the slightest apprehension of sudden superphysical manifestations, yet I cannot help saying that as I met that glance from the pseudo-Tristram's eyes I felt my flesh begin to creep.

He sat for so long in silence that I began to wonder if he ever meant to speak.

"The secret of success in seeing certain classes of apparitions," he said at length, "to a very great extent lies in sympathy. Sympathy! And now for my story. I will tell it to you in the 'third person.'"

I looked at Tristram's face in dismay. "The third person!"

"Yes, the third person," he gravely rejoined, "and under the circumstances the only person. You see it is now close on midnight."

I looked at the clock. Great heavens! What he said was correct. A whole evening had slipped by without my knowledge. He would, of course, have to stay the night. I suggested it to him.

"My dear fellow," he replied, with an odd smile, "don't worry about me. I am not dependent on any trains. I shall be home by two o'clock."

I shivered--a draught of cold air had in all probability stolen through the cracks of the ill-fitting window-frames.

"You have on one of your queer moods, Martin," I expostulated. "To be home by two o'clock you must fly! But proceed--at all costs, the story."

Tristram raised an eyebrow, a true sign that something of special interest would follow.

"You know Bruges?" he began.

I nodded.

"Very well, then," he went on. "Exactly a week ago Martin Tristram arrived there from Antwerp. The hour was late, the weather boisterous, Tristram was tired, and any lodging was better than none.

"Hailing a four-wheeler, he asked the Jehu to drive him to some decent hostel where the sheets were clean and the tariff moderate; and the fellow, gathering up the reins, took him at a snail's pace to a mediaeval-looking tavern in La Rue Croissante. You remember that street? Perhaps not! It is quite a back street, extremely narrow, very tortuous, and miserably lighted with a few gas-lamps of the usual antique Belgian order.

"Tristram was too tired, however, to be fastidious; he felt he could lie down and go to sleep anywhere, and what scruples he might have had were entirely dissipated by the appearance of the charming girl who answered the door.

"It is not expedient to dwell upon her--she plays a very minor part, if, indeed, any, in the story. Martin Tristram merely thought her pretty, and that, as I have said, fully reconciled him to taking up his quarters in the house.

"He has, as you are doubtless aware, a weakness for vivid colouring, and her bright yellow hair, carmine lips, and scarlet stockings struck him impressively as she led the way to his bed-chamber, where she somewhat reluctantly parted from him with a subtly attractive smile.

"Left to himself, Martin sleepily examined his surroundings. The room, oak-panelled throughout, was long, low, and gloomy; an enormous, old-fashioned, empty fireplace occupied the centre of one of the walls; on the one side of it was an oak settee, on the other an equally ponderous black oak chest.

"Heavy oaken beams traversed the ceiling, and the sombre, funereal character of the room was further increased by a colossal and antique four-poster which, placed in the exact middle of the chamber, faced a gigantic mirror attached to grotesquely carved and excessively lofty sable supports.

"Viewed in the feeble, fluctuating candlelight, the latter seemed endowed with some peculiar and emphatically weird life--their glistening, polished surfaces threw a dozen and one fantastic but oddly human shadows on the boards, as at the same time they appeared in bewildering alternation to increase and diminish in stature.

"Tristram hastily undressed, and stretching himself between the blankets, prepared to go to sleep. Like yourself, and for a similar reason, he never sleeps on his left side. Accordingly he occupied the right portion only of the enormous bed.

"Why he did not fall asleep at once he could not explain; he fancied that it might be because he was overtired. This undoubtedly had something to do with it, as also had the remarkable noises--footfalls, creaks, and sighs--that came from every corner of the apartment the moment the light was out.

"He listened to these inexplicable sounds with increasing alarm until the sonorous clock from somewhere outside boomed 'one,' when, quite unaccountably, he fell asleep, awaking on the stroke of two from a dreadful nightmare.

"To his intense astonishment and consternation he was no longer alone in the bed--someone, or something, was lying by his side on the left-hand side of the bed.

"At first his thoughts reverted to the young lady with the scarlet stockings; then, a sensation of icy coldness, whilst speedily reassuring him with regard to her, struck him with the utmost terror. Who or what could it be?

"For some seconds he lay in breathless silence, too frightened even to stir, and panic-stricken lest the violent beating of his heart should arouse the mysterious visitor. But at length, impelled by an irresistible impulse, he sat up in bed and opened his eyes. The room was aglow with a phosphorescent light, and in the depths of the glittering mirror he saw a startling reproduction of the phantasmagoric four-poster.

"He instinctively felt that there was some extraordinary change in the supports, and that the suspicions he had at first entertained as to their semi-human properties had become verified; but, mercifully for his sanity, he found it impossible to look. His attention was immediately riveted on the object by his side, which he recognized with a thrill of surprise was a bronzed and bearded man of rather more than middle age, who appeared to be buried in the most profound sleep.

"The picture was so vividly portrayed in the glass that Tristram could see the gentle heaving of the bedclothes each time the sleeper breathed.

"Fascinated beyond measure at such an unlooked-for spectacle, and desirous of a closer inspection, Tristram, with a supreme effort, managed to tear away his eyes from the mirror and to glance at the bed, where, to his unmitigated astonishment, he saw no one.

"Quite unable to know what to make of the phenomenon, he again directed his gaze to the glass, and there right enough lay the sleeper.

"A cold shudder now ran through Tristram--he could no longer disguise from himself what he had in reality thought all along, that the room was haunted!

"The usual symptoms accompanying occult manifestations rapidly made themselves known. Tristram was constrained to stare at the luminous glitter before him in helpless expectation; to save his soul he could neither have stirred nor uttered the faintest ejaculation. He saw in the mirror the door of the bedroom slowly open, and a hideous, apish face peep stealthily in, not at him, but at the sleeper.

"Next he watched a figure, brown, hairy and lurid--the figure of some huge monkey--come crawling into the room on all-fours, and followed each of its tell-tale movements as, sidling up to its sleeping victim, it suddenly hurled itself at him, choking him to death with its long fingers.

"This was the climax--Tristram saw no more. The phosphorescent light died out, the mirror darkened, and on sinking back on his pillow, he realized with the wildest delight he was once again alone--his bedfellow had gone!

"Tristram was so unnerved by all that had happened that he made up his mind to leave the house at daybreak, a decision which, however, was altered on the appearance of the sun and the charming little girl in the red stockings.

"After breakfasting, Tristram strolled about the town, chancing to meet an old school-fellow, named Heriot, in the Rue de Mermadotte.

"Heriot had only recently come to Bruges; he was dissatisfied with his lodgings, and readily fell in with Tristram's suggestion that they should 'dig' together.

"The maid with the yellow hair was more pleasing than ever, Heriot fell desperately in love with her, and it was close on midnight before he could be persuaded to bid her good night and accompany Tristram to the bed-chamber.

"'I wonder why she told me not to sleep on the left side of the bed?' he said to Martin, as they began to undress.

"Tristram glanced guiltily at the mirror. For reasons of his own he hadn't as much as hinted to Heriot what he had seen there the previous night, and he was not at all sure now that it might not have been a nightmare or an hallucination; anyhow, he would like to put it to the test before mentioning it to anyone, and Heriot, whom he knew to be a sceptic with regard to ghosts, was so strong and hale a man physically that, happen what might, he had no apprehensions whatever concerning him.

"Regretting that he was obliged to disobey the wishes of a lady, Heriot declared his preference for the left side of the bed, adding that if the maiden was so highly enamoured of him, she must put herself to the inconvenience of a few extra yards. 'Infatuation like hers,' he maintained, 'should surely overcome all obstacles.'

"Nothing loth, Tristram gave in to him, and before many minutes had elapsed both men had fallen into a deep sleep.

"On the stroke of two Tristram awoke, perspiring horribly. The room was once again aglow with a phosphorescent light, and he felt the presence next to him of something cold and clammy.

"Unable to look elsewhere, he was again compelled to gaze in the mirror, where he saw, to his consternation and horror, no Heriot, but in his place the man with the bronzed face and bushy beard.

"He had hardly recovered from the shock occasioned by this discovery when the door surreptitiously opened, and the figure of the ape glided noiselessly in.

"Again he was temporarily paralysed, his limbs losing all their power of action and his tongue cleaving to the roof of his mouth.

"The movements of the phantasm were entirely repetitionary of the previous night. Approaching the bed on 'all-fours,' it leapt on its victim, the tragedy being accompanied this time by the most realistic chokings and gurgles, to all of which Tristram was obliged to listen in an agony of doubt and terror. The drama ended, Tristram was overcome by a sudden fit of drowsiness, and sinking back on to his pillow, slept till broad daylight.

"Anxious to question Heriot as to whether he, too, had been a witness of the ghostly transaction he touched him lightly on the shoulder. There was no reply. He touched him again, and still no answer. He touched him yet a third time, and as there was still no response, he leaned over his shoulder and peered into his face.

"Heriot was dead!"

*   *   *   *   *

"'This is the fourth death in that bed within the last twelve months that I can swear to,' the English doctor remarked to Tristram, as they walked down the street together, 'and always from the same cause, failure of the heart due to a sudden shock. If you take my advice, you'll clear out of the place at once.'

"Tristram thought so too, but before he went he had a talk with the girl in the red stockings.

"'I can't tell you all I know,' she said to him, as he kissed her; 'but I wouldn't sleep a night in that room for a fortune, though I believe it's quite safe if you keep on the right side of the bed. I wish your friend had done so, he was so handsome,' and Tristram, not a little hurt, let go her hand, and made arrangements for the funeral."

*   *   *   *   *

"And is that all?" I asked, as Tristram's material body paused.

"It may be," was the reply, "but that is why I've come to you. Don't be gulled by Tristram into any investigations in that house. Enthusiasm for his research work makes him unconsciously callous, and if he once got you there he might, even against your better judgment, persuade you to sleep on the left side! Good night!"

I shook hands with him and he departed. The following evening I heard it all again from Tristram himself--the real Tristram.

Needless to say, his concluding remarks differed essentially. With unbounded cordiality he urged me to accompany him back again to Bruges, and I--declined!

    *   *   *   *   *

He wrote to me afterwards to say that he had discovered the history of the house--a man, a music-hall artist, answering to the description of the figure in the bed--had once lived there with a performing ape, an orang-outang, and happening to annoy the animal one day, the latter had killed him. The brute was eventually shot!

"This experience of mine," Tristram added, "is of the greatest value, for it has thoroughly convinced me of one thing at least--and that--that apes have spirits! And if that be so, so must all other kinds of animals. Of course they must."

Phantasms of Cat and Baboon

A sister of a well-known author tells me there used to be a house called "The Swallows," standing in two acres of land, close to a village near Basingstoke.

In 1840 a Mr. Bishop of Tring bought the house, which had long stood empty, and went to live there in 1841. After being there a fortnight two servants gave notice to leave, stating that the place was haunted by a large cat and a big baboon, which they constantly saw stealing down the staircases and passages. They also testified to hearing sounds as of somebody being strangled, proceeding from an empty attic near where they slept, and of the screams and groans of a number of people being horribly tortured in the cellars just underneath the dairy. On going to see what was the cause of the disturbances, nothing was ever visible. By and by other members of the household began to be harassed by similar manifestations. The news spread through the village, and crowds of people came to the house with lights and sticks, to see if they could witness anything.

One night, at about twelve o'clock, when several of the watchers were stationed on guard in the empty courtyard, they all saw the forms of a huge cat and a baboon rise from the closed grating of the large cellar under the old dairy, rush past them, and disappear in a dark angle of the walls. The same figures were repeatedly seen afterwards by many other persons. Early in December, 1841, Mr. Bishop, hearing fearful screams, accompanied by deep and hoarse jabberings, apparently coming from the top of the house, rushed upstairs, whereupon all was instantly silent, and he could discover nothing. After that, Mr. Bishop set to work to get rid of the house, and was fortunate enough to find as a purchaser a retired colonel, who was soon, however, scared out of it. This was in 1842; it was soon after pulled down. The ground was used for the erection of cottages; but the hauntings being transferred to them, they were speedily vacated, and no one ever daring to inhabit them, they were eventually demolished, the site on which they stood being converted into allotments.

There were many theories as to the history of "The Swallows"; one being that a highwayman, known as Steeplechase Jock, the son of a Scottish chieftain, had once plied his trade there and murdered many people, whose bodies were supposed to be buried somewhere on or near the premises. He was said to have had a terrible though decidedly unorthodox ending--falling into a vat of boiling tar, a raving madman. But what were the phantasms of the ape and cat? Were they the earth-bound spirits of the highwayman and his horse, or simply the spirits of two animals? Though either theory is possible, I am inclined to favour the former.

Psychic Bears

Edmund Lenthal Swifte, appointed in 1814 Keeper of the Crown Jewels in the Tower of London, refers in an article in Notes and Queries, 1860, to various unaccountable phenomena happening in the Tower during his residence there. He says that one night in the Jewel Office, one of the sentries was alarmed by a figure like a huge bear issuing from underneath the Jewel Room door. He thrust at it with his bayonet, which, going right through it, stuck in the doorway, whereupon he dropped in a fit, and was carried senseless to the guard-room. When on the morrow Mr. Swifte saw the soldier in the guard-room, his fellow-sentinel was also there, and the latter testified to having seen his comrade, before the alarm, quiet and active, and in full possession of his faculties. He was now, so Mr. Swifte added, changed almost beyond recognition, and died the following day.

Mr. George Offer, in referring to this incident, alludes to queer noises having been heard at the time the figure appeared. Presuming that the sentinel was not the victim of an hallucination, the question arises as to the kind of spirit that he saw. The bear, judging by cases that have been told me, is by no means an uncommon occult phenomenon. The difficulty is how to classify it, since, upon no question appertaining to the psychic, can one dogmatize. To quote from a clever poem that appeared in the January number of the Occult Review, to pretend one knows anything definite about the immaterial world is all "swank". At the most we--Parsons, Priests, Theosophists, Christian Scientists, Psychical Research Professors,--at the most can only speculate. Nothing--nothing whatsoever, beyond the bare fact that there are phenomena, unaccountable by physical laws, has as yet been discovered. All the time and energy and space that have been devoted by scientists to the investigation of spiritualism and to making tests in automatic writing are, in my opinion--and, I believe, I speak for the man in the street--hopelessly futile. No one, who has ever really experienced spontaneous ghostly manifestations, could for one moment believe in the genuineness of the phenomena produced at seances. They have never deceived me, and I am of the opinion spirits cannot be convoked to order, either through a so-called medium falling into a so-called trance, through table-turning, automatic writing, or anything else. If a spirit comes, it will come either voluntarily, or in obedience to some Unknown Power--and certainly neither to satisfy the curiosity of a crowd of sensation-loving men and women, nor to be analysed by some cold, calculating, presumptuous Professor of Physics whose proper sphere is the laboratory.

But to proceed. The phenomenon of the big bear, provided again it was really objective, may have been the phantasm of some prehistoric creature whose bones lie interred beneath the Tower; for we know the Valley of the Thames was infested with giant reptiles and quadrupeds of all kinds (I incline to this theory); or it may have been a Vice-Elemental, or--the phantasm of a human being who lived a purely animal life, and whose spirit would naturally take the form most closely resembling it.

　　　*　　　*　　　*　　　*　　　*

Judging by the number of experiences related to me, hauntings by phantom hares and rabbits would appear to be far from uncommon. There is this difference, however, between the hauntings by the two species of animal--phantom hares usually portend death or some grave catastrophe, either to the witness himself, or to someone immediately associated with him; whereas phantom rabbits are seldom prophetic, and may generally be looked upon merely as the earth-bound spirits of some poor rabbits that have met with untimely ends.

Hauntings by a White Rabbit

Mr. W.T. Stead, in his Real Ghost Stories, gives an account of the hauntings by a phantom rabbit in a house in ---- Road. He does not, however, mention any locality. After describing several of the phenomena which disturbed various occupants of the place, he goes on to say, in the language of Mrs. A., who narrates the incident:--

"A dog which lay on the rug also heard the sounds, for he pricked up his ears and barked. Without a moment's delay she flew to the door, calling the dog to follow her, intending as she did so to open the hall door and call for assistance, but the dog, though an excellent house dog, crouched at her feet and whined, but would not follow her up the stairs, so she carried him up in her arms, and reaching the door, called for assistance; when, however, the dining-room doors were opened, the rooms were in perfect quiet and destitute of any signs of life."

The behaviour of the dog here accords exactly with the behaviour of dogs I have had in haunted houses, and substantiates my theory that dogs are excellent psychic barometers.

"After the family had been in the house a few weeks, a white rabbit made its appearance. This uncanny animal would suddenly appear in a room in which members of the family were seated, and after gliding round and slipping under chairs and tables, would disappear through a brick wall as easily as through an open door."

This is the invariable trick of ghosts; they seldom, however, open doors. Mrs. A. adds:--

"Some years have now elapsed since the incident I have now related took place, and again, in response to orders given by the enterprising landlord of the property, long-closed doors and windows have been thrown open, and painters and paper-hangers have brought their skill to bear upon gruesome rooms and halls; the house is once more inhabited, this time by a widow lady and some grown-up sons. These tenants come from a distance, and are entirely strangers both to the neighbourhood and the former history of the house, but, to use her own words, the mistress 'cannot understand what ails the house,' her sons insist on sleeping together in one room, and the quiet of the house is constantly being broken by the erratic appearances of a large white rabbit, which the inmates are frequently engaged chasing, but are never able to find."

Mr. Stead offers no explanation. I can see no other conclusion, however, than that this ghost was the actual phantasm of some rabbit that had been done to death in the house, probably by the boy whose apparition was among the other manifestations seen there.

John Wesley's Ghost

In his article "More Glimpses of the Unseen" (Occult Review, October, 1906), Mr. Reginald B. Span writes:--

"During the extraordinary manifestations which occurred in the house of John Wesley at Epworth, the phantom forms of two animals appeared, one being a large white rabbit, and the other an animal like a badger, which used to appear in the bedrooms and run about and then disappear, whilst the various bangings and rappings were at their loudest."

This is the only case I have ever come across of the ghost of a badger. I think it must be unique. Mr. Span adds: "Many strange and inexplicable things occurred in that house which were not due to any natural cause or reason. I remember that loud rappings used to sound round my room at nights, even when I had a light burning. I was often awakened by rappings on the floor of my bedroom, which would then sound on the walls and furniture, and were heard by others occupying rooms some distance off." This, again, is most interesting, as ghosts seldom visit lighted rooms. Mr. Span continues:--

"It was in the afternoon in broad daylight when my brother saw this mysterious animal.

"He was in the drawing-room alone, and as he was standing at one side of the room looking at a picture on the walls, he heard a noise behind him, and found, on looking round, that a sofa which generally lay against one of the walls had been lifted by some unknown power into the middle of the room, at the same time he saw an animal like a rabbit run from under the sofa across the room and disappear into the wall. He searched everywhere for the animal, which could not have escaped from the room, as the doors and window were closed, but was unable to find any sign of one or any hole whereby one might have passed out."

The Psychic Faculty in Hares and Rabbits

Hares and rabbits are very susceptible to the superphysical, the presence of which they scent in the same manner as do horses and dogs.

I have known them to evince the greatest symptoms of terror when brought into a haunted house.

CHAPTER VI
INHABITANTS OF THE JUNGLE

Elephants, Lions, Tigers, etc.

Elephants undoubtedly possess the faculty of scenting spirits in a very marked degree. It is most difficult to get an elephant to pass a spot where any phantasm is known to appear. The big beast at once comes to a halt, trembles, trumpets, and turning round, can only be urged forward by the gentlest coaxing.

Jungles are full of the ghosts of slain men and animals, and afford more variety in hauntings than any other localities. The spirits of such cruel creatures as lions, tigers, leopards, are very much earth-bound, and may be seen or heard night after night haunting the sites of their former depredations.

The following case of a tiger ghost was narrated to me years ago by a gentleman whom I will style Mr. De Silva, P.W.D. I published his account in a popular weekly journal, as follows:--

The White Tiger

"Tap! tap! tap. Someone was coming behind me. I halted, and in the brilliant moonlight saw a figure hobbling along--first one thin leg, then the other, always with the same measured stride--accompanied with the same tapping of the stick. I had no wish for his company, though the road was lonely, and I feared the presence of tigers, so I hurried on, and the faster I went, the nearer he seemed to come. Tap! tap! tap! The man was blind and a leper, and so repulsively ugly that the niggers on the settlement regarded him with superstitious awe. I had a horror of tigers, but of lepers even greater. And I loved my wife with no ordinary love. So I hurried on, and he followed quickly after me.

"The night was brilliant, even more so, I thought, than was ordinary, and the very brilliancy made me fear, for my shadow, the shadow of the trees, shadows for which I had no name, flickered across the road, were lost to sight to return again, and the jungle was getting nearer. The open country on either side ceased, one by one tall blades of jungle grass shook their heads in the gentle breeze, and the silence of the darkness beyond began to make itself felt. A night bird whizzed past me, croaking out a dismal incantation from its black throat; something at which I did not care to look clattered from under a stone I loosened with my foot, and sped into the shade, and I hastened on.

"Tap! tap! tap! Faster and faster, and faster came the blind man. I could smell the oil on his body, hear his breathing.

"'Whoever you are, sahib, stop!'

"There was fear in his voice as he whined out these words, a fear which increased my own; but I pretended not to hear, and pressed on faster.

"The darkness grew; high over my head at either side of the road waved the grass, rustling to and fro, and singing to sleep the insects nestling on its green stalks with its old-time song of the jungle.

"The grass ahead of me slowly parted; my heart beat quicker, the tapping behind me ceased--it was only some small animal. What was it? A small hyaena? No. A jackal, a lame jackal, and it looked at me from out of eyes that for some reason or other made me shiver. I did not know what there was about the jackal that was different from what I had seen in any other jackal, but there was a something. And as I looked at it in awe, it vanished--melted into thin air.

"The moment after a second jackal appeared just where the other one had been standing, but there was nothing remarkable about this one, and on my bending down, pretending to look for a stone to throw at it, it slunk back silently and stealthily whence it had come, and I hurried on faster than ever, knowing a tiger was near at hand.

"Tap! tap! tap! I blessed the presence of the blind man.

"'For God's sake, sahib, stop! For the love of Allah, sahib, stop!' (You know how they talk, O'Donnell.) 'The jackals, did you see them? I knew them by their smell, the smell of the living and of the dead. Walk with me, sahib, for Allah's sake.'

"Presently, O'Donnell, I heard a heavier rustling in the grass than the wind makes; a rustling that kept pace with me and went along by my side, never halting, but faster and faster, and faster.

"A short distance ahead of me was a patch of bright light, where the cross-roads met. A few yards more and the jungle grass would end.

"I thought of this, O'Donnell--the beggar might not know the road so well as I.

He had no wife, no child; he was a leper, only a leper--and my teeth chattered.

"Here the Colonel paused and wiped his forehead.

"I slackened my speed, the rustling by my side slowing down, and the tapping grew faster. I was close to the whitened road.

"'Sahib, the blessing of Allah be on you for stopping. Sahib, let me walk by your side.'

"(To the end of my days, O'Donnell, I shall never forgive myself, and yet I want you to understand it was for my wife--and child.) I slunk into the shade. Two steps more and the tapping would pass me. The stick struck the ground within one inch of my foot; my heart almost ceased to beat; I gazed in fascination at the spot in the jungle opposite. The heavy rustling had stopped; only the gentle sighing of the wind went on. The two steps were taken, the blind man paused on the cross-roads. He was ghastly in the moonlight. I shuddered. His eyes peered enquiringly round on all sides; he was looking for me; he had lost his way; he feared the tiger.

"Suddenly something huge shot like an arrow from the darkness opposite me. I bowed my head, O'Donnell, and muttered a prayer, for I thought my end had come.

"A terrible scream rang out in the clear night air. I was saved.

"'Allah curse you and yours, sahib.'

"I opened my eyes; an enormous tiger was bending over the leper, searching for the most convenient spot in his body to afford a tight grip.

"The man's sightless eyes were turned towards the moon, his teeth shone white and even; with the striped horror purring in his face, he thought of vengeance on me.

"I dared not move. I could not pass, O'Donnell. I had no gun. The big brute found a nice place to catch hold. It opened its mouth so that I could see its glistening teeth. It looked down at its paws, where the cruel claws glittered, and they seemed to afford it keen satisfaction--it was a tigress and vain--then it lowered its head, and the leper shrieked. I watched it pick him up as if he were one of its cubs; saw the blood trickle down its soft white throat into the dusty road, and then it trotted gracefully away, and was lost in the darkness of the jungle. There was a deathlike silence after this. I waited a few minutes, and then I got up.

"I had only a short distance to go, and I no longer feared the presence of man-eaters--there was not likely to be another. Hours afterwards, O'Donnell, when I lay in my hammock as safe as a fortress, I fancied I heard the dead man's cry, fancied I heard his curse. No one was more devoted to a wife than I was to mine. Ours had been purely a love match, and it was against my wish that she had accompanied me to such an out-of-the-way place as Seconee. I told her about my adventure, suppressing the leper's curse; and I was glad I did so, as she was greatly distressed.

"'Thank goodness you escaped, Charlie,' she said. 'I am so sorry for the poor leper. I suppose you couldn't have helped him.'

"'I might have fetched my rifle,' I replied, 'and tried to rescue him, of course. But I fear it wouldn't have been of much avail, as he would have been badly mauled by then.'

"My wife sighed. 'Ah, well,' she said, 'love is selfish! It makes one forget others. Still, I wouldn't have it otherwise.'

"'I wish this railway job here was over,' I murmured, sitting with my elbows on my knees and looking over the flat ground, sun-baked and barren, away towards the dark jungles and the still darker mountains towering above them; and as I gazed a shadow seemed to blur my vision and a voice to whisper in my ears, 'Beware of my curse.'

"I took Cushai, one of the native servants, into confidence.

"'Now, Cushai,' I said, 'you know all the superstitions of the country--the evil eye and the rest of them. Tell me, what can the dying curse of a leper do?'

"Cushai turned pale under his skin.

"'Not of Nahra!' he stuttered, swinging the knife with which he had been cutting maize in his hand, 'not of Nahra, the leper of Futtebah. Sahib, if you were cursed by him, beware. He was learned in the black arts; he could heal ulcers by repeating a prayer, he could bring on fever.'

"At this, O'Donnell, I turned cold. I had lived long in India. I had seen their so-called juggling, had experienced also strange cases of telepathy, and knew quite sufficient of their intimacy with the supernatural elements to be afraid.

"'You must keep the young sahib safe,' Cushai said, 'and the white lady. I wish it hadn't been Nahra.'

"I took his advice. My boy, Eric, was more closely supervised than ever, and as to my wife, I begged and entreated her not to move from the house until the tiger was dead, and I searched for it everywhere.

"The dry season passed, the wet came, and my work still kept me in Seconee. At times there came to us rumours of the man-eater--of another victim--but it never visited our bungalow, where the bright rifle leaned against the wall waiting for it.

"I certainly did meet with slight misfortunes, which the more timid might have put down to the working of the curse.

"My little finger was squashed in the laying down of a rail, and Eric had several bouts of sickness.

"It was nearly a year after the leper's death that alarming rumours of a man-eater having been at work again were spread about us. Several niggers were carried off or badly bitten, and the wounded showed symptoms of the loathsome disease so well known and feared by us all--leprosy.

"I knew from that it must be the same tiger.

"'The tiger is near,' someone would cry out, and a stampede among the native workmen would ensue.

"'Why the white tiger?' I asked Cushai.

"'Because, sahib,' he replied, 'the leprosy has made it so! Tigers, like men, and all other animals, go white even to their hair. I have not told them the story, sahib; they only know it must have caught the leprosy. To them Nahra is still living.'

"Then, O'Donnell, when I thought of what was at stake, and of all the hideous possibilities the presence of this brute created, I took my rifle and went out to search for it. In the evenings, when the dark clouds from the mountains descended and the wind hissed through the jungle grass, I plodded along with no other companion than my Winchester repeater--searching, always searching for the damned tiger. I found it, O'Donnell, came upon it just as it was in the midst of a meal--dining off a native--and I shot it twice before it recovered from its astonishment at seeing me. The second shot took effect--I can swear to that, for I took particular note of the red splash of blood on its forehead where the bullet entered, and I went right up to it to make sure. As God is above us, no animal was more dead.

"'The curse won't come now, Cushai,' I said, laughing. 'I've killed the white tiger.'

"'Killed the white tiger, sahib! Allah bless you for that!' Cushai replied.

"'But don't laugh too soon. Nahra was a clever man, wonderfully clever; he did not speak empty words,' and as his eyes wandered to the dark hills again I fancied a shadow darted along the sky, and the curse came back to my ears.

"I was superintending the line one afternoon; the backs of the niggers were bending double under the burden of the great iron rods when I heard a terrible cry.

"'The white tiger! the white tiger!' Rods fell with a crash, spades followed suit, a chorus of shrieks filled the air, and legs scampered off in all directions. I was fifty yards from my rifle, and a huge creature was slowly approaching between it and me.

"I could hardly believe my eyes--the white tiger, the tiger I knew I had killed! Here it was! Here before me! The same in every detail, and yet in some strange, indefinable manner not the same. On it came, a huge patch of luminous white, noiselessly, stealthily--the mark of the bullet plainly visible on its big, flat forehead. Step by step it approached me, its paws no longer with the colouring of health, but dull and worn. And as it came, the cold shadow of desolation seemed to fall around it. Nothing stirred; there was no noise whatever, not even the sound of its feet crushing the loosened soil. On, on, on nearer, nearer and nearer.

"Shunned by all, avoided by its fellow-creatures of the jungle, a blight to all and everything, it drew in a line with me. Not once did its eyes meet mine, O'Donnell; not once did it glare at the natives who were hiding on the banks of the cutting; but it stole silently on its way with a something in its movements that left no doubt but that it was engaged in no casual venture. I remembered, O'Donnell, that my wife had promised to come with Eric to meet me along the cutting, as she was sure no tiger would be there. I ran as fast as I could, and yet somehow my feet seemed weighted down. I cursed my folly for not forbidding my wife to come.

"It was uphill till I got to the bend, and it might have been a mountain, it seemed so steep. I knew if the thing I had seen met them a little farther on, they would be cornered, as the cutting narrowed very much, leaving not more than twenty yards, and that was a generous estimate. At last, after what seemed an eternity, I reached the summit of the slope; the tiger was a mere speck along the line. I rushed after it as fast as I could go, stumbling, half falling, pulling myself together, and tearing on, and the faster I went the quicker moved the great white figure. A feeling of despair seized me; all my fondness for my wife became intensified tenfold, and was revealed to me then in its true nature; she was the one great tie that made life dear to me. Even my love for Eric paled away before the blinding affection I bore her. I tore madly on, shouting at the same time, anything to make the white tiger aware of my presence, to keep it from seeing her. Another bend in the road hid it from view. The same hideous fears gripped me hard and fast, as I strained every muscle in the mad pursuit. At last I ran round the curve, and saw before me the tableau I had dreaded. The tiger was crouching, ready to spring on the group of three--Eva, Eric and the ayah. They were paralysed with fear, and stood on the rails staring at it, unable to move or utter a sound. I well understood their feelings, and knew they were labouring in their minds as to whether the thing that confronted them was a creature of flesh and blood, or what it was. They could not take their eyes off it, and, as a consequence, did not see me. The white tiger now went through a series of actions, so lifelike that I could not but believe it was real, and that I had been deceived in thinking I had killed it. Its haunches quivered, it got ready to spring, and my rifle flew to my shoulder. I saw it mark Eric, and read the increased agony in my wife's eyes. The critical moment came. Another second, and the thing, be it material or supernatural, would jump. I must fire at all costs. If mortal, I must kill it, if ghostly, the noise of my rifle might dematerialize it. And, as God is my judge, O'Donnell, at that moment I had not the least idea which of it was--tiger or phantom. It sprang--my brain reeled--my fingers grew numb, and as my wife suddenly bounded forward, the shadowy form of Nahra seemed to rise from the ground and mock me. With a supreme effort I jerked my finger back and fired. Bang! The sound of the explosion acted like a safety-valve to the pent-up feelings of all, and there was a chorus of shrieks. I rushed forward--the ayah lay on the ground, face downward and motionless. My wife had hold of Eric, who was shaking all over. Of the tiger there were no signs. It had completely vanished.

"'Thank God,' I exclaimed, kissing my wife feverishly. 'Thank God! It was only a ghost! but it was very alarming, wasn't it?'

"'Alarming!' my wife gasped, 'it was awful! I quite thought it was real! so did Eric, and so did ---- '--then her eyes fell on the ayah, and she gave a great start. 'Charlie!' she cried, 'for mercy's sake look at her! I dare not! Is she all right?'

"I turned the ayah over--she was dead! Fright had killed her!

"I then told my wife of the curse of Nahra, and of the phantom I thought I had seen of him, when the white tiger was springing. When I had finished, my wife hid her face in my shoulder.

"'Charlie!' she said, 'I did something awful. I saw what I then took to be the real white tiger single out Eric, and in my anxiety to save him from the brute, I pushed the ayah in front of him. And the thing sprang on her instead. It was nothing short of murder! And yet--well, there were extenuating circumstances, weren't there?'

"'Of course there were,' I said--for I verily believed, O'Donnell, fear had, for the time being, turned her brain.

"On our way home she suddenly called my attention to Eric.

"'Charlie,' she cried, 'what's that mark on his cheek? He's hurt!'

"I looked--and my heart turned sick within me. On the boy's cheek was a faint red scratch, just as might have been caused by a slight, very slight contact with some animal's claw.

"'Sahib!' Cushai whispered to me, when he saw it and heard of our adventure. 'Sahib! Beware! Nahra was a clever man. He must have used the spirit of the white tiger as his tool. Let the medicine man examine the scar.'

"I did so. I took Eric to a Dr. Nicholson, who lived close by.

"He looked at the wound curiously for a few moments, and then said to me--he was renowned for his plain speaking--'Mr. De Silva, there's no use beating about the bush, and prolonging the agony unnecessarily for you and your wife. The boy's got leprosy--God alone knows how! At the most he may live six weeks.'

"The shock, of course, was terrible. Eric had to be isolated from everyone-- even from those who loved him best--and died within a month.

"'Sahib, I knew!' Cushai said to me the day of the funeral, 'I knew some disaster would befall you. Nahra was a wonderful man, and his curse had to be fulfilled. You may rest assured, however, nothing further will befall you, for I saw Nahra in a vision this morning, and he told me both his and the white tiger's spirit were now on friendly terms, and would trouble you no more.'

"My wife and I left the place at once, and for a long time I lived in a hell of suspense lest she should develop the infernal disease. By a merciful providence, however, she did no such thing, but, on the contrary, picked up in health in the most marvellous fashion; indeed, she only told me yesterday, she felt better than she had done for years. I've told you the story, O'Donnell--and it is true in every detail--because it goes a long way to substantiate your theory that animals, as well as human beings, have a future life."

"I am absolutely sure they have!" I replied.

Jungle Animals and Psychic Faculties

It is, of course, impossible to say whether animals of the jungle possess psychic faculties, without putting them to the test, and this, for obvious reasons, is extremely difficult. But since I have found that such properties are possessed--in varying degree--by all animals I have tested, it seems only too probable that bears and tigers, and all beasts of prey, are similarly endowed.

It would be interesting to experiment with a beast of prey in a haunted locality; to observe to what extent it would be aware of the advent of the Unknown, and to note its behaviour in the actual presence of the phenomena.

PART III
BIRDS AND THE UNKNOWN

CHAPTER VII
BIRDS AND THE UNKNOWN

As Edgar Allan Poe has suggested in his immortal poem of "The Raven," there is a strong link between certain species of birds and the Unknown.

We all know that vultures, kites and crows scent dead bodies from a great way off, but we don't all know that these and other kinds of birds possess, in addition, the psychic property of scenting the advent not only of the phantom of death, but of many, if not, indeed, all other spirits. Within my knowledge there have been cases when, before a death in the house, ravens, jackdaws, canaries, magpies, and even parrots, have shown unmistakable signs of uneasiness and distress. The raven has croaked in a high-pitched, abnormal key; the jackdaw and canary have become silent and dejected, from time to time shivering; the magpie even has feigned death; the parrot has shrieked incessantly. Owls, too, are sure predictors of death, and may be heard hooting in the most doleful manner outside the house of anyone doomed to die shortly.

In an article entitled "Psychic Records," the editor of the Occult Review (in the August number, 1905) supplies the following anecdotes of ghosts of birds furnished him by his correspondents.

"In the autumn of 1877 my husband was lying seriously ill with rheumatic fever, and I had sat up several nights. At last the doctors insisted on my going to bed;

and very unwillingly I retired to a spare room. While undressing I was surprised to see a very large white bird come from the fireplace, make a hovering circle round me, and finally go to the top of a large double chest of drawers. I was too tired to trouble about it, and thought I would let it remain until morning. The next morning I said to the housemaid:

"'There was a large bird in the spare room last night, which flew to the top of the drawers. See that it is put out.'

"The nurse, who was present, said:

"'Oh, dear, ma'am, I am afraid that is an omen, and means the master won't live,' and she was confirmed in her opinion by the maid saying she had searched, and there was no trace of any bird.

"I was quite angry, as my husband was decidedly better, had slept through the night, and we thought the crisis had passed. I went to his bedside and found him quietly sleeping, but he never woke, and in about an hour passed quietly away.

"I thought no more of the bird, fancying I must have been mistaken from being overtired.

"Some months after my husband's death my youngest little one was born; he lived for twelve months, and then had an attack of bronchitis. He slept in a cot in my room, and I was undressing one night, when this same large white bird came from his cot, floated round me, and disappeared in the fireplace. At the time I did not for a moment think of it as anything but a strange coincidence, and in no way connected it with baby's illness.

"The next morning I was sitting by the drawing-room fire with baby on my lap. The doctor came in, looked at him, sounded his chest, and pronounced him much better. As he was a friend of the family, he sat down on the other side of the fireplace and was chatting in an ordinary way, when he suddenly jumped up with an exclamation, 'Why, what does this mean?' and took the child from my arms quite dead!

"For two years we saw nothing more of the white bird, and we had moved to another place.

"One day I was in my room, and my two little girls, aged six and eight, were standing at the window watching a kitten in the garden, when suddenly the youngest cried out:

"'Oh, mamma! Look at that great white bird,' putting her hands as if to catch it, exactly in the way it flies round one.

"I saw nothing, and the elder child said, 'Don't be silly, Jessie; there is no bird.'

"'But there is,' said the child. 'Don't you see? There, look! There it is!'

"I looked at my watch. It was twenty minutes past three.

"Two days after we received the news that a niece of mine had died at twenty minutes past three. The children had never known anything of the former appearances, as we had never talked about it before them. We have seen nothing since of the bird, but have for some years had no death in the family."

So runs the article in the Occult Review, and I can corroborate it with similar experiences that have happened to my friends and to me.

Some years ago, for instance, a great friend of my wife's died, and on the day of the funeral a large bird tried to fly in at the window of the room where the corpse lay; while, shortly afterwards, an exactly similar bird visited the window of my wife's and my room in a house, several hundreds of miles away. If it was only a coincidence, it was a very extraordinary one.

Then again, this spring, just before the death of one of my wife's relatives, a large bird flew violently against the window-pane behind which my wife was sitting--an incident that had never happened to her in that house before.

Undoubtedly, spirits in the guise of birds--most probably they are the phantasms of birds that have actually once lived on the material plane--are the messengers of death.

A Case of Bird haunting in East Russia

Some years ago the neighbourhood of Orskaia, in East Russia, was roused by an affair of a very remarkable nature. The body of a handsome young peasant woman, called Marthe Popenkoff, was found in a lonely part of the road, between Orskaia and Orenburg, with the skin of her face and body shockingly torn and lacerated, but without there being any wounds deep enough to cause her death, which the doctor attributed to syncope.

The people of Orskaia, not satisfied with this verdict, declared Marthe had been murdered, and made such a loud clamour that the editor of the local paper at last voiced their sentiments in the East Russia Chronicle. It was then that M. Durant, a smart young French engineer, temporarily residing in those parts, became interested in the case, and decided to investigate it thoroughly. With this end in view he wrote to his friend M. Hersant--a keen student of the Occult--in Saratova, to join him, and three days after the despatch of his letter met the latter at the Orskaia railway station. M. Durant retailed the case as they drove to his house.

"It is a remarkable affair, in every way," he said. "The woman was leading a perfectly respectable married life; she was hard-working and industrious, and beyond the fact that she was over-indulgent to her children, does not seem to have had any serious faults. As far as I can ascertain she had no enemies."

"Nor secret lovers?" M. Hersant asked.

"No; she was quite straight."

"And you feel sure she was murdered?"

"I do. Public opinion so strongly favours that view."

"Did you see the marks on the woman?"

"I did, and could make nothing of them. After supper I will take you to see her, in the morgue."

"What--she is still unburied?"

"Yes--but there is nothing unusual about that. In these parts bodies are often kept for ten days--sometimes even longer."

M. Durant was as good as his word; after they had partaken of a somewhat hasty meal, they set out to the morgue, where they made a careful inspection of the poor woman's remains.

M. Hersant examined the marks on the woman's body very closely with his magnifying-glass.

"Ah!" he suddenly exclaimed, bending down and almost touching the corpse with his nose, "Ah!"

"Have you made a discovery?" M. Durant enquired.

"I prefer not to say at present," M. Hersant replied. "I should like to see the spot where this body was found--now."

"We will go there at once," M. Durant rejoined.

The scene of the tragedy was the Orenburg road, at the foot of two little hills; and on either side were the sloping fields, yellow with the nodding corn.

"That is the exact place where she lay," M. Durant said, indicating with his finger a dark patch on a little wooden bridge spanning a stream, within a stone's throw of a tumbledown mill-house, all overgrown with ivy and lichens. M. Hersant looked round and sniffed the air with his nostrils.

"There is an air of loneliness about this spot," he remarked, "that in itself suggests crime. If this were an ordinary murder, one could well imagine the assassin was aided in his diabolical work by the configuration of the land which, shelving as it does, slips down into the narrow valley, so as to preclude any possibility of escape on the part of the victim. The place seems especially designed by Providence as a death-trap. Let us have a look at the interior of this building."

"The police have searched it thoroughly," M. Durant said.

"I've no doubt," M. Hersant replied drily. "No one knows better than I what the thoroughness of the police means."

They entered the premises cautiously, since the roof was in a rickety condition, and any slight concussion might dislodge an avalanche of stones and plaster. While M. Durant stood glancing round him rather impatiently, M. Hersant made a careful scrutiny of the walls.

"Humph," he said at last. "As you so rightly observed, Henri, this is a remarkable case. I have finished my investigation for to-night. Let us be going home. To-morrow I should like to visit Marthe's home."

This conversation took place shortly before midnight; some six hours later all Orskaia was ringing with the news that Marthe Popenkoff's three children had all been found dead in their beds, their faces and bodies lacerated in exactly the same manner as their mother's. There seemed to be no doubt now that Marthe had been murdered, and the populace cried shame on the police; for the assassin was still at large. They agreed that the murderer could be no other than Peter Popenkoff, and the editor of the local paper repeating these statements, Peter Popenkoff was duly charged with the crimes, and arrested. He was pronounced guilty by all excepting M. Hersant; and of course M. Hersant thought him guilty, too; only he liked to think differently from anyone else.

"I don't want to commit myself," was all they could get out of him. "I may have something to say later on."

M. Durant laughed and shrugged his shoulders.

"It, undoubtedly, is Peter Popenkoff," he observed. "I had an idea that he was the culprit all along."

But a day or two later, Peter Popenkoff was found dead in prison with the skin on his face and hands all torn to shreds.

"There! Didn't we say so?" cried the inconsequent mob. "Peter Popenkoff was innocent. One of the police themselves is the murderer."

"Come, you must acknowledge that we are on the right track now--it is one of the police," M. Durant said to his friend.

But M. Hersant only shook his head.

"I acknowledge nothing of the sort," he said. "Come with me to the mill-house to-night, and I will then tell you what I think."

To this proposition M. Durant willingly agreed, and, accompanied by his friend and the village priest, set off. On their arrival, M. Hersant produced a big compass, and on the earth floor of the mill-house drew a large circle, in which he made with white chalk various signs and symbols. He then sat in the middle of it, and bade his two companions stand in the doorway and watch. The night grew darker and darker, and presently into the air stole a something that all three men at once realized was supernatural. M. Hersant coughed nervously, the priest crossed himself, and M. Durant called out, "This is getting ridiculous. These mediaeval proceedings are too absurd. Let us go home." The next moment, from the far distance, a church clock began to strike. It was midnight, and an impressive silence fell on the trio. Then there came a noise like the flutterings of wings, a loud, blood-curdling scream, half human and half animal, and a huge black owl, whirling down from the roof of the building, perched in the circle directly in front of M. Hersant.

"Pray, Father! Pray quickly," M. Hersant whispered. "Pray for the dead, and sprinkle the circle with holy water."

The priest, as well as his trembling limbs would allow, obeyed; whereupon the bird instantly vanished.

"For Heaven's sake," M. Durant gasped, "tell us what it all means."

"Only this," M. Hersant said solemnly, "the phantasm we saw caused the death of the Popenkoff family. It is the spirit of an owl that the children, encouraged by their parents, killed in a most cruel manner. As soon as I examined Marthe's body, I perceived the mutilations were due to a bird; and when I visited this mill on the eve of my arrival, I knew that a bird had once lived here; that it had been captured with lime and murdered, and that it haunted the place."

"How could you know that?" the priest exclaimed in astonishment.

"I am clairvoyant. I saw the bird's ghost as it appeared to us just now. Afterwards I enquired of the Popenkoffs' neighbours, and the information I gathered fully confirmed my suspicions--that the unfortunate bird had been put to death in a most barbarous manner. The deaths of the three children laid to rest any doubt I may have had with regard to the superphysical playing a part in the death of Marthe. Then when her better-half had been served likewise, I was certain that all five pseudo-murders were wholly and solely acts of retribution, and that they were perpetrated--I am inclined to think involuntarily--by the spirit of the owl itself. Accordingly, I decided to hold a seance here--here in its old haunt, and if possible to put an end to the earth-bound condition and wanderings of the soul of the unhappy bird. Thanks to Father Mickledoff we have done so, and there will be no more so-called murders near Orskaia."

Hauntings by the Phantasms of Birds

One of the most curious cases of hauntings by the phantasms of birds happened towards the end of the eighteenth century in a church not twenty miles from London. The sexton started the rumours, declaring that he had heard strange noises, apparently proceeding from certain vaults containing the tombs of two old and distinguished families. The noises, which generally occurred on Friday nights, most often took the form of mockings, suggesting to some of the listeners--the enaction of a murder, and to others merely the flapping of wings.

The case soon attracted considerable attention, people flocking to the church from all over the country-side, and it was not long before certain persons came forward and declared they had ascertained the cause of the disturbance. The churchwarden, sexton, and his wife and others all swore to seeing a huge crow pecking and clawing at the coffins in the vaults, and flying about the chancel of the church, and perching on the communion rails. When they tried to seize it, it immediately vanished.

An old lady, who came of a family of well-to-do yeomen, and who lived near the church about that time, said that the people in the town had for many years been convinced the church there was haunted by the phantom of a bird, which they believed to be the earth-bound soul of a murderer, who, owing to his wealth, was interred in the churchyard, instead of being buried at the cross-roads with the customary wooden stake driven through the middle of his body. This belief of the yokels received some corroboration from a neighbouring squire, who said he had seen the phantasm, and was quite positive it was the earth-bound soul of a criminal whose family history was known to him, and whose remains lay in the churchyard.

This is all the information that I have been able to gather on the subject, but it is enough to, at least, suggest the church was, at one time, haunted by the phantom of a bird, but whether the earth-bound soul of a murderer taking that guise, or the spirit of an actual dead bird, it is impossible to say.

The Ghost of an Evil Bird

Henry Spicer, in his Strange Things Amongst Us, tells the story of a Captain Morgan, an honourable and vivacious gentleman, who, arriving in London in 18--, puts up for the night in a large, old-fashioned hotel. The room in which he slept was full of heavy, antique furniture, reminiscent of the days of King George I, one of the worst periods in modern English history for crime. Despite, however, his grimly suggestive surroundings, Captain Morgan quickly got into bed and was soon asleep. He was abruptly awakened by the sound of flapping, and, on looking up, he saw a huge black bird with outstretched wings and fiery red eyes perched on the rail at the foot of the four-poster bed.

The creature flew at him and endeavoured to peck his eyes. Captain Morgan resisted, and after a desperate struggle succeeded in driving it to a sofa in the corner of the room, where it settled down and regarded him with great fear in its eyes. Determined to destroy it, he flung himself on the top of it, when, to his surprise and terror, it immediately crumbled into nothingness. He left the house early next morning, convinced that what he had seen was a ghost, but Mr. Spicer offers no explanation as to how one should classify the phenomenon.

It may have been the earth-bound spirit of the criminal or viciously inclined person who had once lived there, or it may have been the phantom of an actual bird. Either alternative is feasible.

I have heard there is an old house near Poole, in Dorset, and another in Essex, which were formerly haunted by spectral birds, and that as late as 1860 the phantasm of a bird, many times the size of a raven, was so frequently seen by the inmates of a house in Dean Street, Soho, that they eventually grew quite accustomed to it. But bird hauntings are not confined to houses, and are far more often to be met with out of doors; indeed there are very few woods, and moors, and commons that are not subjected to them. I have constantly seen the spirits of all manner of birds in the parks in Dublin and London. Greenwich Park, in particular, is full of them.

Addendum to Birds and the Unknown

Though their unlovely aspect and solitary mode of life may in some measure account for the prejudice and suspicion with which the owl, crow, raven, and one or two other birds have always been regarded, there are undoubtedly other and more subtle reasons for their unpopularity.

The ancients without exception credited these birds with psychic properties.

"Ignarres bubo dirum mortalibus omen," said Ovid; whilst speaking of the fatal prognostications of the crow Virgil wrote:

"Saepe sinistra cava praedixit ab ilice cornix."

A number of crows are stated to have fluttered about Cicero's head on the day he was murdered.

Pliny says, "These birds, crows and rooks, all of them keep much prattling, and are full of chat, which most men take for an unlucky sign and presage of ill-fortune."

Ramesay, in his work ***Elminthologia*** (1688), writes:

"If a crow fly over the house and croak thrice, how do they fear they, or some-one else in the family, shall die."

The bittern is also a bird of ill omen. Alluding to this bird, Bishop Hall once said:

"If a bittern flies over this man's head by night, he will make his will"; whilst Sir Humphry Davy wrote:

"I know a man of very high dignity who was exceedingly moved by omens, and who never went out shooting without a bittern's claw fastened to his button-hole by a riband, which he thought ensured him 'good luck.'"

Ravens and swallows both, at times, prognosticate death. In Lloyd's Stratagems of Jerusalem (1602) he says:

"By swallows lighting upon Pirrhus' tents, and lighting upon the mast of Mar. Antonius' ship, sailing after Cleopatra to Egypt, the soothsayers did prognosticate that Pirrhus should be slaine at Argos in Greece, and Mar. Antonius in Egypt."

He alludes to swallows following Cyrus from Persia to Scythia, from which the "wise men" foretold his death. Ravens followed Alexander the Great from India to Babylon, which was regarded by all who saw them as a fatal sign.

"'Tis not for nought that the raven sings now on my left and, croaking, has once scraped the earth with his feet," wrote Plautus.

Other references to the same bird are as follows:

"The raven himself is hoarse
That croaks the fatal entrance of Duncan
Under my battlements."--(***Macbeth.***)

"It comes o'er my memory
As doth the raven o'er the infected house,
Boding to all."--(***Othello.***)

"That tolls
The sick man's passport in her hollow beak,
And in the shadow of the silent night
Doth shake contagion from her sable wings."
(Jew of Malta.)

"Is it not ominous in all countries where crows
and ravens croak upon trees?"--(***Hudibras.***)

"The boding raven on her cottage sat,
And with hoarse croakings warned us of our fate."(The Dirge.)

"In Cornwall," writes Mr. Hunt, in his work on popular beliefs, etc., of the West of England, "it is believed that the croaking of a raven over the house bodes evil to some of the family. The following incident, given to me by a really intelligent man, illustrates the feeling:

"'One day our family were much annoyed by the continual croaking of a raven over the house. Some of us believed it to be a token; others derided the idea. But one good lady, our next-door neighbour, said:

"""Just mark the day, and see if something does not come of it."

"'The day and hour were carefully noted. Months passed away, and unbelievers were loud in their boastings and enquiries after the token. The fifth month arrived, and with it a black-edged letter from Australia, announcing the death of one of the members of the family in that country. On comparing the dates of the death and the raven's croak, they were found to have occurred on the same day.'"

In an old number of Notes and Queries a correspondent relates that in Somersetshire the appearance of a single jackdaw is regarded as a sure prognostication of evil. He goes on to add that the men employed in the quarries in the Avon Gorge, Clifton, Bristol, had more than once noticed a jackdaw perched on the chain that spanned the river, prior to some catastrophe among them.

Dead magpies were once hung over the doorways of haunted houses to keep away ghosts; it being almost universally believed that all phantasms shared the same dread of this bird. Ghosts of magpies themselves are, however, far from uncommon; on Dartmoor and Exmoor, for example, I have seen several of them, generally in the immediate vicinity of bogs or deep holes.

Witches were much attached to this bird, and were said to often assume its shape after death.

"Magpies," says Mr. William Jones, in his Credulities, Past and Present, "are mysterious everywhere. A lady living near Carlstad, in Sweden, grievously offended a farm woman who came into the court of her house asking for food. The woman was told 'to take that magpie hanging upon the wall and eat it.' She took the bird and disappeared, with an evil glance at the lady, who had been so ill-advised as to insult a Finn, whose magical powers, it is well known, far exceed those of the gipsies." (Other authorities corroborate this statement; and I have heard it said that the Finns can surpass even the famous tricks of the Indians.) Mr. Jones, in the same story, says: "Presently the number increased, and the lady, who at first had been amused, became troubled, and tried to drive them away by various devices. All was to no purpose. She could not move without a large company of magpies; and they became at length so daring as to hop on her shoulder." (This reads like hallucination. However, as I have heard of similar cases, in which there has been no doubt as to the objectivity of the phenomena, I see no reason why these magpies should not have been objective too.) "Then she took to her bed in a room with closed shutters, although even this was not an effectual protection, for the magpies kept tapping at the shutters day and night." Mr. Jones adds: "The lady's death is not recorded; but it is fully expected that, die when she may, all the magpies of Wermland will be present at her funeral."

There is a house in Great Russell Street, W.C., where the hauntings take the form of a magpie that taps at one of the windows every morning between two and three, and then appears inside the room, perched on what looks like a huge alpine stick, suspended horizontally in the air, about seven feet from the floor. The moment a sound is made the apparition vanishes. It is thought to be the spirit of a magpie that was done to death in a very cruel manner in that room many years ago. There is a story current to the effect that a lady, when visiting the British Museum one day, happened to pass some slighting remark about one of the Egyptian mummy cases (not the notorious one), and that on quitting the building she felt a sharp peck on her neck. She put up her hand to the injured part, and felt the distinct impression of a bird's claw on it. She could see nothing, however. That night--and for every succeeding night for six weeks--she was awakened at two o'clock by the phantom of an enormous magpie that fluttered over the bed, and was clearly visible to herself and her sister. The phenomenon worried her so that she became ill, and was eventually ordered abroad. She went to Cairo and enjoyed a brief respite; the hauntings, however, began again, and this time became so persistent that she at last lost her reason, and had to be brought home and confined in a private asylum, where she shortly afterwards died. Though I cannot vouch for the truth of this story, I do think it is somewhat risky to make fun of certain of the Egyptian relics in the Museum. They may be haunted by something infinitely more alarming than the ghosts of magpies. There are many sayings respecting the magpie as a harbinger of ill luck. In Lancashire, for example, there is this rhyme:

> "One for anger, two for mirth,
> Three for a wedding, four for a birth,
> Five for rich, six for poor,
> Seven for a witch, I dare tell you no more."

From further north comes this couplet:

> "Magpie, magpie, chatter and flee,
> Turn up thy tail, and good luck fall me."

Rooks, again, are very psychic birds; they always leave their haunts near an old house shortly before a death takes place in it, because their highly developed psychic faculty of scent enables them to detect the advent of the phantom of death, of which they have the greatest horror. A rook is of great service, when investigating haunted houses, as it nearly always gives warning of the appearance of the Unknown by violent flappings of the wings, loud croaking, and other unmistakable symptoms of terror.

Owls, though no less sensitive to superphysical influence, are not scared by it; they and bats, alone among the many kinds of animals I have tested, take up their abode in haunted localities, and with the utmost sang-froid appear to enjoy the presence of the Unknown, even in its most terrifying form.

The owl has been associated with the darker side of the Unknown longer than any other bird.

"Solaque, culminibus ferali carmine bubo. Saepe queri et longas in fletum ducere voces," writes Virgil.

Pliny, in describing this bird, says, "bubo funebris et maxime abominatus"; whilst Chaucer writes: "The owl eke that of death the bode ybringeth."

In the Arundel family a white owl is said to be a sure indication of death.

That Shakespeare attached no little importance to the fatal crying of the bird may be gathered from the scene in *Macbeth*, when the murderer asks:

"Didst thou not hear a noise?" and Lady Macbeth answers:

"I heard the owl scream and the crickets cry"; and the scene in Richard III, where Richard interrupts a messenger of evil news with the words:

"Out on ye, owls! Nothing but songs of death?"

Gray speaks of "moping" owls; Chatterton exclaims, "Harke! the dethe owle loude dothe synge"; whilst Hogarth introduces the same bird in the murder scene of his Four Stages of Cruelty.

Nor is the belief in the sinister prophetic properties of the owl confined to the white races; we find it everywhere--among the Red Indians. West Africans, Siamese, and Aborigines of Australia.

In Cornwall, and in other corners of the country, the crowing of a cock at midnight was formerly regarded as indicating the passage of death over the house; also if a cock crew at a certain hour for two or three nights in succession, it was thought to be a sure sign of early death to some member of the household. In Notes and Queries a correspondent remarks that crowing hens are not uncommon, that their crow is very similar to the crow of a very young cock, and must be taken as a certain presagement of some dire calamity.

It was generally held that in all haunted localities the ghosts would at once vanish--not to appear again till the following night--at the first crowing of the cock after midnight. I believe there is a certain amount of truth in this--at all events cocks, as I myself have proved, are invariably sensitive to the presence of the super-physical.

The whistler is also a very psychic bird. Spenser, in his Faerie Queene (Book II, canto xii, st. 31), alludes to it thus:--

"The whistler shrill, that whoso hears doth die";

whilst Sir Walter Scott refers to it in a similar sense in his Lady of the Lake.

The yellow-hammer was formerly the object of much persecution, since it was believed that it received three drops of the devil's blood on its feather every May morning, and never appeared without presaging ill luck. Parrots do not appear to be very susceptible to the influence of the Unknown, and indicate little or no dread of superphysical demonstrations.

Doves, wrens, and robins are birds of good omen, and the many superstitions regarding them are all associated with good luck. Doves, I have found in particular, are very safe psychic barometers in haunted houses.

It is almost universally held to be unlucky to kill a robin. A correspondent of Notes and Queries (Fourth Series, vol. viii, p. 505) remarks:

"I took the following down from the mouth of a young miner:

"'My father killed a robin and had terrible bad luck after it. He had at that time a pig which was ready for pipping; she had a litter of seven, and they all died. When the pig was killed the two hams went bad; presently three of the family had a fever, and my father himself died of it. The neighbours said it was all through killing the robin.'"

George Smith, in his Six Pastorals (1770), says:

"I found a robin's nest within our shed,   And in the barn a wren has young ones bred;   I never take away their nest, nor try   To catch the old ones, lest a friend should die.   Dick took a wren's nest from the cottage side, And ere a twelvemonth pass'd his mother dy'd!"

In Yorkshire it was once firmly believed that if a robin were killed, the cows belonging to the family of the destroyer of the bird would, for some time, only give bloody milk. At one time--and, perhaps, even now--the robin and wren, out of sheer pity, used to cover the bodies of those that died in the woods with leaves.

Webster, in his Tragedy of Vittoria Corombona (1612), refers to this touching habit of these birds thus:

"Call for the robin redbreast and the wren, Since o'er the shady groves they hover, And with leaves and flowers do cover   The friendless bodies of unburied men."

Not so harmless is the stormy petrel, whose advent is looked upon by sailors as a sure sign of an impending storm, accompanied by much loss of life.

The vulture and eagle, obviously on account of their ferocious dispositions, often remain earth-bound after death, and usually select as their haunts, spots little frequented by man. From what I have heard they are by far the most malignant of all bird ghosts, and have even been known to inflict physical injury on those who have had the misfortune to pass the night within their allotted precincts.

CHAPTER VIII
A BRIEF RETROSPECT

If I have failed to convince my readers as to the reality of a future existence for all species of mammalia, I trust I have at least suggested to them the idea of probability in such a theory; for did the belief that all animals possess imperishable spirits similar to mankind only become general, I feel quite sure that a marked improvement in our treatment of all the so-called "brute" creation--and God alone knows how much such an improvement is needed--would speedily result. It is still only the comparative few who are kind to animals--the majority are either wholly indifferent or absolutely cruel. But if children were made to realize that even insects have spirits, they, at least, let us hope, would cease to take delight in pulling off the wings and legs of flies.

Man has hitherto entertained the ridiculously unjustifiable idea that all the animal and insect world has been created solely for his benefit, to be killed or to be kept alive entirely at his discretion. Such an absurd and presumptuous belief ought to be exploded once and for all. The animal world, so all sane people must agree, was undoubtedly created to lead the same, free, untrammelled life as does man himself. Man--save in cunning--is nothing superior either to the dog, horse, or other mammalia; indeed, he is not infrequently so inferior that one cannot help thinking that possibly the higher spiritual planes are not for him at all, but for those who--misnamed the lower creation--have surpassed man in spirituality. Let those who doubt this study the superphysical all around them. Let them carefully watch animals, and observe their propensities, their psychic faculties of scent, sight, and hearing. They can easily test them in any house or locality which has a well-established reputation for being haunted. They will then see how close a relationship there really is between the animal and superphysical worlds. And if they want further proof,--proof of a more material nature,--let them search around for some spot stated to be haunted by a ghostly phenomenon in the form of a dog, horse, cat, or other animal,--and investigate there themselves.

Such investigations have convinced me, and surely, by using these same methods with patience and perseverance, other people might also be convinced. At all events, let them try. For, a conviction like mine--a conviction that an eternity exists for our canine pets and dumb friends--is certainly worth a lot of striving after. At least so I think.

The Codes Of Hammurabi And Moses
W. W. Davies

The discovery of the Hammurabi Code is one of the greatest achievements of archaeology, and is of paramount interest, not only to the student of the Bible, but also to all those interested in ancient history...

Religion   **ISBN: *1-59462-338-4***

QTY

Pages:132
MSRP $12.95

The Theory of Moral Sentiments
Adam Smith

This work from 1749. contains original theories of conscience amd moral judgment and it is the foundation for systemof morals.

Philosophy ISBN: *1-59462-777-0*

QTY

Pages:536
MSRP $19.95

Jessica's First Prayer
Hesba Stretton

In a screened and secluded corner of one of the many railway-bridges which span the streets of London there could be seen a few years ago, from five o'clock every morning until half past eight, a tidily set-out coffee-stall, consisting of a trestle and board, upon which stood two large tin cans, with a small fire of charcoal burning under each so as to keep the coffee boiling during the early hours of the morning when the work-people were thronging into the city on their way to their daily toil...

Childrens   ISBN: *1-59462-373-2*

QTY

Pages:84
MSRP $9.95

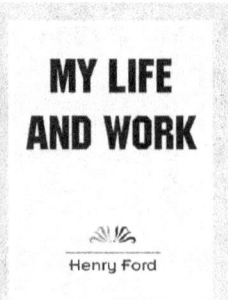

My Life and Work
Henry Ford

Henry Ford revolutionized the world with his implementation of mass production for the Model T automobile. Gain valuable business insight into his life and work with his own auto-biography... "We have only started on our development of our country we have not as yet, with all our talk of wonderful progress, done more than scratch the surface. The progress has been wonderful enough but..."

Biographies/   ISBN: *1-59462-198-5*

QTY

Pages:300
MSRP $21.95

The Art of Cross-Examination
Francis Wellman

QTY

I presume it is the experience of every author, after his first book is published upon an important subject, to be almost overwhelmed with a wealth of ideas and illustrations which could readily have been included in his book, and which to his own mind, at least, seem to make a second edition inevitable. Such certainly was the case with me; and when the first edition had reached its sixth impression in five months, I rejoiced to learn that it seemed to my publishers that the book had met with a sufficiently favorable reception to justify a second and considerably enlarged edition. ..

Reference   **ISBN:** *1-59462-647-2*

Pages:412

MSRP $19.95

On the Duty of Civil Disobedience
Henry David Thoreau

QTY

Thoreau wrote his famous essay, On the Duty of Civil Disobedience, as a protest against an unjust but popular war and the immoral but popular institution of slave-owning. He did more than write—he declined to pay his taxes, and was hauled off to gaol in consequence. Who can say how much this refusal of his hastened the end of the war and of slavery ?

Law   **ISBN:** *1-59462-747-9*

Pages:48

MSRP $7.45

Dream Psychology Psychoanalysis for Beginners
Sigmund Freud

QTY

Sigmund Freud, born Sigismund Schlomo Freud (May 6, 1856 - September 23, 1939), was a Jewish-Austrian neurologist and psychiatrist who co-founded the psychoanalytic school of psychology. Freud is best known for his theories of the unconscious mind, especially involving the mechanism of repression; his redefinition of sexual desire as mobile and directed towards a wide variety of objects; and his therapeutic techniques, especially his understanding of transference in the therapeutic relationship and the presumed value of dreams as sources of insight into unconscious desires.

Dream Psychology
Psychoanalysis for Beginners

Sigmund Freud

Psychology   **ISBN:** *1-59462-905-6*

Pages:196

MSRP $15.45

The Miracle of Right Thought
Orison Swett Marden

QTY

Believe with all of your heart that you will do what you were made to do. When the mind has once formed the habit of holding cheerful, happy, prosperous pictures, it will not be easy to form the opposite habit. It does not matter how improbable or how far away this realization may see, or how dark the prospects may be, if we visualize them as best we can, as vividly as possible, hold tenaciously to them and vigorously struggle to attain them, they will gradually become actualized, realized in the life. But a desire, a longing without endeavor, a yearning abandoned or held indifferently will vanish without realization.

Self Help   **ISBN:** *1-59462-644-8*

Pages:360

MSRP $25.45

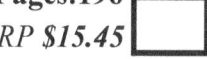

The Rosicrucian Cosmo-Conception Mystic Christianity by *Max Heindel*　ISBN: *1-59462-188-8*　**$38.95**
The Rosicrucian Cosmo-conception is not dogmatic, neither does it appeal to any other authority than the reason of the student. It is: not controversial, but is: sent forth in the, hope that it may help to clear..　New Age/Religion Pages 646

Abandonment To Divine Providence by *Jean-Pierre de Caussade*　ISBN: *1-59462-228-0*　**$25.95**
"The Rev. Jean Pierre de Caussade was one of the most remarkable spiritual writers of the Society of Jesus in France in the 18th Century. His death took place at Toulouse in 1751. His works have gone through many editions and have been republished...　Inspirational/Religion Pages 400

Mental Chemistry by *Charles Haanel*　ISBN: *1-59462-192-6*　**$23.95**
Mental Chemistry allows the change of material conditions by combining and appropriately utilizing the power of the mind. Much like applied chemistry creates something new and unique out of careful combinations of chemicals the mastery of mental chemistry...　New Age Pages 354

The Letters of Robert Browning and Elizabeth Barret Barrett 1845-1846 vol II　ISBN: *1-59462-193-4*　**$35.95**
by *Robert Browning* and *Elizabeth Barrett*　Biographies Pages 596

Gleanings In Genesis (volume I) by *Arthur W. Pink*　ISBN: *1-59462-130-6*　**$27.45**
Appropriately has Genesis been termed "the seed plot of the Bible" for in it we have, in germ form, almost all of the great doctrines which are afterwards fully developed in the books of Scripture which follow...　Religion/Inspirational Pages 420

The Master Key by *L. W. de Laurence*　ISBN: *1-59462-001-6*　**$30.95**
In no branch of human knowledge has there been a more lively increase of the spirit of research during the past few years than in the study of Psychology, Concentration and Mental Discipline. The requests for authentic lessons in Thought Control, Mental Discipline and...　New Age/Business Pages 422

The Lesser Key Of Solomon Goetia by *L. W. de Laurence*　ISBN: *1-59462-092-X*　**$9.95**
This translation of the first book of the "Lernegton" which is now for the first time made accessible to students of Talismanic Magic was done, after careful collation and edition, from numerous Ancient Manuscripts in Hebrew, Latin, and French...　New Age/Occult Pages 92

Rubaiyat Of Omar Khayyam by *Edward Fitzgerald*　ISBN:*1-59462-332-5*　**$13.95**
Edward Fitzgerald, whom the world has already learned, in spite of his own efforts to remain within the shadow of anonymity, to look upon as one of the rarest poets of the century, was born at Bredfield, in Suffolk, on the 31st of March, 1809. He was the third son of John Purcell...　Music Pages 172

Ancient Law by *Henry Maine*　ISBN: *1-59462-128-4*　**$29.95**
The chief object of the following pages is to indicate some of the earliest ideas of mankind, as they are reflected in Ancient Law, and to point out the relation of those ideas to modern thought.　Religion/History Pages 452

Far-Away Stories by *William J. Locke*　ISBN: *1-59462-129-2*　**$19.45**
"Good wine needs no bush, but a collection of mixed vintages does. And this book is just such a collection. Some of the stories I do not want to remain buried for ever in the museum files of dead magazine-numbers an author's not unpardonable vanity..."　Fiction Pages 272

Life of David Crockett by *David Crockett*　ISBN: *1-59462-250-7*　**$27.45**
"Colonel David Crockett was one of the most remarkable men of the times in which he lived. Born in humble life, but gifted with a strong will, an indomitable courage, and unremitting perseverance...　Biographies/New Age Pages 424

Lip-Reading by *Edward Nitchie*　ISBN: *1-59462-206-X*　**$25.95**
Edward B. Nitchie, founder of the New York School for the Hard of Hearing, now the Nitchie School of Lip-Reading, Inc, wrote "LIP-READING Principles and Practice". The development and perfecting of this meritorious work on lip-reading was an undertaking...　How-to Pages 400

A Handbook of Suggestive Therapeutics, Applied Hypnotism, Psychic Science　ISBN: *1-59462-214-0*　**$24.95**
by *Henry Munro*　Health/New Age/Health/Self-help Pages 376

A Doll's House: and Two Other Plays by *Henrik Ibsen*　ISBN: *1-59462-112-8*　**$19.95**
Henrik Ibsen created this classic when in revolutionary 1848 Rome. Introducing some striking concepts in playwriting for the realist genre, this play has been studied the world over.　Fiction/Classics/Plays 308

The Light of Asia by *sir Edwin Arnold*　ISBN: *1-59462-204-3*　**$13.95**
In this poetic masterpiece, Edwin Arnold describes the life and teachings of Buddha. The man who was to become known as Buddha to the world was born as Prince Gautama of India but he rejected the worldly riches and abandoned the reigns of power when...　Religion/History/Biographies Pages 170

The Complete Works of Guy de Maupassant by *Guy de Maupassant*　ISBN: *1-59462-157-8*　**$16.95**
"For days and days, nights and nights, I had dreamed of that first kiss which was to consecrate our engagement, and I knew not on what spot I should put my lips..."　Fiction/Classics Pages 240

The Art of Cross-Examination by *Francis L. Wellman*　ISBN: *1-59462-309-0*　**$26.95**
Written by a renowned trial lawyer, Wellman imparts his experience and uses case studies to explain how to use psychology to extract desired information through questioning.　How-to/Science/Reference Pages 408

Answered or Unanswered? by *Louisa Vaughan*　ISBN: *1-59462-248-5*　**$10.95**
Miracles of Faith in China　Religion Pages 112

The Edinburgh Lectures on Mental Science (1909) by *Thomas*　ISBN: *1-59462-008-3*　**$11.95**
This book contains the substance of a course of lectures recently given by the writer in the Queen Street Hall, Edinburgh. Its purpose is to indicate the Natural Principles governing the relation between Mental Action and Material Conditions...　New Age/Psychology Pages 148

Ayesha by *H. Rider Haggard*　ISBN: *1-59462-301-5*　**$24.95**
Verily and indeed it is the unexpected that happens! Probably if there was one person upon the earth from whom the Editor of this, and of a certain previous history, did not expect to hear again...　Classics Pages 380

Ayala's Angel by *Anthony Trollope*　ISBN: *1-59462-352-X*　**$29.95**
The two girls were both pretty, but Lucy who was twenty-one who supposed to be simple and comparatively unattractive, whereas Ayala was credited, as her Bombwhat romantic name might show, with poetic charm and a taste for romance. Ayala when her father died was nineteen...　Fiction Pages 484

The American Commonwealth by *James Bryce*　ISBN: *1-59462-286-8*　**$34.45**
An interpretation of American democratic political theory. It examines political mechanics and society from the perspective of Scotsman James Bryce　Politics Pages 572

Stories of the Pilgrims by *Margaret P. Pumphrey*　ISBN: *1-59462-116-0*　**$17.95**
This book explores pilgrims religious oppression in England as well as their escape to Holland and eventual crossing to America on the Mayflower, and their early days in New England...　History Pages 268

QTY

The Fasting Cure by *Sinclair Upton*   **ISBN:** *1-59462-222-1*   **$13.95**

In the Cosmopolitan Magazine for May, 1910, and in the Contemporary Review (London) for April, 1910, I published an article dealing with my experiences in fasting. I have written a great many magazine articles, but never one which attracted so much attention... New Age/Self Help/Health Pages 164

☐

Hebrew Astrology by *Sepharial*   **ISBN:** *1-59462-308-2*   **$13.45**

In these days of advanced thinking it is a matter of common observation that we have left many of the old landmarks behind and that we are now pressing forward to greater heights and to a wider horizon than that which represented the mind-content of our progenitors... Astrology Pages 144

☐

Thought Vibration or The Law of Attraction in the Thought World   **ISBN:** *1-59462-127-6*   **$12.95**

by *William Walker Atkinson*   Psychology/Religion Pages 144

☐

Optimism by *Helen Keller*   **ISBN:** *1-59462-108-X*   **$15.95**

Helen Keller was blind, deaf, and mute since 19 months old, yet famously learned how to overcome these handicaps, communicate with the world, and spread her lectures promoting optimism. An inspiring read for everyone... Biographies/Inspirational Pages 84

☐

Sara Crewe by *Frances Burnett*   **ISBN:** *1-59462-360-0*   **$9.45**

In the first place, Miss Minchin lived in London. Her home was a large, dull, tall one, in a large, dull square, where all the houses were alike, and all the sparrows were alike, and where all the door-knockers made the same heavy sound... Childrens/Classic Pages 88

☐

The Autobiography of Benjamin Franklin by *Benjamin Franklin*   **ISBN:** *1-59462-135-7*   **$24.95**

The Autobiography of Benjamin Franklin has probably been more extensively read than any other American historical work, and no other book of its kind has had such ups and downs of fortune. Franklin lived for many years in England, where he was agent... Biographies/History Pages 332

☐

Name	
Email	
Telephone	
Address	
City, State ZIP	

☐ **Credit Card**   ☐ **Check / Money Order**

Credit Card Number	
Expiration Date	
Signature	

Please Mail to: *Book Jungle*
PO Box 2226
Champaign, IL 61825
or Fax to: *630-214-0564*

ORDERING INFORMATION

web: *www.bookjungle.com*
email: *sales@bookjungle.com*
fax: *630-214-0564*
mail: *Book Jungle PO Box 2226 Champaign, IL 61825*
or PayPal *to sales@bookjungle.com*

Please contact us for bulk discounts

DIRECT-ORDER TERMS

**20% Discount if You Order
Two or More Books**

Free Domestic Shipping!
Accepted: Master Card, Visa,
Discover, American Express